IF I GO

my friend when she was 75.

IF I GO

A NOVEL

DIANE R. MOLBERG

SAGIT
PUBLICATIONS

IF I GO. Copyright © 2014 by Diane R. Molberg. All rights reserved. Printed in the United States of America. No part of this book may be used or reproduced in any manner whatsoever without written permission except in the case of brief quotations embodied in critical articles and reviews.

ISBN: 978-1-63443-532-1

1. Families—Colorado—1956 2. San Francisco Bay Area-Fiction 1959–60 3. Social Life and Customs-Colorado, 1956-57 San Francisco Bay Area-Fiction. 4. Parenting-Colorado-Fiction 1956 5. Domestic Violence-Colorado-Fiction 6. Alcoholism-Colorado-Fiction

FOR MY MOTHER, EVELYN

Youth with its insupportable sweetness,
Its fierce necessity,
Its sharp desire,
Singing and singing
Out of the lips of silence,
Out of the earthy dusk.
—*O Pioneers!* Willa Cather

"What's in store for me in the direction I don't take?"
—*The Subterraneans*, Jack Kerouac

THE DANCE

CHAPTER ONE

He was late. He got to the edge of the dance platform just as Lorrie Rathburn, Miss Rodeo Queen of 1956, waltzed by in the arms of the square dance caller, Mitch Yates. The charms on her bracelet jingled as she gave Buck Malone a withering smile. Lorrie wasn't his steady girl, but he'd promised her the first dance, and now he was late.

Buck liked watching Lorrie dance, but he wasn't in any hurry to dance with her. Something about the way she tilted her head, making sure people were watching her, embarrassed him. Like now. She smiled at Yates and acted as if she didn't care whether Buck was there, but when she saw him, she stumbled.

He didn't trust dancing. He'd always felt there was more going on than just shuffling across the floor. Before long, a girl had her arms locked around her partner's neck and there'd be nothing for him to do but wrap his arms around her waist, and right there something else was going on. His buddy, Ray Perez, said Buck had a dirty mind, but Buck said he'd like to see Ray dance.

The waltz ended and he looked for Lorrie. She was standing in the shadows near the edge of the band shell with Yates, but instead of enjoying his attention, as Buck might have expected her to do, she looked nervous.

He started toward them just as Yates tossed his cigarette to the ground, leaned down, gave Lorrie a kiss on the cheek, and then swung easily back onstage to call the next dance. He was already leaning into the microphone, arms loose at his sides, right leg angled away from his body and ready for the next call, by the time Buck reached her.

"Hey, Lorrie. Yates do something to bother you?"

"No. What would you care if he did?" She was blushing, and from the look in her eyes, she was struggling to hold back tears.

"I care. After he calls this dance, I can talk to him."

"What would you say? It's over with, anyway. Besides, you promised to be here for the first dance."

Whatever the reason for his failure to waltz Lorrie through the first dance, it wouldn't matter to her now. She'd already turned back to watch the dancers, her hands clasped behind her back, swaying to the music. He watched them circle the floor, following Yates's call. It looked so easy, the patterns of the dance coming together with such order. Maybe that's what bothered him: the order of it.

He spotted some trouble in the shadows on the other side of the dance floor, and narrowed his eyes for a better look. Arturo Perez, Ray's father, had a grip on the arm of a young woman, who was struggling to pull away.

Every dance floor's got a story, he thought. *I'd sure like to know what this one is.*

He watched the girl push hard at Perez and run out of the park. The man stumbled backwards before making a feeble attempt to go after her, then pausing and leaving the park in another direction.

"What on earth are you thinking about?"

He hadn't even realized Lorrie was talking to him.

"Mr. Packer wants me to write up something about the dance for the *Gazette*," he said quickly. "About you being Rodeo Queen." He looked into the shadows near the street where the girl had run.

"Really?"

"Yep. Says he'll put it in Friday's edition."

"How can you write about it if you weren't here? You're just going to make something up, I suppose."

He'd thought she'd be satisfied to have her name in the paper, but that would be too easy. "Well, I'm here now. Let's go for pizza like we planned."

She didn't move, but looked down at her pale yellow flats. "I don't want to go to Giuseppe's with dirty shoes."

Buck jammed his hands in the back pockets of his jeans, and rocked back and forth on his cowboy boots. He felt the small notebook in his hip pocket and wondered what to write about

Lorrie. Maybe how she looked like a spring garden in her yellow print dress, or how she'd let Yates kiss her cheek with mud on her shoes, but wouldn't go with him for pizza until he cleaned them.

"They look okay to me."

"Hey, Buck. Miss Rodeo Queen."

Ray came up behind them and gave a little bow to Lorrie. Buck thought he caught a shine of excitement in her eyes that hadn't been there a minute ago.

"Hey, Ray," Buck said. "Didn't know you were going to be here tonight."

"Wasn't. Just stopped to see what all the fuss is about."

"What do you mean, fuss?" Lorrie snapped.

Ray lit a cigarette and glanced at the dancers, and Buck wondered if he'd come because he knew Lorrie would be here.

"Buck's going to write a story about me for Friday's paper." Lorrie started slowly swaying again.

"Well, Lorrie. You couldn't ask for a better deal than that." Buck wished she'd stop swaying.

"We're going to Giuseppe's for pizza," she said. "Do you want to come along?"

Ray gave Buck a sideways look. "Okay with you?"

"Why not? " Buck shrugged.

"Come on and clean my shoes, Buck, and we can all go for pizza."

They walked toward Buck's car just as the band started to play another waltz.

"Like I said, Lorrie. I think your shoes look fine."

She stared at him, her eyes wide. Ray took a jolt of tequila from a battered flask he pulled from his hip pocket, and watched Buck.

"You said you'd clean them."

He took a couple of deep breaths. "Giuseppe's is going to be crowded tonight. I think we should get there. Besides, no one's going to be looking at your shoes."

He held the door for her. Ray smiled and sat in the backseat, snapping his fingers to Elvis Presley singing "Heartbreak Hotel" on the tinny radio.

*   *   *

The highway south toward Eagle Springs, Colorado was narrow and deserted except for an occasional big-rig that passed them heading north toward Denver. It sent a blast of air through the open window and shook the car as it went by.

"Appreciate you taking me home." Ray slumped against the back of the front seat. "Sorry I didn't ride my motorcycle instead of hitching a ride where he'd moved when they had taken Lorrie home. You paid off this car yet?"

"Yeah. Did some extra research for Art and he paid me. It's mine now, free and clear."

Ray looked at the straight line of highway ahead. "Ever want to just keep going? California maybe?"

"I plan to go there. San Francisco, I think."

"Can't you see us hanging around 'Frisco?' I hear it's pretty free and loose."

They rode in silence, the dark prairie stretching west toward the Front Range.

"My editor at the *Gazette*, Art—Art Packer—has the idea that the climate there might ease up my asthma."

"Lorrie didn't exactly like you not shining her fancy yellow shoes," Ray said.

"If there's one thing I don't need to go on about, it's Lorrie. We're just friends. Besides, once at Giuseppe's she forgot about the shoes." He coughed. "Actually, she seemed more interested in you."

A police cruiser's siren whined behind them.

"Geez," Ray said. "Ain't no signals to run out here. You hit something?"

Buck pulled to the side of the highway and turned off the ignition. "Not that I know. You got that flask stashed away?"

Ray patted his back pocket.

In the rearview mirror, Buck watched Officer West walk slowly toward them.

"Evening, boys." West leaned against the car, and lowered his head to look inside. "Out a little late?" His eyes focused on Ray, slumped dark and sullen against the door.

"Hey, Officer West. Just taking my friend here home."

"Saw you just last night, didn't I, Buck?"

"Yessir. My folks don't exactly lock me up."

Officer West looked at him, perhaps contemplating his next step as he had no evidence any laws had been broken. "Don't figure you've been working at the paper this late."

"No sir. Just came from the dance in Kiowa Park." Buck felt Ray settle low against the seat.

Officer West hadn't moved.

"I'm just going to drop my friend here home," Buck repeated.

"Uh huh . . ." West cocked his head and eyed Ray before tipping his finger to his hat. "You take care now, boys." He stepped back and Buck pulled onto the highway, watching again in the rearview mirror as the figure of Officer West grew smaller.

"Goddamn this town." Ray rolled down the window.

"It's not the town, just some of the people in it. Besides, nothing happened. Probably stopped us because we're the only car on the road."

However minor, the incident had triggered nervousness and Buck felt the tightness building in his chest. His breathing became forced and he reached in the glove compartment, taking out an awkward-looking inhalator, and giving two quick puffs.

"Not the town? You have any evidence that Eagle Springs believes teenagers are even people? Besides, you notice he kept eyeballing me but talking to you?"

Buck had noticed. Pull over two boys in a car: if one boy is white and the other is brown, they'd speak to the white boy, but keep their eye on the Mexican.

They drove in silence, until he turned down the dirt road toward the trailer park. His headlights caught the yellow eyes of a prairie dog that had stopped, frozen in the glare. Buck pulled to a stop on the dusty incline and killed the engine. To their right, the land spread flat and dark until it reached the highway they'd just turned from, now marked by a random, thin line of flickering headlights.

Ray kept looking toward the distant ridge, and Buck relaxed his head against the car seat. "Thought I saw your dad at the dance tonight."

"That's hard to believe."

"On the far side of the park, kind of back in the shadows. Looked like he was with a girl, a little older than us, with long black hair. Reminded me that you said an Indian girl helped get you started drawing back when you were a kid. I wondered if that was her."

Ray looked at him. "You thought you saw my old man with a girl who taught me how to draw eight years ago." It was a statement, not a question. He opened the door and walked to Buck's side of the car. "I didn't see any girl such as you describe, at the dance, and I sure can't picture my old man there. Your writer's imagination is getting too active. Catch you somewhere tomorrow?"

"I have to do some work at the paper, otherwise I'll be at the library."

Ray gave a wave of his hand and walked down the short, rocky, incline to the entrance of the trailer park. Buck turned on the ignition just as he heard a loud crack, like something being whacked hard. A large rock sailed through the air, landing just in front of the car. He turned off the engine and jumped out.

"Jesus!" Ray crouched behind a tree. "What the hell you doing, you crazy drunk?" he yelled.

Buck slid down the rocky slope. "Ray?" he shouted.

"Get outta here, Buck."

In the darkness, Buck saw Ray's father coming toward them, swinging a baseball bat against his leg.

"You little punk," he slurred. "You think you can steal my booze and get away with it? What else you been taking that don't belong to you?" He staggered toward Ray, who was still crouched behind a tree. "I oughta beat the hell outta you."

He bent to pick up another rock, tossing it into the air and swinging at it with the bat.

"Get down, Buck," Ray yelled.

Buck ducked just as the rock sailed past his ear. "Damn." He looked up and saw Ray making a run at his father. He rammed him in the stomach. Perez slumped to the ground and passed out. Ray kicked the bat away as Buck ran toward his friend, now looking down at his father with a disgusted expression. Across the weedy spit of land that separated the trailers, a light sprang to life.

"Come on, Ray. Let me help you get him inside."

"Just as soon let him lay where he is."

"Ray? Arturo?" A small figure stood silhouetted in the doorway of the trailer across from them. He looked impossibly unreal.

"Just what I need." Ray lifted his father from the shoulders and Buck took Perez's feet.

"Who the heck is that?" Buck's voice was a squeak, his breath coming in short, anxious gasps.

"Sam Lightfoot," Ray said. "Everything's okay, Sam. A friend's helping me out here. Go back inside."

"Is Misae with you?"

"No." Ray backed toward the trailer, Perez swaying heavily between the two boys. "I suspect she's safe at home."

Buck braced Perez against the side of the trailer until Ray managed to push open the door. It was a balancing act with both boys half pulling, half dragging the man up three steps and into the living room.

For a moment neither boy could speak. Ray dragged his father into a small bedroom on the other side of a narrow kitchen and pushed his father onto the bed.

Buck bent over in a spasm of coughing, wheezing, and gasping for breath. The inhalator was in the glove compartment and the way he was breathing now, he didn't think he'd even make it to the car. At the kitchen sink he gulped water from the faucet and wiped his mouth on his sleeve. He had half a pill in his shirt pocket and he swallowed it. He leaned over the sink, coughing up the phlegm that clogged his breathing into a paper towel. When he straightened up, he noticed, on the grimy counter, a slim package wrapped in white tissue with a maroon ribbon around it. It looked out of place, just as being sick here felt out of place. He waited for the wheezing to subside and cursed the asthma that disabled him at the worst possible times.

He peeked into the bedroom. Ray had tossed his father's boots on top of a pile of clothes at the foot of the bed. Perez mumbled and turned over.

Buck waited. He wasn't sure what for, but he didn't want to leave without making sure his friend was safe. This was only the second time he'd been in Ray's trailer and that had been to pick him up. Ray had never asked him in again. Looking around he wondered where Ray slept. Most likely it was on the worn sofa, riddled with so many stains the red and yellow splotches looked part of the overall design. Newspapers were piled haphazardly in the only chair. The whole place smelled of overcooked beans, stale cigarette smoke, and beer. Only the push of wind against the front-door screen cleared the air.

"Thought you left." Ray's voice was flat, his eyes dark and without expression. A shaft of black hair angled above his right eye. His body, lean and taut, looked strained as though ready to spring. "I can get you a picture," Ray said. "It'd last longer."

"No need to talk like that."

"What're you waiting for? Thanks? Well, thanks for helping me haul my old man's drunk ass inside. Sorry my home conditions ain't what you're used to." He pushed open the screen door, and stepped aside.

The grim reality of Ray's situation ached inside Buck's chest as much as the asthma. He jammed his hands in his pockets and pushed through the door. "See you tomorrow, Ray." He crossed the rough patch of ground and headed toward his car.

Outside, everything hung suspended in the dry night air. Halfway down the two rows of trailers, a mangy dog straggled toward a stand of evergreen, its eyes gleaming in the darkness. Buck threw some stones and the dog darted into the brush.

He got into his car but didn't start it immediately. The trailer where the slight figure had stood was dark now. Ray had called the man Sam. He'd never heard Ray mention him before.

He looked at Ray's trailer. He wanted a light to go on, or Ray to come up the incline and say it was all a mistake.

"Things ain't as bad as they look, Buck," he'd say.

But Buck knew they were.

CHAPTER TWO

Buck looked out the window of the *Gazette*. Across the street, the Chief movie theatre had run the evening's last showing of *High Noon*, and people sauntered down the main street, perhaps surprised at the unexpectedly warm wind coming off the Front Range. It was too early for a Chinook.

He returned to the stack of police blotters on his desk. For the last hour, he'd been scanning them for anything about a woman being pushed around in the park the night of the dance, but there was nothing. If a teenager was involved, or anyone from the dark cluster of Mexican kids standing in the shadows that night, it would be front-page news.

He put the police blotters back in the binder, locked up the *Gazette* office, and walked north toward Kiowa Park and his car. At seventeen, Buck was tall and lean, with dark red hair.

The cowboy boots he wore made him taller and often called attention to him, but that didn't bother him. His mother had given him the boots when he'd turned sixteen, and the minute he'd put them on, they felt right.

Light from the Wheaton & French drugstore fell across the sidewalk ahead. He'd have time for a cup of coffee before they closed. The warm breeze brushed against the back of his neck as he pushed open the door. Inside, a beautiful young woman, dark—maybe Mexican or Indian—sat alone at the counter, nursing a cup of coffee and a battered face.

Horace Wheaton was cleaning the glass display case and keeping an eye on her. He waved the cloth when Buck came in, and the air took on the mingled scents of Windex and 711 Eau de Cologne. "Hey, Buck."

"Hello, Mr. Wheaton."

"How's that asthma?"

"No problems, thanks." He eased onto the wobbly red vinyl stool a few seats down from the girl, who still stared at the coffee cup in front of her. This close, he saw what might be the imprint of a ring on her cheekbone. She'd been struck hard and something ached inside him. He'd never seen a woman beaten before.

"Enjoyed your story about Queenie Dawson in the *Gazette*."

"Thanks."

"Guess you'll be writing about Lorraine being crowned Miss Rodeo Queen last night."

"Yessir."

Buck looked in the long mirror behind the fountain and saw that besides the girl's bruised cheek, one eye looked like sunset after a bad storm, all dark purples and blues. A pale blue crescent-shaped discoloration circled part of her wrist. *Whatever happened, it just happened*, he thought.

She looked older than him, but not by much. Maybe college age, and she had long black hair that lay across her shoulders like a shawl.

Laverne Foote stood in front of him, snapping her gum. "Almost closing time." She glared at Buck.

"Not ten yet. Believe I'll have a cup of coffee."

"Ten cents." Laverne shoved the coffee toward him, sloshing some onto the saucer.

He put a dime on the counter and sipped the coffee. It was hot and it tasted good. He wanted to ask the girl if he could help her even if he couldn't imagine what he could do, but just then she turned to leave and her eyes caught his. He felt a catch in his chest, like he felt before an asthma attack took his breath away. It was the girl he'd seen last night at the dance in the park—the girl struggling with Ray's father.

She stood and moved toward the door, pushed it open and stepped outside.

"You believe that?" Laverne snapped her gum. "Coming in here looking like that. Indian girl."

Buck stood and slid his book bag slantwise across his body. "Ever think to ask her if she needed help instead of staring at her, hurt like that?"

Laverne's mouth fell open, which he thought was a general improvement on her looks. He opened the door.

"So long, Buck." Mr. Wheaton waved the cloth.

The Indian woman stood in the shadows near the entrance, snapping the buttons on her jean jacket. He looked in the shadows to see if anyone might be around, and kicked nervously at the sidewalk with the toe of his cowboy boot. She glanced at him.

"Hey," he said. "My name's Buck Malone." He tipped his fingers to the rim of his cowboy hat.

She smiled a little, but he detected a wince. Even in the shadows, he could see she had the high cheekbones and features of women in the Ute Tribe. "Pauline," she said.

"Hey."

Officer West's police cruiser slowly rounded the corner at the end of the block. It would be best if he could get them both away before West reached them. A seventeen-year-old white boy and an Indian woman standing in the middle of town at ten at night would be sure to cause questions. "If you need a lift, my car's on the other side of the park."

She put her hands into her jacket pocket and looked in the direction he pointed, away from the cruiser. "Thank you, but that won't be necessary." She stepped to the curb and then turned back. "Well, my pickup is just down the block."

He steered her across the opposite intersection and away from the slowly approaching police cruiser. They walked in silence. Buck was sure this was the woman he'd seen in the park, but how, or why, could he bring that up? She'd probably say nothing, drive off, and he'd never know if his suspicions were right or wrong.

"What are you going to write about?" she said. "The man in the drugstore said you were going to write about someone."

"Last night was the last square dance of summer. Lorrie Rathburn was crowned Miss Rodeo Queen. I'm a part-time reporter for the *Gazette* and cover local events, so I did a write-up on that." He took a deep breath and said, "Did you happen to be in the park last night? At the dance, that is? Maybe you saw her crowned?"

They reached the corner and she stopped next to a black pickup.

"No. I wasn't in the park last night."

"The paper printed a story I wrote about Queenie Dawson." He wanted to delay getting to her truck. "She was an eccentric woman who had her husband build a castle up near Mesa Road. It's called the Seminary now."

"Yes. I think I've seen it from a distance." She got in and started the truck. "I'll look for your articles. Thanks for walking me to my truck, Buck."

She pulled from the curb and he stood, watching the red glow of the taillights turn north, and he knew he'd seen something that didn't look right. Something he wanted to make right, but he knew there was nothing he could do to change it, until it was gone.

He knew she was the girl he'd seen in the park with Perez. After seeing Perez drunk and mean last night, ready to beat his own son with a baseball bat, he wondered if

Ray's father had something to do with the way Pauline looked.

"Evening, Buck." Officer West's cruiser pulled to the curb.

"Officer."

"Working late at the paper tonight?"

"Yessir. Heading home now."

West didn't move. "Be careful. Dark around the park."

"Yessir. I'll do that."

Buck turned quickly and crossed to his car on the other side of the park next to the high school. He was wheezing from asthma brought on by the chill air, and nervousness from seeing Pauline, and the thoughts about Ray's father. He took the inhalator from the glove compartment and gave two deep puffs, and tossed it back in. He circled the blocks half hoping to spot a black pickup parked at the curb. The streets were deserted. He circled several blocks, but even if he spotted her truck, or saw her walking into her house, what would he do?

A full moon had risen above the high range when he moved quietly into his house and to his room. He lay on his bed, remembering that Art had told him Eagle Springs had plenty of stories. "Just look around," he'd said. "You'll find one."

He'd found one tonight. But what was it, and what did it mean?

CHAPTER THREE

He couldn't stop thinking about Pauline. He woke the next morning to the memory of her battered face and the determination to find out not just what had happened, but also more about her. He'd have to do it without Ray until his friend would open up. The house was quiet except for the sound of Charles Malone busy in his basement workshop. Buck's mother had left a plate of cinnamon rolls on the kitchen table.

Buck moved quietly to open the screen door but his father called him.

"That you, Buck?"

"Yessir." He took a few steps down, and sat on the stair.

"Where are you off to so early?"

"The *Gazette*. Following up on some leads for a story."

"What kind of leads?"

He paused trying to think of a possible story Art would assign.

"Art wants something on the Youth Retreat at the Seminary."

His father reached for a square of sanding paper and started smoothing out a plank of blond-colored wood.

"You call your boss by his first name?"

"It's just the two of us. It's pretty informal since I'm not a regular employee, just an intern."

An old song was playing on the radio. "Nice music," Buck said.

"Brings back memories," his father said.

"Yeah? What exactly?"

"Oh, you know how it is with me. My memory isn't always clear."

"Maybe makes you remember Hawaii?" He knew his father had served in the Merchant Marines shortly after Pearl Harbor.

"Yeah. Must be Hawaii."

The sweet odor of cedar wafted through the room. Buck thought about how, as a child, he'd stack blocks of wood, or make a pile of wood shavings, always watching his father's careful hands smoothing the wood into shape. When he began coughing, and his breath came out as a drawn-out wheeze, his mother took him to the doctor.

"It's asthma," the doctor said flatly. "It's incurable but if he's careful and takes care of himself, he might outgrow it."

Buck left with a prescription and instructions to take a pill daily, and an awkward, oversized inhalator to use as needed.

"I know it's clumsy," the doctor said. "But you should have this with you in case you have an attack and you're away from home. It doesn't matter what your friends might think. A full-blown asthma attack is something you don't want to have. I hate to say this, but you shouldn't spend too much time in your Dad's workshop. Wood scents and dust can trigger an attack."

The effect of his illness created a distance between Buck and his father that neither could bridge. It became a source of guilt for Charles Malone, who blamed himself for bringing the disease on. Buck resented the restrictions the illness had forced on him. That's when he made plans to become a writer.

"You have pictures of Hawaii?" He changed the subject quickly.

"Just one of me and my buddies, but not in Hawaii. It's in Long Beach, California."

"I didn't know you were in California."

"Just for a few months." His father's back was to Buck as he bent low over the table. "I liked it there."

"I think I'm going to California." Buck immediately regretted speaking.

His father stood and closed a tool drawer with more force than necessary. "When do you plan to do that?"

"I'm only thinking about it." Buck held back a cough. "I'm doing good at the *Gazette*, Dad. Art's already printed a short piece I wrote about the Castle. Besides, lots of writers started out as reporters."

"Doesn't seem like *work*," his father emphasized the word. "You expect to support yourself writing books?"

The wheeze started building deep in Buck's chest, and he took short breaths.

"I suppose it's because of your sickness," his father continued. "Afraid you can't do anything but sit and write all day. That just isn't true, Son. You've got medications and you might even outgrow the asthma. The doctor said so. Give yourself a chance."

Buck began to feel the pent-up anger that could trigger an attack.

"Doesn't seem like much of a job," he said again. "Writing."

"It isn't a job like you do, but . . ." He stopped. It was a losing argument. Writing was something he could control, a way he could steady himself, but he couldn't say that to his father.

"It's honest work, and it's a way I want to live, Dad. See things, meet people, have my ideas come to life."

His father hung a small saw and a hammer on hooks on the wall, and put a box of nails in a drawer.

"I'm likely to be at the Seminary most of the weekend working on the article."

"Your mother worries, especially when you miss meals."

"I'll leave her a note." He started up the stairs, turning at the top. "The table looks real nice, Dad."

He left a note for his mother on the kitchen table that he might not be home for dinner. Outside, he felt the urge to drive aimlessly down the streets, through shadow and sunlight, and then onto the highway stretching north through the flat, tedious, and tiresome expanse of lion-colored prairie until he arrived in Denver. He wanted to drive down streets there, past other houses, and if they weren't part of his own town, that would be fine.

* * *

He parked near the corner of Wheaton & French before going to the newspaper. No one was at the fountain and he wondered if Pauline was all part of his imagination, part of a story he'd written in which he saved the girl.

Inside, Lorrie stood at the glass-topped display case, her head lowered, intently considering some object Horace Wheaton had put on a square of black cloth.

"Hello there, Buck," he said. "You're getting to be a regular here."

"Hey, Mr. Wheaton. Buy you a Coke, Lorrie?"

"Sure. I'll be right there."

He ordered a Coke and package of cheese crackers. Reflected in the mirror, he saw Mr. Wheaton pat Lorrie on the shoulder absentmindedly and move to the back of the store. Lorrie continued to stare at whatever lay on top of the display case. She lifted it and Buck saw it was a round, gold compact that glittered in the light when she opened and closed it. As he watched, he caught the quick movement of her hand as she slipped the compact into her skirt pocket. The black cloth on which it had rested was empty. Her eyes were bright and a blush had come to her cheeks, and he wondered if the petty theft had in some way excited her.

She sat on the stool next to him and started looking at a copy of *Photoplay* magazine left on the counter, and ordered a lime Coke.

"Mr. Wheaton always calls me Lorraine. I just hate it." She started looking at the magazine. "Why are you here, Buck?"

He'd stopped here to try and think through Pauline's possible relationship with Arturo, but instead of sorting through his confusion, he'd caught Lorrie stealing.

"I'm on my way to work. Got some copy to type up." He watched her profile for some expression of guilt, but she continued nonchalantly skimming the movie magazine.

"About my being crowned Miss Rodeo Queen?"

Maybe something about Miss Rodeo Queen lifting a compact, he thought.

It was like a story, and he was the author trying to figure out an ending that wouldn't hurt anyone. Maybe the heroine would see the wrong she'd done and return the stolen object. He thought of myths and stories he'd read in which a beautiful object often triggered a disastrous outcome, usually one that revealed the character as conceited or vain, their self-preoccupation hurting everyone around them.

"I'm working on a story about the Castle," he said. "Art might see if he can help me get it published, maybe in the *Denver Post*."

"You mean the Seminary? Why on earth would you write about that?"

"When Queenie Dawson lived there."

She sipped her Coke. "I have her room. Did you know that?"

"No, Lorrie. I didn't know that."

"You're coming to the Retreat this weekend aren't you?"

He groaned. "I hadn't planned on it."

Mr. Wheaton had returned to the counter, now frantically looking on the floor and around the display case.

"Oh come on, Buck. You can write about the Retreat and get more information about Queenie. I'll even show you my room." She kept flipping the pages of the movie magazine.

I should say something now. Ask her if she picked the compact up by mistake, or have her give it to me and I'll pretend I just found it and give it back to Wheaton.

Mr. Wheaton was walking toward them. Buck coughed, trying to ease his breathing.

"I'll think about it," Buck said.

"I told my parents you'd come."

"Why did you do that? Maybe I've got plans for the weekend."

Lorrie closed the magazine and smiled brightly at him. "How would you like to take me to Ruby's Cantina in Three Corners tonight? There's a new rock'n'roll band there."

"In case you've forgotten, we're underage. Besides, only cowboys and beat-up rodeo guys go there."

She shrugged. "We won't drink liquor. Anyway, from what I hear, Ruby isn't too particular." She smiled at Horace Wheaton, who had come up behind them.

"Lorraine, Buck. I'm sorry to interrupt you two. I can't find the compact we were looking at, Lorraine. Did you by any chance notice where I left it?"

Maybe he knows and he's trying to give her a chance to give it back.

"Well, on the counter I think, Mr. Wheaton. It's sure beautiful. I hope you find it. Pick me up at eight, Buck?" Lorrie hopped off the stool. "It'll be fun, I promise."

It seemed she had no grasp of the wrongness of her petty theft or of her deceit with Mr. Wheaton, who had returned to the display case.

"I hope you know what you're doing, Lorrie." But she was out the door without a backward glance.

Buck wanted to say something, but he'd have to be deliberately vague. "Hey, Mr. Wheaton." He approached the counter, where the man was rearranging items to make up for the empty space. "I'll keep an eye out for the compact; let you know if I see anything."

The man looked even more bewildered. "Well, thank you, Buck. I probably misplaced it, but I'd appreciate your help."

Once in his car, he pumped the inhalator. He was sick of feeling this way. Whenever something happened, his lungs would tighten and he'd freeze, afraid that any action would bring on an attack. He should have told Lorrie that he saw her take the compact. He should have told her he'd take it to Mr. Wheaton and say he found it. Why hadn't he?

Art Packer looked up when Buck came in, tossed his satchel on his desk, and sat down.

"Problem?" Art understood the pressures Buck was under with his health and his family.

"Yeah. My dad's on my case again about my wanting to be a writer."

"That's it?"

A black-and-white photo of Lorrie was on the corner of Art's desk, the Rodeo Queen banner across her chest and a small tiara on her blond curls.

"You hear anything about a girl being pushed around?" Buck asked Art.

"Pushed around? You mean hit? Beaten?"

"Art, I saw a girl in the park the night of the dance and she was with someone I know and he was shoving her around. Later that night I saw him again, and he was going after my buddy, Ray."

"Have you talked to Ray?"

Buck waited before answering. "Not exactly. The man pushing the girl around in the park was Ray's dad. The next night, when I left here about ten, I saw this same girl sitting alone in Wheaton & French. Her face was banged up and she had a black eye. She was an Indian girl."

He moved to the window and looked at the wide street that ran through the center of town and ended at the elegant Twin Towers Hotel. He'd taken for granted these quiet streets and his frustration with their sameness, the sense that nothing could go wrong. Now in the space of two days, all his ideas were beginning to change.

"You saw an Indian woman who'd been beaten, in Wheaton & French at ten at night?" Art lit a cigarette. "The way the police treat Indians in this town she must have been darn scared or very brave to be there late and alone."

"I went outside when she did and we talked a little bit. She told me her name is Pauline and I walked her to her pickup. I had to know if it was her I saw the night before, so I asked if she'd been in the park."

"Why is this important to you? You think there's a story?"

"Sure. Isn't a woman getting beat up a story?"

"Are you sure that's the real reason?"

"It's important if my buddy's dad beat her up." Another pause. "The girl was beautiful. I felt real sorry for her and wanted to help."

Art started to sort through copy on his desk. "I want you to do a little more on your piece about Lorrie Rathburn being crowned Rodeo Queen. It's too thin."

"I'm not real happy with it either."

"If you know something is off, keep hammering to get it right. Even a boring newspaper article. If you want to be a writer, you need to get under the skin of the people you're writing about, in this case, Lorrie. You're already friends with her. How did being Miss Rodeo Queen make her feel? Was she proud? Maybe a little nervous? She must have felt special in some way."

Buck wondered if finding out how she felt about being Rodeo Queen might help him understand why she lifted the compact. "Okay if I get it in tomorrow morning?"

Art leaned forward. "Monday morning is fine. I want you to cover the Retreat this weekend and maybe that will beef up the story."

Buck groaned. "I get asthma every time I think about that damn Retreat."

"You say you hate the way your asthma holds you back. Well, take control of it. Go to the Retreat; talk to Lorrie. Follow up with your buddy Ray and find out if his father has any connection to the girl, but go slowly and figure out what you think the story is. What do you want to tell? I'm going to give you some advice, though you won't like it. Keep your emotions out of it."

Buck rested his head on his desk. He knew Art was right.

"One more thing. If an asthma attack comes, deal with it, don't give in. I know that's easy to say. I've seen you have a minor attack and I can only imagine how it must feel to be that helpless. But the longer you have to deal with this illness, the more I see it dragging you down."

CHAPTER FOUR

Above the high range the early night sky was turning the color of marmalade, covering the Rathburn house in a warm, peach-tinged light. It was a modest house near the center of town, provided for the family of the assistant pastor by the church. A gardener came weekly to take care of the yard, and the church also provided a car for the family.

Lorrie hated living in a house paid for by the church. She thought it made them seem poor, as though they couldn't pay for their own house. As the assistant pastor of First Presbyterian, her father was also required to arrange events for the Seminary located in the front range of the Rockies just outside Eagle Springs, and his family had living space there.

"I'm just glad we don't have to be there too often," she'd told Buck.

"I like it," he'd said. "Art Packer wants me to do a story about the Seminary."

Buck remembered Lorrie's conversation as he pulled to the curb and parked. A slight parting of the curtain in the front room caught his eye. Someone was watching him. He pumped his inhalator just to be safe and tipped his Stetson low over his eyes. He stepped on the porch and the curtains fell back into place. Lillian Rathburn opened the door before he could ring the bell.

She stood behind the screen without speaking, looking at Buck as if he were a stranger—maybe a college student earning money, here to sell her a subscription to *Good Housekeeping*.

"Evening, Mrs. Rathburn."

She seemed to expect him to say more. One hand was against the inside of the screen door she hadn't opened yet. Her hair, usually carefully arranged, looked as if she'd been running her hands through it, and her blue dress was slightly wrinkled. She pushed the door open and stepped back slightly. Buck edged in. The air hung heavy with the smell of perfume and cigarettes.

She moved to the end of a beige couch and patted the cushion next to her. "Sit here, Buck." He moved to the other end.

"You certainly look nice. The way Lorraine is fixing herself, I'd never think you two were just going to the movies." She lit a cigarette and took a drink of orange juice, and he remembered hearing his parents talk about the minister's wife mixing alcohol in her fruit juice.

He leaned forward and spun his hat nervously between his

legs, and considered the fact that Lorrie had lied about where they were headed tonight. In a way, he could understand it. The minister's daughter at some honky-tonk bar in the foothills would create a scandal, but then why had Lorrie chosen it?

"Is anyone else going with you tonight?"

He tried to imagine what other lies Lorrie might have told.

"To the movies?" Mrs. Rathburn added.

Before he could stumble out an answer, Reverend Rathburn came in. "Hello, Buck." His eyes always had an expression that Buck could only describe as melancholy and pensive.

"Hello, sir."

"Youth Retreat starts tomorrow. You're coming for the weekend? We start at six Friday evening. Hamburgers and hot dogs in the community kitchen, that sort of thing. Then a prayer meeting and singing."

"Sounds fine, sir."

"We have close to a hundred young folks signed up. Be happy to add your name to the list."

"I don't know if I can be there for the whole weekend, but Art Packer wants me to do a short piece for the *Gazette*, so I'll likely spend some time there."

Suddenly Lorrie was there in the doorway. Buck stood and held back a little gasp. She wore a brown-and-white scoop-neck dress that revealed, however slightly, the rise of her breasts.

"Lorraine," her father said. "I thought you were going to the movies."

"Oh, Robert. They might want to stop for a soda afterwards."

Lorrie grabbed Buck's hand and headed for the door.

"Don't forget you have Retreat work tomorrow." Her father's tone was resigned.

*   *   *

Buck turned west and the town grew small in the rearview mirror as the foothills came into view ahead. He turned onto Mesa Road.

"Someday," he said, "I'm going to write about all this."

"All what?" Lorrie looked out the window. "Tumbleweeds and dust?"

He swerved to avoid hitting a jackrabbit. He knew he should be talking to her about being chosen as Rodeo Queen, but her petty theft of the compact was on his mind. He should have told Art about that. Now his mind had become a confusion of images and emotions. A frustrating lack of clarity bothered him as incidents ran together and he would mistake one for another.

Lorrie, who had been humming along with the music from the car radio, suddenly spoke. "This used to be the only road to Queenie Dawson's Castle," she said. "Before it became the Seminary. Did you know she gave elegant and fancy parties and people came from San Francisco, New York, and Denver? Fancy buggies carrying men and women all dolled up had to creep behind a mule led by an old miner. Why don't you write about that?"

"I will. Art Packer's interested."

Lorrie shifted sideways to face him. "Ray rides his motorcycle up here, doesn't he?"

"Now and then."

"Do you come with him?"

"Now and then."

Scattered lights from Three Corners glowed in the near distance.

"My father would bring us up here summer nights," she said. "We'd go to the red-brick arcade in the center of town and watch the Indian boys dance. They had tiny silver bells around their bare ankles marking time." She looked out the window at the Front Range. "They were so pretty." Her voice was soft.

"Say what?"

"The dancers. Their skin looked so smooth and they seemed strange and mysterious. Buck!" she said. "You missed the turn."

He made a sharp U-turn and drove down a steep gravel driveway to the small parking area. Cars, pickups, and motorcycles were parked at crazy angles beneath a lime-green-and-fuchsia neon sign flashing "Ruby's Cantina." He pulled into a semicircular space near a stand of evergreen trees and parked. The steady rhythm of drums, a guitar being played hard and fast, and the baritone of the lead singer filtered into the night.

Lorrie shivered.

"You cold? You can put on my jacket if you want."

"That's okay." She slipped into the pink sweater she'd had on her lap.

He kept the radio on.

"Aren't we going in?" Her fingers tapped lightly on her knee.

He turned the radio off. "Actually, Lorrie, I wanted to ask you about this morning in Wheaton & French."

She looked straight ahead at the dark stand of evergreen trees, and ran her fingers through her hair. "About what?"

"That compact Mr. Wheaton asked us about."

A spark of defiance flashed in her eyes.

"I saw you slip it into your skirt pocket." He coughed.

She shifted her position with a quick intake of breath. The high mountain air carried the scent of pine through the window. A cowboy went into Ruby's, his arm around a pretty girl.

"I don't believe you saw anything, Buck. And I don't know why you're saying all this now when you know I've been looking forward to tonight."

He remained silent.

"Honestly, Buck. Look at all the stuff Mr. Wheaton has there. Do you believe for a minute those college girls don't take things?"

"That doesn't make it right, Lorrie. Besides, you don't know they take anything."

More cars were filling the lot. They needed to get in before it got too crowded.

"Tell me the truth," she said. "Haven't you ever thought about slipping one of those paperback books you're always looking at into your satchel? I'll tell you something, Buck, if you promise not to tell."

His breathing tightened. "I'm not good at secrets."

"You'd keep a secret for Ray." She sat still and looked at him. "I suppose that's different, though."

Buck shrugged. To his recollection, Ray hadn't confided anything to him, but he would keep a secret about the trailer and Ray's father.

"I've taken things before." She spoke with no hesitation. "Just little things. Small glass bottles, scarves, and once a bracelet. I suppose you think I'm awful."

The truth was he didn't know what to think. "Why? You have more than most girls in Eagle Springs. What if you were caught?"

"That's just it, Buck. I'm the minister's daughter. Who'd ever think I'd steal anything?"

She had it all figured out. If she did something, it was all right.

"So you do it just because you can? Even if you know it isn't right?"

"Well, I never thought of it that way. But the minute I slipped that compact into my pocket, I wasn't scared about getting caught. I was more sure of myself than I was seconds before I took it. Besides, I can lie as good as I can steal."

He couldn't believe what he was hearing. "Have you ever tried to put back whatever you took?"

"Well, that would be silly, wouldn't it?" She sighed in irritation. "Why take it if I'm just going to give it back?"

The night moved around them, the trees dark and the stars bright in the high mountain sky, and Buck didn't want to hear any more. He got out and took a few steps toward the front of the car, where he waited for Lorrie.

"What about promising to keep this a secret?" She moved toward him.

"No need to make me promise, but I wish you'd stop before you get in trouble."

They walked to the entrance of the Cantina and took the three narrow steps into the entrance, and Buck pushed open the door. Cigarette smoke shrouded the air in a haze. The wood floor was scuffed and scarred, and burgundy leather booths lined one wall. College students gathered at one of three tables scattered at the edge of the small bandstand, and cowboys and a trucker or two sat hunched at a long wood bar directly opposite the door. Above the bandstand a silver ball rotated slowly.

A thirty-something-year-old cowboy with a voice scratchy from too many cigarettes stepped to the mic. "Taking a little break, folks. I'm Zeke, and these good ole boys are the Pioneers."

The cowboys at the bar stuck their fingers between their teeth and let loose with loud whistles.

"Y'all order up another round," Zeke said. "And don't nobody throw out that pretty little blonde who just came in the door." He nodded at Lorrie, who flashed him a bright smile.

Despite the smoke-filled air that had triggered a brief coughing spell, Buck felt the energy. He'd always wondered what these little mountain bars were like, and now that he was in one, it didn't disappoint. The perfect setting for a story.

"Oh look, there's Ray."

Lorrie pulled at Buck, who was surprised to see his friend sitting alone at a table off to the side.

"Hey, Lorrie. Buck." Ray stood up. "Whyn't you guys sit here?"

Buck stopped without speaking, amazed the way a child is amazed to discover his feet are off the ground after a Ferris wheel has lifted him into the air. Pauline stood across from him at the edge of the table.

"Hello, Buck."

"Hey," he said. Some of the bruises had faded slightly, but her sunset eye was still discolored. He looked away, not wanting to stare.

"Can I get you all something to drink?" Pauline asked.

"Any chance Ruby'll let us have a beer?" Ray said.

"Hi," Lorrie interrupted. "I'm Lorrie Rathburn."

Buck noticed something immediately different about Lorrie around Pauline. *Like she feels herself slipping into Pauline's shadow, the way who you are slips away in a dream.*

"Hello, Lorrie. Miss Rodeo Queen, right? I'm Pauline. Congratulations. Let me get you all something to drink."

She moved to the bar, said something to Ruby, and started talking with a cowboy sitting at the end of the bar.

"Believe you can sit down now, Buck." Ray had been watching him.

He hadn't realized he'd been standing the whole time, and sat on the chair next to Lorrie.

"You two are about the last people I'd figure to see here," Ray said.

"Reckon it's your lucky night."

"Do you come here a lot, Ray?" Lorrie asked.

Buck looked at her. Her eyes were too shiny, the way they'd been after she'd swiped the compact.

"Now 'n' then," Ray said. He leaned his arms on the table and looked sideways at her. "I didn't figure a preacher's daughter would like rock 'n' roll."

"Maybe there's a lot about me you don't know, Ray."

Pauline came over with a tray of drinks. Two beers, one for Buck and another for Ray, and a Coke for Lorrie. She put a small bowl of popcorn and another one of peanuts on the table.

"Do you have any 7Up?" Lorrie said.

Buck rolled his eyes and Ray shook his head.

"Why sure, Lorrie. I'll be right back." Pauline smiled and took back the Coke, and Buck watched her walk away, the wide, full skirt of her red dress billowing like a fan around her slim, brown legs.

Someone slid a quarter into the jukebox and a cowboy led a girl onto the small dance floor. She leaned her head on his shoulder and he held her hand against his chest. It was nothing like square dancing.

Pauline gave Lorrie her 7Up. "Everything all right?" She smiled.

Buck wanted to ask her to dance, to hold her the way the cowboy had held the girl, but she walked back to the bar, and started talking to a cowboy sitting there. He said something and she laughed and suddenly Buck wanted to say something that would make her laugh.

"Dance with me, Buck. It's a slow number." Lorrie's voice startled him.

"Go ahead," Ray said. "It's a damn sight easier than those square dances."

"I'm not much for dancing, Lorrie." He stared at the initials carved into the table, some with a heart around them. *Stories*, he thought. *Stories are everywhere all of a sudden.*

"Well, ladies and gents." Zeke took the stage again. "Now that you're all warm and fuzzy, let's cut loose with something to work up a sweat." Loud cheers and whistles, and the band started with "Blue Suede Shoes."

Buck smiled at Ray. "How about you and Lorrie dancing? It's not slow, but you can handle it."

"Want to dance, Lorrie?" Ray stood, and with no hesitation took her hand and led her to the dance floor.

Buck watched as they moved easily into the deeper rhythms, backing away and coming together again. Ray moved with a grace that surprised Buck. No one noticed them here, but if a Mexican boy were dancing with a white girl any place downtown, there would be a fight.

"That was fun." When the song ended Lorrie sat and fanned herself with her hand. "Did you watch us, Buck?"

"Hard to miss. Where'd you learn to dance like that, Ray?"

"That ain't dancing. Just moving around. You should've asked Pauline to dance. Ruby wouldn't care as long as she keeps up with the customers. Pretty much anything goes here."

Lorrie grabbed Ray's beer and took a long swallow.

"Damn it all, Lorrie. Don't be drinking here."

"Why not?" She was defiant. "We're the same age, but she brings you beer and me a 7Up." She looked to Buck for support. "What if I ordered a beer? Would she bring me one?"

"Lorrie," Buck said. "I wouldn't push your luck here, especially if you want to come back." He had the feeling she did.

She rested her hand in her chin and smiled at the guitar player, who smiled back. "I bet Zeke would buy me a beer."

Both boys groaned. "Here." Buck looked to be sure Ruby was busy before he moved the beer toward Lorrie.

Buck watched Pauline as she waited on a boisterous group of college students taking over one of the booths and then returned to the bar.

"The pretty Pauline has made a request for a nice slow number," Zeke said, "so pick your best girl and get ro-man-tic."

They started playing "Love Me Tender." Buck stood and in three strides was at the bar. Pauline was talking to the cowboy, who gave Buck a sideways look.

"Hi, Buck." She smiled.

"Think it'd be okay for a dance?"

"Sure. Okay, Ruby?"

Ruby nodded and took over the conversation with the cowboy.

Buck took Pauline's hand and led her to the dance floor. She turned to him easily, and he slipped his arm around her waist and after a minute or two, she rested her head on his shoulder. The warmth of her body came almost as a shock.

He took her right hand and laid it against his chest like he'd seen the cowboys do. Her hair smelled of lavender, and a thin red strap of her dress lay across her shoulder that looked soft as suede.

"I hope you're okay." She moved slightly in his arms.

"Say what?"

"I can feel your heart beating away."

"Guess I'm nervous dancing."

"How long have you had asthma?"

"How'd you know I have asthma?"

"I thought the man at the drugstore said something." She patted his shirt pocket where half a pill still rested. "I thought I saw you take a pill too."

"Got it when I was a kid. Pretty much growing out of it."

The music stopped.

"Thank you, Buck." She stepped back. "You're a good dancer."

He held her hand and walked her back to the bar. Ruby was already putting drinks on the tray.

He stood awkwardly, not wanting to leave. "What time does this place close?"

Pauline smiled. "Ruby might not want underage customers when it gets too late. But you can always come again."

Back at the table a college boy was asking Lorrie to dance. "Is it okay with you?" She looked at Ray.

"Fine with me," he said.

They watched her for a minute until Ray spoke. "For somebody who doesn't dance, you were doing fine with Pauline."

"You have a problem with that?"

"Why is it whenever we talk about girls we turn cantankerous on each other?" He took a swallow of beer.

"Don't mean to." He watched Pauline serving a table in the rear. "Lorrie's more complicated than you might imagine."

"Ain't we all?" Ray paused. "You care to explain that?"

The song ended and Lorrie came back. She reached for Ray's beer. Out of the corner of his eye, Ray saw Ruby watching.

"Believe we need to be getting out. In case Officer West drops in," Ray said.

Buck groaned. "Don't tell me he shows up here, too."

Lorrie's shoulders slumped. "Just because I had a couple of sips of beer?"

"No reason we can't come back some other night."

Lorrie didn't move.

"You're all leaving?" Pauline stood beside Buck.

"Looks like it," he said. "Thanks for the beer and all."

"Sure. Thanks for the dance, Buck."

Outside, the night was cold. Lorrie hurried to Buck's car, got in, and slammed the door.

"Looks like you'll have a nice ride taking her home," Ray said.

Buck walked with him to his motorcycle. Behind them, the Cantina door opened and the college kids left, laughing into the darkness. Lorrie tapped the horn.

"Like to talk to you later, Ray."

Ray climbed on his bike. "Sure. Let's catch up tomorrow."

Before Buck could say more, Ray gunned the motor of his bike and ground up the gravel incline and onto the highway.

Lorrie started arguing the minute he got in. "I have never known you to be this way, Buck. We hardly spent any time here. I thought you wanted to come with me." She moved closer to the door and concentrated on the flat prairie out the side window. "I have half a mind never to talk to you again."

Buck turned up the road and onto the highway, which was dark and empty of traffic. His mind was on Pauline, and why Ray was there.

"Is that Ray's girlfriend?" Lorrie said.

"Her name is Pauline. How would I know if she's his girlfriend?"

"She's older than we all are, isn't she?"

Instead of the familiar tightness he felt in moments of frustration, this time he felt anger. "Lorrie, how would I know how old she is? This is only the second time I've seen her."

"Second? When was the first?"

Buck concentrated on his driving until he pulled to the curb in front of her house. He turned off the engine, his hands gripping the steering wheel in frustration. The evening had started with his plea to Lorrie to do the right thing regarding the compact, and it ended in confusion and more unanswered questions. "Looked like you had a good time dancing with Ray."

"Of course I had a good time. I just don't see why we had to leave." She was quiet before speaking again. "Did you mind if I danced with Ray?"

"Why would I mind? You two can do whatever you want." He didn't mean to sound harsh. He took two deep breaths and relaxed his grip. He remembered what Art had told him, to get control when he thought asthma was winning.

"We're still friends, aren't we Buck?"

"Sure. Why ask me that?"

"Because of the stuff we talked about. What I told you."

"If it's about the compact, I think it's wrong and that you should do the right thing."

A light went on in her house. Lorrie leaned over and kissed him on the cheek, and putting her hands on his face and turning him to face her. She kissed him on the lips before getting out of the car and walking away.

He watched until she went in. As he drove away he saw a long road of sorry stretching out before him.

CHAPTER FIVE

It was after midnight. Buck followed the street that ran high above the banks of the Eagle River, which was running low. Everyone hoped for a snowy winter to avoid drought. The streets were deserted, the alleys and side streets dark. Lorrie had just kissed him, something he couldn't help but think of as a bribe for him to keep quiet, but it didn't matter. His thoughts were on Pauline, and the press of her body against his when they danced, the curve of her spine beneath his hand. He'd felt more in that dance than in Lorrie's kiss.

He turned south on 87 until he came to 115, where he turned east toward the trailer park. He needed to talk to Ray. He stopped on the rise. The trailer was dark and Perez's black Dodge was parked at the side, but there was no sign of Ray's motorcycle. Buck killed his engine and turned off the headlights. Ray should be here by now.

Just then Perez came out. He walked steady and wore a black cowboy hat, dark Western-style shirt, boots, and jeans. He started the Dodge and Buck watched the red taillights disappear around a curve ahead. He was tempted to follow him. His hand was on the ignition when in his rearview mirror he saw Ray's motorcycle crest the hill and coast toward the shoulder, where he stopped and got off the bike. He came up beside Buck's open window. "Hey," he said, his hands in his pockets.

"Hey."

"Like to think you came by to say you ain't rankled with me anymore."

"Guess you can think whatever you want."

Ray lit a cigarette and turned back toward his bike.

"Hold on, Ray." Buck got out. "I'm not aggravated with you. There are things I don't have answers to and I thought you could help."

Ray leaned against his bike. "What kind of things?"

A dog barked in the distance. The end of Ray's cigarette glowed in the dark night.

"I want to know more about Pauline, and you being friends with her, I thought you might help me." That hadn't come out right, and his lungs were getting tight. "To tell you the truth, I plan to see more of her."

Ray flicked the cigarette down and ground it into the dirt.

Buck reached into the car and grabbed the inhalator from the glove compartment and took two short puffs.

"Seeing more of Pauline might not be a good idea, Buck."

Buck was wheezing like a steam engine, and his stomach was in knots. Everything he said next came from that sick place. "When I saw her at the square dance, she was having trouble with your dad, and later that night, I see him coming at you with a baseball bat. The next night I see her sitting in Wheaton & French looking beat-up, and it set me wondering."

"So you put two and two together and it comes out my old man beat up Pauline. Is that the *thing* that's troubling you so?"

Buck opened the car door, but Ray jumped toward him and slammed it before he could get in. They were close enough to feel each other's breath on their faces.

"Just what are you doing out here, Buck? You planning on speaking to my old man about Pauline, setting him straight about beating up girls and all? Hell"—he slapped the car with his hand—"you have any idea what he'd do to someone like you? Who couldn't fight if your life depended on it?"

"Shut up." Buck shoved at his friend and reached for the car door.

Ray blocked it again. "Sure. In just a minute. My old man is no good, no way I'm denying that. Growing up he didn't have a rat's chance of making it out of Mexico. He never got above the seventh grade; he barely learned to read from auto mechanic magazines left at the station where he pumped gas. My mother used to tell me how my old man's dad drank himself stupid and told my dad he'd never make it in the world. Are these the little things you need to know, Buck?"

Buck kicked the side of his car and walked down the road. It had turned colder, and his breathing was still ragged. He slid to the ground, his back against a pine tree. Ray sat on a pile of bricks facing him.

"Didn't mean to be telling you so rough. I never meant for you to know any of this. But if you're developing an interest in Pauline, you're buying into a load of trouble."

"How so?" Buck's voice was low.

"My old man never hit my mother, but he'd trash the house, throwing dishes, slashing clothes. He'd whack me around and call it discipline. I was the one who brought Pauline to our house. She'd been teaching me to draw and I invited her to dinner. Her uncle Sam had an old pickup that sat in their yard. Useless piece of junk, but Pauline liked to sit in it and draw. One day we cleaned and polished it, and my old man repaired the engine almost as good as new. I was proud of him."

In the silence an owl hooted. Lights in the trailers were going out.

"Teaching Pauline to drive was the best time in his life. Mine too. I sat in the truck bed and sang Mexican songs at the top of my voice, and my old man sat up front showing Pauline how to shift gears. She'd strip 'em so bad and jam on the brakes and the three of us would fly forward and then back, and laugh like fools. Whenever she got into the truck, he'd put his hand over her head so she wouldn't bang it on the doorjamb." He shook his head. "Crazy. But he eased up on Mom and me."

Buck watched a lizard scuttle across the ground. There was a persistent buzzing in the night air that made him uncomfortable. He hadn't wanted to know all this, after all. He just wanted to know if Perez had hit Pauline the other night; not if he loved her, or if they had a past together. Most of all, he didn't want someone else's memories.

Buck stood and moved toward Ray. "So your old man was in love with Pauline?" Ray shrugged and stood, and Buck shoved at him, knocking him backwards. Ray landed on his butt but scrambled up quickly, crouching as though ready to fight.

"You ain't never hit at me before, Buck."

"There's a first time for everything." He strode toward his car. "I didn't ask for all these details."

"Just a damn minute. I ain't through talking."

"You're through talking to me, you son of a bitch," Buck shouted.

Ray followed him slowly. "You never asked me what you really want to know. If my old man hit Pauline the other night."

"I don't give a good goddamn." He got in the car but Ray was at the door, reaching through the open window and grabbing the steering wheel.

"I don't know what happened to Pauline." His voice was low and steady. "My old man caught up with her when she was leaving Sam's. I heard her tell him to leave her alone, that she wanted a new start." He paused as though envisioning the scene. "That might have been Tuesday, I can't remember."

He moved his hand and stepped back. "He grabbed her arm. That was all. It's none of my affair what you do, Buck. But you better be damn careful."

He stepped back, and Buck took off, spinning the wheels on the gravel road as he headed back to town. In the rearview mirror he saw Ray still standing by his motorcycle. He drove through the empty streets of Eagle Springs, and coasted to a stop in the alley behind his house. He got out quickly, bent over, and puked. Lying awake that night, he hoped he'd have the nerve to tell Ray none of it mattered. But right now, it did.

THE SEMINARY

CHAPTER SIX

It had rained in the night and the smell of wet morning grass was sweet. Buck dressed and left the house quietly, coasting his car out of the garage and down the alley. Nothing was simple or steady anymore. In one ordinary day, everything had changed and he needed to understand.

The streets were quiet, and shadows from the morning sun glanced through the leaves of giant oak trees. Shades on the windows pulled half-down, or drapes half-closed, despite the fact that bright sunlight couldn't penetrate the thick-limbed trees enough to pierce through the sheltered windows.

A bus rounded the corner. The traffic lights were still flashing yellow before the regular pattern started. The simple things that had grounded him—street signals, a bus coming on time, Eagle Springs, even Ray and Lorrie—were all at the edge of a circle and he stood in the middle, able only to observe what had once held meaning for him, but unable to reach the edges of his life.

He opened the *Gazette* office and left the window shades down. Art had left a note on his desk: *Buck, I'll be in late. Meeting with some folks at the Chamber of Commerce. If everything is quiet, go ahead and take the day off. Don't worry about the phone. Maybe you can get started on that piece about the Retreat at the Seminary this weekend.*

He rolled a sheet into the typewriter and sat back, staring at it. He sharpened pencils, the shavings piling on the desk, and typed a note to Art saying he'd work up some copy about the Retreat. He wanted to find Pauline, but first he needed to clear things up with Ray. He locked the office and pulled his Chevy from the curb, heading to the trailer park again.

Gray clouds hung over the eastern plains. Sooner or later, a storm would hit. At the edge of the road he stopped, out of sight of Ray's trailer. His grip was tight on the steering wheel and his chest pressed against it. He turned off the engine and watched the grasshoppers spitting their ugly brown juice against his car, their odd primordial shapes springing through the haze. Where was the sense of purpose he'd had when he woke this morning? Now, thoughts darted through his mind like the idiot grasshoppers leaping randomly in front of him. A brown splotch of goo at eye level where a grasshopper had hit his windshield startled him.

"Damn." He flicked the wipers on and a long brownish-green streak arced across the windshield. He got out and walked down the slope, slipping on the gravel. He saw no sign of Ray's bike or Perez's Dodge. Would Ray leave his motorcycle somewhere else? If so, where? Maybe he was inside. Buck stopped at the bottom step in front of the door. Blood smears, dry and faded, streaked across the top step, and the door handle had a bronzy-blood imprint. Buck looked down. There were dark spots on the ground.

"God Almighty," he whispered. He started to walk around the trailer when he heard a solemn voice, flat and monotone, behind him.

"No one there."

The old Indian, Sam, sat perched on a wooden crate just outside the door of his trailer. He wore a plaid flannel shirt buttoned at neck and wrists, faded jeans, worn cowboy boots, and a straw cowboy hat.

"I'm looking for my buddy, Ray Perez." Buck walked toward the old man.

"Gone. Haven't seen him for one night." Sam held up a bony finger.

The muscles in Buck's neck tightened more.

Sam's eyes half closed. "Perez as well."

Buck thought of the blood smears.

"I'm Buck Malone." He extended his hand, but Sam didn't move.

"Sam Lightfoot." He closed his eyes again and became so still that Buck thought he'd fallen asleep. Buck shuffled, dust quickly covering his boots.

"Feels like Chinook," Sam said.

"Say what?"

Sam opened his eyes a crack and looked at Buck. "Chinook," he said, using the Indian name for the wind. Crooked fingers pointed at the trees swaying in the dry wind. The scene looked like a dusty set from a long-ago movie.

"Arturo was very drunk." Sam sat suddenly erect on the crate, his hands resting like gnarled roots on his knees.

There must have been a fight, Buck thought. *Especially if Perez was drunk, and it must have been bad because of the blood.* "Did you hear any trouble around here last night?" He kicked at the ground and looked sideways under the brim of his Stetson at Sam.

Sam sat mute. Buck rocked back and forth on his heels, hoping to wait out the old man for an answer. None came.

He was turning to leave when Sam suddenly spoke. "Ray is a like a coyote who wanders in the hot wind. His journey is long and lonely." Sam's thin chest rose and fell in as deep a sigh as he could seem to manage.

The longer Buck stood there, the more questions he had and the fewer answers he was likely to get. He wanted to get in the trailer, see if there was a sign of a fight, or more blood. But not with Sam watching.

"Pleasure to meet you, Mr. Lightfoot." He tipped his hat. "Believe I'll see if I can find my buddy."

"To be a friend is to fly above the mountains." Sam nodded.

The old man touched on something meaningful and human, even if Buck couldn't understand it now. He walked back up the incline and started his engine, double-clutching the Chevy and raising so much dust that Sam and the trailer park were left in a reddish haze. He turned west, toward the foothills and Mesa Road.

* * *

Mesa Road was tinged a dark reddish-brown from the rain. A prairie dog darted across the road and Buck swerved to avoid it, forcing a grinding stop to his car.

The road was forbidding in its isolation. Listening to the wind in the canyons just to the west of him, he understood that the mystery, the inaccessibility of the road, could be intriguing. This was where Ray came when something went wrong, and Buck felt it might be where he'd come last night.

He drove slowly around the wide curves that were rough from potholes dug by the animals. In the distance, a spire from the Seminary poked above the expanse of the small, dark-green forest in front of the main building. A prairie dog scuttled across the road in front of him and he braked hard again. This time the engine died.

"Damn it all." He got out and kicked at the road. Wind from the canyons pushed against his back when he bent to check the tires. The left front tire was dug in to the moist soil.

The only signs of life were the animals scurrying across the dry earth, and the tumbleweeds twirling along the ground. Heat prickled against the back of his neck. He saw something and bent over studying the ground. Skid marks traced an uneven path to the left, across the road in the opposite direction, then veered west, to the left. Two tires, not four. A motorcycle. He set the gear in neutral and pushed his car to the side of the road, moving the gear back to park and pulling on the hand brake. He turned back and crossed Mesa Road, following the tracks toward the rise that led into some rough terrain.

"Ray?" He moved toward the opposite side of the road. "You around here?" Not even an echo.

He moved into the brush, still following the skid marks. They looked deeper, as if the rider had tried to stop the skid. At the top of a rise he saw Ray's bike, wrecked and upended, but no sign of Ray. The ground to Buck's left sloped suddenly and he lost his footing, sliding halfway back down, toward Mesa Road, on his backside and skinning his palms until a boulder stopped his fall.

He shook his head, his breath now forced and coming in short gasps. He felt in his pocket. No inhalator. He'd left it in the car. He braced himself against the rock and stood, unsteady, and that's when he saw a trail of uneven footprints leading back down to Mesa Road. They must belong to Ray.

"Ray?" he tried to call again, but his voice was barely audible.

Distant thunder rumbled to the east, across the plain, and the wind cooled.

He started back down toward the road, his breathing becoming more painful and shallow.

Mesa Road is always deserted. I could die up here as easy as not if I can't stop an asthma attack. He saw his car in the distance and someone standing beside it waving. He picked up some pebbles, wiped them on his shirt, and sucked on them, working up saliva to settle the dryness in his throat and give him something to cough up and clear his lungs. For a moment he thought it was Ray waving, until he heard Pauline's voice carry across the draw. She was calling his name.

He spit out the stones. No longer following Ray's footprints he focused on Pauline's figure in the distance. The uneven terrain sloped again and he tripped sliding down the rocky incline until he landed, gasping, on his hands and knees at the side of the road.

He sat back on his haunches and tried to catch his breath, when he saw Pauline running toward him. He heard the wheezing deep in his chest, and he knew from the pressure he felt that his lungs were filling with sticky, thick phlegm clogging his airway. Then he felt the light pressure of Pauline's hand on his neck, which ached from the coughing. He was trembling, his body heaving with each strained breath. If he were in town, he'd be on his way to the emergency room.

"Buck. You need help." Pauline patted his shirt pocket, feeling for a pill, anything that would help. "Where's your inhaler?"

He shook his head, and then motioned to his car. He felt the familiar, frightening panic that came when he struggled to breathe.

"In your car? It's in your car?"

He nodded.

Pauline ran to his car. "Where, where?" She searched in the glove compartment and ran her hands over the seats, knocking the cylinder onto the floor. She grabbed it.

"Don't collapse on me," she whispered to herself and ran back toward Buck where he still knelt, head low. "Don't collapse, don't collapse . . ." She bent down, looking at his now pale face as he strained for breath.

He took the inhalator, and gave two puffs. He felt her hand on his neck again, the strain of breathing throbbing in his neck. As his breathing eased, he tried to calm himself. He was exhausted, and there was no place close where he could go for help, except maybe the Seminary. They stayed at the side of the road and he braced himself against Pauline.

Thunder rumbled in the distance.

"We should get to your car. Can you stand? Walk? Do you want me to bring my pickup and get you to your car?"

"Gimme a minute. You happen to have any water on you?" His voice was still a whisper.

She sat back on her heels. "No. Sorry."

"'S'kay. Where's my hat?"

"Up there, I guess." She pointed to the boulder he'd fallen against. It looked more deadly looking up at it from Mesa Road. "Can you make it?" Storm clouds were building.

"Yeah." He stood with his arm around her shoulders until he felt steady. The asthma attack had weakened him and his shoulder hurt. His hands stung from trying to brace his fall when he slid down the path toward Mesa Road, but what hurt worse was Pauline seeing the helplessness of his situation, and his dependence on her help.

"I hate this goddamn road," he grumbled.

"What were you doing up there?" She looked toward the path he'd just tumbled down.

"Looking for Ray. His motorcycle's crashed up there. I saw skid marks along the road and followed them. Looks like he rolled away from the bike when it started to slide. Maybe landed hard against that same boulder I banged up against."

He felt her body against his, and caught the scent of lavender the wind carried from her hair, and all he could think of was the way she felt when he'd danced with her. Suddenly the parts of this day weren't fitting together.

Jackrabbits and prairie dogs hurried into the cool, dark recesses of the foothills, anticipating the storm, while shadows turned the landscape softer and less angled, and although he didn't know what it would be, he wanted so much from this moment.

"Oh." She steadied him and moved forward. "There's your hat." She stepped into the brush and picked it up. "Bit dusty." She brushed it and put it on her head and smiled. He would think, later, how infrequently playful gestures came to Pauline and how important they became to him. "Here you go." She put it on his head and stepped back, jamming her hands in her jean pockets.

"Looked better on you," he said.

They were at his car. Lightning flashed bright and jagged in the eastern sky. "That storm's been threatening all day," she said.

They got in his car just as raindrops, big and hard, pounded the roof and slammed against the windshield; he liked the sounds.

"Your windows closed?" He looked at her truck in the distance behind him. She nodded.

Pauline touched his shoulder lightly. "Are you feeling better now?"

He nodded but didn't speak, afraid to bring on another attack. He could hear the deep wheezing in his chest.

"That must be so terrifying, to lose your breath that way. I can't imagine it."

"Thanks for helping me. I'm not sure I could've made it back to my car, at least not for a while."

"Shouldn't you get to a hospital? I can still hear your breath rattling in your chest."

He should go to the hospital, but said, "I'll go later. I need to see if I can find Ray. What brought you up this way, Pauline?"

The storm had moved across the Front Range and was dissipating.

"Sometimes I take Mesa Road when I'm going to Ruby's."

He cracked the window open slightly and the car filled with the sweet, damp fragrance of evergreen and pine.

"Where do you think Ray is?"

"Before I fell, I was following footsteps that looked like he might have headed toward the Seminary. Hard to tell now that the rain's washed everything away."

"Why would he go there?"

"Reckon he'd head for the Seminary as the nearest place to find help, but it's tough to believe anyone there would help a beat-up Mexican kid. More likely they'd call the police." He was quiet, thinking. "There's something else. I saw bloodstains on the door of his trailer, and a couple drops on the stairs. Sam said Perez was pretty drunk and took off in the night, just after Ray left."

She was looking straight ahead, her hair falling forward and shielding all but a glimpse of her profile, just as he'd first seen her at Wheaton & French.

"You talked to Sam?"

"Yeah. He was sitting on the porch and called out to me. He said there was no one at the trailer. Ray never talked about his dad. Even when I'd drive him home, he never wanted me to come into the trailer. I never knew why until the other night."

He started coughing and leaned against the steering wheel. Pauline rubbed the back of his neck and he felt his muscles loosen.

"What night? What are you talking about, Buck?"

"The night of the square dance. I drove him home and next thing I knew, his dad's coming toward Ray, swinging a baseball bat. Mad, he said, because Ray took a bottle of tequila."

She lowered her head and covered her face with her hands, and he didn't want to go on but he did.

"Ray ran at his old man and knocked him out. I helped get him into the trailer. The thing is, Ray told me you go out there every week to help your uncle and being so close to their trailer, just got me worrying."

He stopped. She was watching him, waiting for what he'd say next.

"I saw Perez pushing you around at the dance in the park the other night, Pauline." He tried to sound confident, but wasn't sure he should say anything.

The sky had brightened. He waited for her to speak.

"You don't have to worry about me, Buck, and thank you for helping Ray. His father." She hesitated. "He's fine when he's sober, but he can't control his drinking, so he's not sober very often. Anything can set him off. He works as a mechanic at the army base a few days a week." She looked out the side window. "Just enough to buy booze and some food for Ray and himself."

"Sorry, Pauline. It's none of my business."

She put her hand on the door handle. "Well, that might be true, but I suspect you're telling me all this because you're concerned. Is that right?"

He pictured her standing by the side of the road only a short time ago, calling his name. The way she patted his shirt pocket for a pill, knowing that's what he needed, and then running to the car to find his medicine, and running back with it. Her hand on his neck then, calming him, as if she knew how to help him when he needed it most.

It's more than concern. I don't want her to get hurt again, and I want to protect her, but can't figure out how that can happen. I know that what I feel is more than casual. I've never had these feelings for any girl before.

"Might be a little more to it than that." He paused, trying to collect his thoughts. "You're right. I don't want you to get hurt again. Thought maybe I could check in now'n then to be sure you're safe and all?"

She opened the door, got out, and came to his side of the car. The window was open, and she rested her hand on the window frame. "You had a bad fall, Buck, plus a serious asthma attack. Maybe you need to catch your breath a little more. Mesa Road can do funny things to people. The wind is here one minute and still the next, the road curves through the pines and rocks so you're not always sure what's ahead, and you can always count on a storm."

Buck took a few deep breaths. Each second was so important that it felt like a lifetime, like there'd never been a moment in his life that mattered as much as this. "You saved me here, Pauline. Getting my inhalator, helping me like you did, staying with me to make sure I'm all right. There's no difference in my wanting to be sure you're okay."

She looked east toward the plains, the sky above now clear. "I'm glad I was there when you needed help, but you've only known me for a few days. Why would you think I need protection?"

"You looked like you'd had some trouble when I saw you at Wheaton & French. The night of the dance in the park, I saw Perez push you and I know he has a mean streak in him." He touched her hand where it still rested on the rim of the window.

"I think I understand, but for now you need to help Ray."

"I'll find him, but I don't plan on spending my time thinking about Ray and his problems. I'm just asking that you understand what I'm saying."

The wind lifted her hair away from her neck, exposing another small bruise he hadn't seen before.

She looked at him, almost smiling. "Maybe we can talk later."

"Once I find Ray and get him out, where's he going to go? He sure can't go back to the trailer."

She stepped back. "I'll talk to Lyle Samuels. He'll help Ray out for a while."

"The art teacher? Why would he take Ray in?"

"He's Ray's teacher, and he's been trying to encourage Ray to take his painting more seriously, plus he knows about Ray's home life."

"How is it you know Samuels?"

"I studied with him." She looked toward the foothills. "Do you know Spirit Rock?"

"Yeah. Big red rock monument behind the Seminary?"

"I go there now and then. I climb to the top where it's flat and I can lie on my back and watch the sky. Sometimes, I try to hear the chants that Sam always talks about."

He looked at the monument and back at her. He couldn't imagine climbing it.

"It's safe. Just a lizard or two."

"Why are you telling me this?"

"There's a road that turns off from Seminary Drive. It goes to the base of Spirit Rock. I'll talk to Lyle first, and come back and meet you and Ray there. How will you find him, and how long will it take you to get him out?"

"I have an idea where he might be. I'll scout things out, but if something goes wrong it could be longer."

"It'll work out. Just be careful." She touched his hands, now resting lightly on the steering wheel, before turning and walking to her pickup parked behind him.

In his rearview mirror he watched as she pulled forward slowly and then stopped, a film of exhaust escaping, the only clue she had hesitated.

He took his cowboy hat from the dashboard and put it on. His gaze hadn't moved from the image of her pickup in his rearview mirror.

"Come on, Pauline." He blinked dust from his eye. "Come on. Just a quick U-turn, and follow me." The truck lurched. "Come on," he whispered again, his eyes watering from staring so hard.

She shifted gears and he watched her drive away, down Mesa Road, until the pickup became a small black shape in the distance, turning right on Canyon, toward Ruby's Cantina.

CHAPTER SEVEN

The grand foyer of the Seminary was cool and silent. A wide staircase led to the mezzanine, where a lantern-shaped chandelier hung from the high ceiling. On the marble floor where he stood, shards of colored light reflected the sun's rays shining through stained-glass windows behind him. There was no sign that Ray could even have gotten in this way.

"Good Lord. Buck Malone?" The quick staccato steps of high heels on marble hurried toward him. He turned and was face-to-face with Mrs. Rathburn. "My goodness, Buck! Have you been hurt?"

Up until that moment he'd forgotten his dusty jeans and the tear in the sleeve of his shirt. He hid scratched hands behind his back before she could see them.

"Let me help you."

"No ma'am. I'm all right. Guess I'm a little shaky. Had a tumble up the road there." He was sorry the minute the words were out.

"Up what road?"

"Mesa Road."

"What were you doing up there? That road's a wreck."

He shifted from foot to foot, gauging her stare, measuring if she was genuinely concerned but reasoning that she had no reason not to be. "Just took it for a change. Is Lorrie around?" He had to have some reason to be here. Coming to see Lorrie was the first thing that came to mind.

"Why are you hiding your hands?"

"Just scratched a little from a fall."

"Let me see them, Buck."

Deep scrapes, some with tiny bits of gravel embedded, marked his palms.

"Come with me."

He followed her down a narrow hall and into a large, communal kitchen filled with young people, most from the high school, gathered around an oak table big enough to seat at least fifty. He recognized a few of his classmates, which only increased his tension.

"Everyone, most of you know Buck Malone. It seems he's a bit of a rebel, driving on Mesa Road, and he had a little spill. Any iodine around?"

"No need for that, Mrs. Rathburn." Buck moved to the sink. "A little soap'll clean them fine." He bent his head so she wouldn't see him wince when the water hit the fresh scrapes. On the counter he saw drops of blood and a scattering of small rocks and gravel in the sink. He took a swipe at the debris with the towel, and washed the gravel down the drain.

"Don't blame you, Buck," a student he vaguely recognized said with a laugh. "Iodine gives a mean sting."

Buck picked up a glass for a drink of water. He was starting to wheeze.

A deliveryman came in. "Looks like enough hamburger and hot dogs to feed all of Eagle Springs." He laughed. "Say, Mrs. Rathburn, the basement window by the service entrance looks broke in. Might want to have the Reverend take a look-see."

"How on earth could that happen?"

Buck looked around for a door that might lead from the kitchen to the basement. Had Ray gotten in that way? Was the residue he'd seen in the sink left by Ray maybe trying to clean up? Judging by his own experience in the rough ground on the west side of Mesa Road, and Ray's wrecked motorcycle, he must have been hurt. If so, where was he now?

"Maybe an animal. We'll look at it. Keep on, everyone." She took Buck's arm and led him out the door, back toward the grand staircase. "Let's get you to Lorraine. I bet she'll make you feel better."

The old feeling returned. The way she always called Lorrie *Lorraine*: the way she made assumptions about Lorrie and Buck to fit her idea of their relationship: the way no matter how innocent something was, she'd make it sinister.

The second floor held the Seminary residences for the assistant pastor and his family. The heavy smell of candle wax that hung in the air made everything solemn, and Buck felt strangely calm. Light from the chandelier and high windows twisted in the two panels of pier glass on the door, and now, with each step, Buck tried to calculate what to say to Lorrie.

"Buck." Mrs. Rathburn stopped suddenly. "Maybe you should call your parents?"

"I'm thinking I won't be able to stay for all the doings tonight. I'll get on home soon as I see Lorrie."

Her eyes took on a shine that made Buck nervous all over again. "I understand." She started down the narrow hall again.

She was saying something about how she hoped he could come to the Retreat tomorrow, but he didn't hear; he was cursing himself for barging forward without thinking. He should have figured on Lorrie's folks being here. Now that the broken window had been discovered, he was more sure than ever that Ray was somewhere in the Seminary.

She stopped in front of a door at the end of the hall. "By the way, Buck. Were you alone when you had your accident?"

"Ma'am?" His stomach sank. Did she know more than she was letting on? She hadn't seemed overly worried about a break-in. Had she seen Ray?

"With the basement window broken in, I wondered if you saw anyone else around. If we should be worried."

He coughed, a deep wheeze aching in his chest. "No ma'am. I didn't see anything but prairie dogs and jackrabbits. That's what caused my car to skid and me to get skinned up this way." She watched him. "Dodging jackrabbits," he added.

"Is your car all right?"

He nodded.

"Where are you parked?"

"Across the road. Near the stand of trees."

"Well." She knocked lightly on the door. "That's good to know."

The minute Lorrie opened the door, the scent of Lily of the Valley drifted out. She looked first at her mother, then Buck.

"Well, Lorraine, look who's come to help us out after all." Mrs. Rathburn watched her daughter through narrowed eyes.

Lorrie stared at Buck in his torn shirt and dusty jeans.

"I forgot to tell you, Mother. Buck's doing an article for the *Gazette* about the Seminary. I thought this would be a good time for him to look around and get more information."

Buck felt the tension in his shoulders ease, and fought leaning against the wall in relief.

"Yes. Well," Mrs. Rathburn said. "I'm sure you'll bring him up-to-date. Don't forget, your father's expecting you to help with the registration." She smiled at Buck and looked back at Lorrie. "I'll tell him you might be a little late." The heels of her pumps clicked against the floor as she walked away.

Buck felt a shiver down his spine as he stepped into the room. "Sometimes your mother makes me real nervous."

Lorrie closed the door. "How do you think *I* feel?"

He glanced at a clock on the small table next to the bed. He had to find Ray fast if they were going to meet Pauline in an hour, and now that he was in Lorrie's room, he had to make an excuse to get out, or find out if she might have heard anything about Ray. He shoved his hands in his jeans pockets and winced, immediately pulling them out and shaking them to ease the sting.

"What's going on, Buck? What happened to you?" She took his hands. "Your hands are all scratched and bleeding."

"It's nothing." He pulled his hands back just as the white louvered doors leading to the bathroom opened and Ray stepped out. He held his T-shirt in one hand. Bruises and scratches showed plainly on his bare chest and arms.

Buck sat on the edge of the bed staring at his friend, while Ray pulled his shirt on and sat in a flowered chair near a small window.

"Ray had an accident on Mesa Road," Lorrie announced as if she'd just discovered it. She paused, waiting for one of them to speak, but Ray was looking at the floor and Buck was looking at Ray.

"He was in here when I came in this morning." She offered further explanation that Buck hadn't asked for.

Buck tried to calculate. Had Ray been in Lorrie's room overnight? He glanced at the clock again and that's when he saw, half hidden behind a table lamp, the slim gift box he'd seen on the kitchen counter in Ray's trailer. Buck assumed it belonged to Perez, but was it Ray's? Had he intended it for Lorrie all along? It had been opened, the maroon ribbon draped over the edge of the table, which made it more likely Ray intended Lorrie to have it, but that didn't add up.

Buck couldn't tell the extent of Ray's injuries, or even if he had any. "How bad you busted up?" he said.

"Mostly scratches. Some bruising." He looked at Buck. "What's wrong with your hands?"

"I fell up on Mesa Road looking for you."

"Sorry."

"Your bike is up there. Wouldn't it run?"

Ray shook his head.

"You walked here from the accident?"

Ray nodded. "Half crawled some of the time."

"You by any chance spend some time in the basement?"

Lorrie looked around quickly from where she'd been standing in front of a small wall mirror.

Ray looked at Buck. "Yeah, why?"

"Seems a broken window was discovered there."

Ray stared at Buck while Lorrie looked from one to the other.

"Damn dumb thing to do. Guess I wasn't thinking."

"And you are now? Thinking, that is?"

"Your shirt's on backwards," Lorrie said to Ray. "Look what Ray gave me." She turned and Buck saw a double-strand pearl choker gleaming against her tan throat.

"Nice," he said, looking briefly at Lorrie. "So, Ray, feeling okay to leave now?"

Ray was concentrating on a white envelope near his feet. Had the jewelry box belonged to him all along? Buck wondered. Where would Ray get money for a pearl necklace? What if Perez bought them for Pauline and she'd refused them, and that's why Perez was so angry that night? Did he push her in the park because she wouldn't take the pearls?

"Anyway," Lorrie said. "Don't you need some kind of escape plan, or are you going back out through the basement window?"

Lorrie sat on the edge of a white shelf, swinging her legs back and forth. "I mean, you must have come up with something down there in the basement." She looked at Ray. "Isn't that why you're here, Buck? To help get Ray out?"

Buck coughed and phlegm rattled in his chest.

"Forget your medicine again?" Ray said.

Buck nodded. "In my car."

"Damn fool."

"I think," Lorrie persisted, "the best idea is to get you out through the front door. At six, when everyone will be eating."

"Just how's that going to work?" Buck looked at the clock again. They couldn't wait until six. "At the very least," Buck said. "Your mother will be sure to spot us. You have a plan to distract her?"

Lorrie was quiet.

"Any chance we can bust out sooner?" Ray said. "Maybe avoid all these people?"

"No. Anyway, where are you going to take him? Are you going to take him to the hospital? What about you, Buck? Don't you need to see about your hands?"

The boys were silent. Any response would likely cause more arguments from Lorrie as to why they should stay.

"Besides," she said, "Ray almost fell a few minutes ago."

"That so, Ray? Want to stay put here for a spell?" Buck felt a pill in his pocket and needed some water. "Mind if I use the bathroom, Lorrie?"

It was spotless except for a white hand towel soiled with dried blood and a smudge of dirt. Lorrie and Ray were talking in the other room. He turned the cold water on, washed the pill down, and splashed his face, holding the already used towel to his face. As he draped the towel over the rack he saw the compact Lorrie had taken from Wheaton & French next to a fancy cut-glass perfume bottle. Buck put the compact in his shirt pocket, snapped the flap closed, and went into the bedroom.

"Best we leave now, Ray. Unless you're planning on hanging around for the prayer meeting?"

"We could both use a little divine help, but better we skedaddle out of here." Ray picked up the white envelope and handed it to Lorrie. *Pasadena Playhouse* was lettered on the outside.

She put the envelope on a small table against the wall. Suddenly she looked flushed and began shifting nervously from foot to foot. Buck wondered if something had happened between Lorrie and Ray when they were alone here in Lorrie's room. Ray had been shirtless when he came out of the bathroom, and quickly had put his shirt on—backwards, and now the revelation that he'd given Lorrie a pearl necklace.

"He's got a place to stay." Buck said, avoiding Ray's startled expression..

"Where?" Lorrie persisted. "Besides, what if Mother comes back and wonders where you are, Buck?"

Both boys sighed. Buck said, "Tell her I had to see about my hands. Mind helping us out?"

"Well, I have been helping out I thought."

Ray poked Buck in the ribs.

"Lorrie," Buck said. "We couldn't do anything without you, and for sure you've helped Ray out. Soon as I get him back to town and settled, I'll call you."

Ray took a deep breath. It seemed all Lorrie's efforts to keep Ray with her were gone for the moment.

"Where are you parked?" she asked.

"Front."

"There's a side door just behind the main staircase. You can take it. It will be safer since some of the kids might be hanging around the front. I'll go with you."

"That ain't necessary, Lorrie," Ray said.

"Oh, yes it is. If Mother comes along, I can distract her."

They walked quietly and slowly down the main stairs, turning quickly toward the right at the foot of the stairs. All was quiet in the foyer as well as outside.

"Thanks, Lorrie." Ray touched her arm. "You don't want your mother coming in on all of us here." They hurried out the door.

CHAPTER EIGHT

The plains stretched east toward the horizon. A clean, flat, measured line in space. Buck wanted to drive to the edge of that line, stop where the blue ended close to the earth in the palest shade he could imagine, where it would be cool, and they could rest.

"Where you going?" Ray asked.

"Pauline's going to meet us at Spirit Rock."

"Mind telling me how that came about?"

"Yeah, I mind." He concentrated on trying to find the turnoff. A few feet later, he saw a dirt path that turned left and away from Seminary Drive. He pulled into a small clearing where his car would be out of sight, and got out. A high, flat-topped, red-tinged butte rose above the plain. It had a presence, a sense of power, or maybe authority, that unnerved him. A chill ran down his back.

"Pauline said she climbs that thing to the top. You ever climb it with her?" The butte cast a shadow that moved toward them as the sun began to lower in the sky.

"Hell no. It's some kind of ritual thing she does now and then to get close to her ancestors."

They moved to a stand of trees and sat on the ground, leaning against the narrow spines of the aspen. Buck pitched small rocks against the boulders opposite. "Any idea what to do if Pauline doesn't show up?"

"No reason to think she won't," Ray said. He pulled his knees to his chest and lowered his head so his forehead rested on his arms. A vein pulsed in his neck, so even and steady that Buck could count the beats. For a minute he thought his friend looked old, but then he only looked young and worn down.

"Wouldn't want to sit out here too long." It wasn't the isolation, though, or the inherent danger of their situation should they be discovered that worried him. He wanted to see Pauline.

"You don't have to wait, Buck. You've done enough. I can wait here on my own for Pauline."

Buck stood and walked to the edge of the gravel road. "You think I came through all this to leave you sitting alone on your skinny Mexican butt?" He kicked the ground and looked down the road.

Ray gave a low laugh. "Ever notice when you get riled at me, you stab at the ground with those cowboy boots?"

"Think she'll drive up this way, or come down Mesa?"

"The main road. Faster 'n Mesa."

Buck moved to the boulder and sat down. The sun had moved behind the high range and the air was already growing chill. Buck knew they'd have to do something soon. He cursed himself for not wearing his jacket and looked at Ray, looking cold and miserable, across from him. He got up again and pulled the blanket out of the trunk. "Here." He put it around Ray's shoulders.

"Thanks."

Buck sat down next to him and pulled some of the blanket over his own lap. "Want to tell me about the pearl necklace?"

Ray paused, perhaps hoping silence would make the question go away.

"I did a dumb thing, Buck. I saw the box after we'd come home from Ruby's. I couldn't figure him buying anything so fancy, so I opened it and saw the pearls. I held them up to the light and they shimmered against my hand, and all I could think of was Lorrie and how much I wanted to give her something beautiful like that."

"So you stole them," Buck said. *Like Lorrie stole the compact, that I just stole back.* "Did your old man buy them for Pauline?"

When he spoke, Ray's voice was tired. "Probably. When he found them in the pocket of my jacket he came at me with a knife. I was damn scared. He called me a *spic,* and said I'd wind up in jail the way I was headed." His voice cracked.

"That explains the blood," Buck said. "I saw dried blood on the door handle, and some on the stairs. Do you know where your dad went after the fight?"

"No. I just took off."

"That's okay. You best take it easy now." He wanted to say something to make Ray feel better somehow. "Besides, I won't let you get tossed in jail."

The wind and the scurry of animals were the only sounds as Buck began to consider how the consequences of their situation became more serious with each passing moment. What if he had to explain his absence to his parents? What if Perez came after him, maybe even after Lorrie? How would Lyle fit in to all this?

"You see any sign of my old man?" Ray asked suddenly.

Buck shook his head. "Art wants me to check out some trouble near the Bluffs."

"Pauline lives at the edge of the Bluffs," Ray said.

That was the punch Buck had not been expecting. He sucked in his breath hard a couple of times before standing and walking to the base of the monument.

Who are we? he thought. *Here in this dry, narrow place with rabbits and wild things, and a huge red rock towering over us with hints of spirits?* A lizard scuttled away. Now he was more worried about Pauline. What if Perez had followed her here and saw her helping them? He needed a plan to protect her.

Ray pulled a half-flattened cigarette from his pocket. "Any chance you got a match?"

"Nope."

Ray rolled the cigarette between his fingers. "Wish you'd take up at least one of my bad habits." The sound of a car coming from the cutoff toward them caught their attention.

Pauline's car turned off the road and pulled into the clearing. Buck supported Ray as they watched her walk through the fading light toward them. Buck felt Ray's body leaning on him. He didn't want his injuries to be serious; all he wanted now was a plan keep Pauline safe.

The wind brushed Pauline's hair away from her face, and Buck felt the same catch in his chest that he had when he'd first seen her. What he wanted seemed out of his control.

"I appreciate your helping me out here," Ray said. "Just be careful."

"Same to you."

Pauline folded her arms in front and considered both boys.

"How did you manage to get into this mess?"

"Wasn't my fault, Pauline," Ray said. "Damn prairie dog scuttled in front of me and I—"

"Why were you riding on Mesa at night? That's what I'd like to know."

Ray stared at the ground and hung on to Buck. They were both silent.

"You look terrible," Pauline said. "To tell the truth, neither one of you look too good. You can explain later. All of it." She put one arm around his shoulder and together with Buck, they helped settle Ray in her pickup.

She walked back with Buck to his car.

"I don't think he needs a doctor," Buck said. "He has some scratches might need tending to."

"Thanks for all you did for Ray today."

Buck got in his car and rolled down the window. "Did you talk to Lyle Samuels? Does he know Ray's coming?"

She touched his hands. "Are your hands okay? Can you drive?"

"Yep." He looked at her.

She smiled. "What were you thinking about?"

"When?"

"When I got out of my truck, you were watching me."

"I was thinking about how much I want to always see you walking toward me."

She was quiet, looking at him. "That's a very sweet thing to say."

"Don't know as I mean it sweet."

"I know how you mean it."

Ray blasted the horn and she waved. "Lyle lives on Miguel Avenue, near the college. You'll go by and see Ray, won't you? He needs you."

"Like to come by and see you if that's okay."

The sound of distant laughter from the Seminary drifted toward them.

"We'll see," she said.

"You live up by the Bluffs?"

She nodded, and then hesitated as though some thought flashed through her mind. "Maybe it's just as well you don't come by, Buck."

His heart thumped. "I have to scout out a story up there. Rumors about somebody sneaking around. You'll be careful, okay?" He felt helpless. Other than staking out her house, he didn't have a plan to protect her.

"Sure." She started toward her pickup. Buck leaned his head against the steering wheel briefly, and then looked straight ahead. It was almost dark. Ray gave a push on the horn.

Pauline called to him to wait a minute, and came back to Buck's car.

"Why are you so worried? People are always telling stories about the Bluffs. Everything from wild coyotes to drunk cowboys."

"It's Ray's old man. I'm just worried he'll be taking things out on Ray's friends." The memory of Pauline's battered face haunted him.

She waited and watched him, then spoke. "You can come by if you want. Gray frame house at the beginning of the road to the Bluffs. You can't miss it. Pink and purple geraniums in front." She walked back to her truck.

The whomp he'd felt in his stomach eased. He watched the red taillights of her truck turn left at the end of the cutoff. What were they talking about? What secrets were they sharing with each other, while he tried to understand how quickly the desire to be part of another person's life had surfaced? Driving home, he wondered if Ray would tell Pauline about the pearls.

CHAPTER NINE

He couldn't go home and he couldn't return to the Seminary. He drove downtown, and pulled to the curb next to the park to settle his mind. He needed to be careful, but of what he wasn't sure. He rested his forehead against the steering wheel, the motor idling. Now his head ached as much as his body still did.

A tap on the half-open car window startled him and he jumped. "Geez!"

"Sorry, son." It was Officer West. "Didn't mean to startle you." Buck rolled the window all the way down and hoped the policeman couldn't see his dirty shirt and jeans. "Any particular reason you're resting here?"

"Thought I heard my engine knocking."

West looked at his car. "Appears to sound okay now."

Buck hadn't realized he'd left the motor running. He shut it off.

"Seem to run into you a lot lately, Buck."

He wanted to say West should mind his own business, and poised himself for handcuffing on the charge of being too visible. "On my way to the *Gazette*. Have some catching up to do."

West stepped back. "You feel okay? You look a little pale."

"Just get out of breath now and then."

"Still troubled by that asthma?"

Eventually everything that happened in town got back to Wheaton & French, so half the town knew he had bad asthma. He started his car.

West said, "Give my regards to Art Packer."

"Yessir. Say, Officer, you hear of any trouble down by the trailer park south of town?"

"There's always some kind of trouble down there, usually between the Mexicans and white trash. Why?"

Buck swallowed the sick feeling rising from the policeman's words. "Just following up on a story."

He drove to the *Gazette* office and went in through the rear door. Art sat on a high, three-legged stool at his slanted worktable, laying advertising copy. He took in Buck's ragged appearance and Buck was sorry he hadn't gone home to clean up first.

"What the devil happened to you?" Art turned off the light and stared at Buck.

Buck considered telling him he'd had to change a flat up in the foothills, but Art was a fair man and deserved the truth.

Besides, he was sick of half-imagined stories floating in his brain. He poured a cup of water from the cooler. His wheezing was loud enough to hear in the whole office.

"Gotta get my inhalator." He went out the back door and returned with the canister.

They waited for Buck's anxiety to ease, his breathing to clear. Art sat at his desk and watched Buck "Maybe you should run by the emergency room, Buck. I can drive you if you're not feeling up to it." He paused. "Shouldn't you call your folks?"

"No to both ideas. I've had spells like this before."

"You hear of any trouble in town lately?" Art changed the subject.

"Trouble?"

"Horace Wheaton's worried that some petty theft might be going on in the drugstore. Nothing certain, but that's Horace for you. I'd like you to talk to him, see if there's anything there."

Buck nodded.

Art waited. "Did you make it to the Seminary?"

Buck nodded again.

"The police blotter has a report of a break-in up there. Did you see anything when you were there?"

Buck paused, knowing he could trust this man, but not wanting to involve him. He wanted to solve things himself, but he was having trouble sorting through it all. First the petty theft, and then the break-in.

"My buddy, Ray Perez, was banged up pretty bad in a

motorcycle crash on Mesa Road. He went to the Seminary for help, but the way he looked and being Mexican and all, he figured they'd call the cops instead of helping him. So he broke in."

Art waited.

"It's a mess, Art. Ray hid out in Lorrie's room—"

"Wait," Art interrupted. "Lorraine Rathburn?"

Buck nodded. "Ray's interested in her."

"So that's why he went to the Seminary?" His tone was incredulous.

"I don't think that was his idea in the beginning, but now, I don't know. All I know is when Lorrie's mother took me to Lorrie's room, Ray was there, and he'd given her a pearl necklace."

Art stood up, walked to the file cabinet, and pulled out a bottle of Scotch. "You're too young to drink this stuff and I'm too old to take in your story."

"It's no story, Art. It's the truth." He watched Art pour some of the liquor into a glass and wondered why adults always seemed to think that alcohol was the answer to problems. "I believe I can handle a little of that." He might as well try it.

The older man poured a short amount in a coffee cup. "Take it easy. If it starts you coughing, I'm taking you to the ER."

They sat in the dim newspaper office, sipping.

"Tell me about the pearl necklace."

"Ray's old man . . . father . . . bought it to give to Pauline. "

Art held up his hand for Buck to stop. "Just who is Pauline?"

"Sorry," Buck said. "Pauline is the girl I told you about; the one I saw beat up in Wheaton & French the night after the dance." He skipped the details about his emerging feelings for her.

Art had another drink and poured a bit more for Buck. "You have some decisions to make, Buck, and they're not going to be easy. Maybe Ray and Lorrie need to solve their own problems, but I'm worried about you getting involved with an Indian woman, not to mention one who's older than you and who might have a relationship with Perez. I've heard about him, seen police pickup reports on him. You need to think about her, too. From what you say, apart from the fact she's beautiful, she sounds kindhearted. You don't want to put her in danger."

"There's one more thing." He told Art he'd seen the compact in Lorrie's bathroom and taken the compact back.

Art sighed. "When you go to interview Horace Wheaton, tell him you found it and return it." He stood and put on his jacket. "Connect with what you know, Buck. Go from there. I'd like to think there's a newspaper story in this mess, but right now I'm tempted to say you have the beginning of a tragic novel. Maybe it's part of growing up, but it seems to me you're making it pretty hard on yourself. Sleep on everything. Stay away from everybody and we'll talk tomorrow." He turned to the door, then back to Buck. "If you want a place to clean up before you go home, you can swing by my house."

"Thanks. I figure I'll head home."

"Fit the piece about Lorrie in with the Retreat," Lyle said. "And remember your objectivity needs some focus. So far you've concentrated on research, but if you want to be a writer you need to consider deadlines. I've been too easy on you. Have the article copy ready by noon tomorrow."

Alone, Buck felt like he couldn't do the simplest thing. He wasn't able to keep track of what he felt, let alone what was happening. He wanted to write about things to see them more clearly, but all he had were bits and pieces of stories that he was helpless to put together and now he had a deadline to meet.

He called her house first, hoping she'd left the Seminary. Lorrie answered on the second ring.

"Hey," he said. "Art wants more for the article about you as Miss Rodeo Queen." She said nothing. "Sorry. I don't mean to be rude. It's just that I have a deadline."

"More? I thought you had everything. Is that all you're going to talk to me about?"

He didn't want to talk to her about this or anything right now. "I haven't got all day, Lorrie." He took a raspy breath. "Just tell me how you felt."

Another long pause. "How I felt? What on earth do you mean?"

He was about to tell her to forget it, when she answered: "I felt like it was the beginning."

"Say what?"

"Of my acting career. Just like you working at a newspaper now so you can write later. Miss Rodeo Queen was a way to show that I could win." She paused. "And I loved the attention, too."

He hung up before she could pin him down about anything else. After all Art was doing for him, at least he could come up with something.

Western Rodeo Week Celebrations in Eagle Springs

A major event in Eagle Springs' annual Western Rodeo Week was the crowning of Lorrie Rathburn as Miss Rodeo Queen of 1956. "It was an honor," Lorrie said. Lorrie is a drama major at Mountain States High and hopes for a career in acting.

Summer Youth Retreat a Success
Another annual event was the Youth Retreat held by First Presbyterian at the Seminary, known to residents of Eagle Springs as the Castle. Close to twenty-five students from Mountain States High attended and joined in songs, prayer, and good food. This event is a nostalgic farewell to summer and opens the door to fall classes and renewing friendships.

There was a report of a break-in at the Seminary, but after a brief investigation it was determined that an animal may have broken a basement window. No one was injured and no theft was discovered.

He couldn't stop thinking about Pauline; about her beauty and the sense of calm and confidence she had. Even if he could find a way to protect her, would she let him? He knew with certainty that his life would change from this point on; whatever he had to do to be near Pauline, he'd find a way.

He drove through the familiar streets of town and onto the tedious strech of highway between Eagle Springs and Denver.

He didn't want to go home, so he went to Wheaton & French. A housewife was choosing a perfume, a businessman was picking up a prescription, and a soldier stood looking at paperbacks. There was no sign of Horace Wheaton. That interview could wait.

"Coffee and a package of cheese crackers," he said to the kid behind the fountain. He put his journal on the counter without opening it. He wanted to write something, anything, but his hands hurt too much, and all that came to mind was Pauline's truck driving away and how long it might be until he could see her again.

"Too early for a Chinook," a deep, serious voice said. Arturo Perez sat down on the stool next to him. "Coffee," he said, and the kid behind the fountain peered at him through lowered eyes, as though calculating how fast to run if he had to.

"Yessir. Guess so."

"Never understand why these mountain winds gets folks so riled up. You?"

"No sir. Doesn't rile me at all." Buck coughed.

"Ain't you Buck, Ray's friend?"

He nodded. His breathing was becoming wheezy. He'd had a chance to take medicine at the *Gazette* but he hadn't.

"Call me Arturo. Any friend of Ray's is a friend of mine."

Buck remembered the dead weight of the man, the smell, when he'd helped Ray haul him into the trailer. He pictured Ray standing over this man, the baseball bat swinging loosely from his hand. He took a swallow of coffee.

Perez had rolled his shirtsleeves up to his elbows and Buck saw a wide, thick band of gauze wrapped around his forearm. He looked sideways and saw one cheek was bruised and the trace of a black eye was visible. *At least Ray didn't kill him.*

"You ain't seen Ray lately, have you?"

"No sir." His heart thumped. "Saw him at the square dance the other night."

Perez nodded and tapped a long finger against the journal.

"That something you scribble in?"

"Yes. It's my journal, sir . . . Mr. Perez."

Perez stared at him, uncomprehendingly.

"I want to be a writer, so now and then I just write down my ideas."

"Writer? Don't say. What ideas do you write down?"

"Nothing much. Some poems." He paused. "I'm starting to get some assignments from the *Gazette* though."

Perez lit a cigarette. There were scratches on the tops of his hands, and he looked as if he hadn't slept for a while. He blew a thin trail of cigarette smoke in front of him. In the mirror Buck saw other customers glaring at him, and Mr. French watched from the back of the store. For a moment Buck felt a quick surge of sympathy for Perez, for the unwanted attention he drew, for his failed relationship with Ray, for whatever bitterness made him so mean and angry.

"You happen to know a Pauline Moon, Buck?"

A slow shudder started low in Buck's solar plexus. This was the first time he'd heard her last name. He started coughing and drank some water. His breathing turned shallow and it seemed everyone was looking at him.

"She's a friend of me and Ray. Thing is"—Perez took a swallow of coffee—"I bought her this pretty little pearl necklace, a choker they call it. Bought it right across the street at Beckman's Fine Jewelry. They looked at me like I was an escapee from the state pen. Like all these white folks are lookin' at me now. Hope I'm not embarrassing you, Buck?"

"No, Mr. Perez. You're not embarrassing me." His heart sank at the confirmation that the pearls were meant for Pauline.

"No. 'Course not. Ray's your best friend." He took another gulp of black coffee. "Seed pearls, the clerk called 'em, but I knew she was wondering what a *spic* like me was doing in a fine jewelry store like Beckman's buying tiny pearls."

Buck jammed his journal into the canvas bag and slipped the strap across his chest.

"Wrapped in white paper with a maroon satin ribbon."

"Sounds nice."

"Well, Buck. They're gone." Perez looked down at the counter as though considering whether or not to bang his fist on it.

Buck's breath was coming in short gasps. He had to get home or to the ER, and neither option was what he wanted.

"The box was on the kitchen counter and poof!" Perez snapped his fingers and the kid behind the counter gave a little jump. "Just like that, I can't find the damn necklace anywhere. Funny thing, I can't find Ray anywhere either." His eyes narrowed.

"When, that is if, I see him, Mr. Perez, I'll tell him he better get on home."

Perez nodded again and stood as if waiting for Buck. A hush shifted through the drugstore.

Mr. French, the pharmacist, suddenly appeared next to him. "Buck, I've been watching you. I can hear you wheezing. If you don't get to the emergency room, I'll have someone take you there. Do you want me to call your folks?"

"I'll call 'em from the hospital."

"Do you have enough medicine? I can give you something now to get you by for the moment."

"No, thanks." Buck headed for the door with Perez behind him.

"Damn wind sure makes people crazy," Perez said again. He kept walking beside Buck as he turned the corner.

Anxiety triggered the coughing again and he bent over, coughing up phlegm into a wad of napkins he'd grabbed.

"Careful there." Perez grabbed Buck's arm. "You almost fell."

"Tell you the truth, Mr. Perez, I need to get to the emergency room."

Perez stared at Buck as though not comprehending.

"Asthma attack," Buck croaked.

"Be pleased to go along with you if you need help. There's a bus stop by the hospital. Maybe I can ride that far with you?"

"Sure." His voice was a squeak and he was too weak to protest.

The hospital was several blocks north, near the college. Buck took the street with the least traffic, but had only gone a few blocks before he had to pull over. He was paicked, not sure if he could drive himself. He gripped the steering wheel and rested his forehead on his hands. He could feel the sweat. Next to him, Perez was still and watching him.

"Mr. Perez," he gasped, "if you don't mind, would you drive me to the emergency room?" He slid across the seat while Arturo Perez walked around the car and got in. Perez didn't speak, and drove carefully as though the slightest bump would injure Buck, who was now slumped against the window. He parked near the ER entrance and supported Buck as they walked along a curved driveway to the door

One person was in the waiting room, reading a magazine. Perez led Buck to a chair and Buck immediately bent over, his head almost between his knees, his breath coming in loud gasps.

"This boy's having a real hard time," he said to the registration nurse. "He says it's asthma. His name's Buck Malone."

"And you are?"

"He's a friend of my son."

He sat on the edge of the chair next to Buck as though unwilling to leave until he was sure Buck was taken care of. He took car keys from his pocket and gave them to Buck.

"Put these in your pocket. Your car's parked on the corner near Navajo Street. Think you'll be okay now," and without a word to the nurse, he left.

The nurse recorded the fact that a Mexican man had, rather gently, helped a young white boy into the ER and immediately left. Although Buck was wet with sweat from coughing and anxiety, in the artificial glare of the ER room, everything seemed clearer to Buck.

When the doctor asked if he'd already called his parents, Buck lied and said yes. He was admitted him to intensive care, given an IV, and had to breathe through a nebulizer until his lungs cleared. Only then did he realize that Perez had left and he hadn't thanked him.

When he was discharged two hours later, the ER doctor gave him a small plastic device, a rescue inhalator he called it.

"It's more portable than the one you've been using, and can fit in your pocket. Always carry it with you. If you would have had this today, you could have avoided this attack."

His car was just around the corner. There was no sign of Perez, but Buck had assumed he'd be long gone by now. He felt the inhalator in his pocket and was instantly relieved.

Having this would spare him the panic of not being able to control an attack.

Above the mountain range, the western sky had taken on the dark and mottled look of an old bruise, and as Buck headed through town and north to the Bluffs, the image of Arturo Perez driving him to the hospital, as well as the information he'd revealed, lay fresh in Buck's mind.

THINGS ONCE BRIGHT

CHAPTER TEN

The Bluffs rose like a vague accumulation of ash at the end of the road. When he was a kid, Buck had ridden his bike here, excited by the eerie, dune like shapes of ancient volcanic powder mixed with prairie dust. The wind shifted their shapes, so the dunes looked different each time he came here. Looking around now, he realized how easy it would be for someone to sneak around and hide in the shadows.

He'd been sure to put the portable inhalator in his pocket, glad for the sense of security it gave him. He spotted the small, gray frame house near the corner. Flower boxes of marigolds, and of pink and purple geraniums, hung from the narrow porch rail. At the end of a path worn through the grass, a black pickup was parked beneath an elm tree.

He killed the engine and sat in his car. What was he thinking? Why had he come here? She'd said they could talk again, but did she mean this soon after they'd met? What would he say? He only knew he didn't want to turn back. He got out and walked around the truck toward the backyard, where a stand of aspen trees, their leaves twittering in the wind, stood against a wood fence.

He stepped around the truck and stopped. Straight ahead, Pauline stood looking at him. She was holding a sheet that billowed at one corner where she was about to hang it on a clothesline.

"Hey," he said, his voice cracking.

"Hey, yourself. I didn't hear you."

"Parked in front. Didn't mean to get you at a bad time."

She stared for another minute before stretching the sheet across the line and securing the end with a clothespin.

"This is a good time." She picked up a large wicker basket. "I just finished the laundry." She shaded her eyes and looked at him; his heart started beating lickety-split. "What brings you up here, Buck?"

"You mentioned we might have a little talk." He shuffled, raising a haze of reddish dirt. She still watched him, the basket balanced on her hip. He tipped the brim of his hat back and looked at her. "Truth is, I came to see you." He cleared his throat. "Can I take that basket for you?"

She didn't speak at first. "No. Can I offer you a lemonade?" She headed to the back porch.

"That'd be swell."

She went inside and Buck sat on the back porch swing, watching the wind kick up small whorls of dust near the cluster of aspen trees. He wanted to remember the smallest details so when he wrote about this moment years later it would be as real in his memory as it was now. He stretched his legs in front of him, feeling the motion of the swing's slight movement from the wind. He tried to understand his feelings, but only one thing was clear. For the first time in his life, he wanted someone all his own. He wanted Pauline.

She pushed the screen door open with one arm, put two tall glasses of lemonade on the small wood table in front of them, and sat next to him. He watched her until she turned and looked at him.

"You're staring."

"Sorry." He kept looking at her.

"Have you seen Ray yet?" She pushed the swing and it began to sway again.

"Not yet. He doing okay at Mr. Samuels' place?"

She paused. "It's hard to tell. Ray tends to keep things inside."

Buck leaned forward and looked at the wood planks on the porch floor. They were swept clean. A spider crept through a crack and stopped. "Wonder why Ray's like that?" The spider crawled along the floor. From the corner of his eye, he saw Pauline's bare foot pushing the swing. When he sat up, he saw she'd been watching him.

"What do you mean?"

He leaned back. "The way he goes to Mesa Road alone, running that bike almost like he's trying to hurt himself."

"Ray pretends to be tough but underneath he's . . ." She hesitated. "Uncertain, I guess I'd call it." She looked at the distant ridge of mountains. "Or scared."

"Scared of what?" Scared of his father, or scared of the town and its attitude toward Mexicans? Was he scared of getting involved with Lorrie?

The wind turned warm and he remembered Perez talking about the Chinook and the pearls, and he knew he should say something to Pauline, but he didn't know how to bring it up. Besides, Ray was the one who had swiped them and given them to Lorrie—he should say something.

"People can be scared about a lot of things that seem harmless," she added.

She watched him closely and then stood, looking at the mountains silhouetted in the distance. "I was just going to fix a sandwich. Are you hungry?"

"Don't mean to put you to any trouble."

"You're not putting me to any trouble. It's nice to have somebody to talk to." She held the screen door open for him. "Keep me company?"

The kitchen was a large room with a wide, square table in the center and four chairs around it. A bowl of apples sat in the middle. From the window above the sink the mountains rose in a blue haze. The room was clean and spare and he thought of the rows of spice jars, and tins with cookies and coffee and sugar lining his mother's kitchen counters.

A radio played softly in the background and he watched her until she put down two plates, each with a cheese sandwich, and a bowl of chips on the table. She brought them each a cold beer. It tasted good.

"Ray wants to be a painter," she said. "What are you interested in?"

"Writing. I want to write novels."

"That's exciting. Does working at the paper help you?"

"The editor supports me. I don't get a lot of understanding at home, from my dad anyway. It doesn't help that I can't come up with a clear idea on how to be a writer. A lot of writers got started writing for newspapers." He paused. "My dad pretty much likes things all laid out."

"And dreams are hard to lay out." She took a drink of the beer.

Outside, the wind was picking up. "Maybe. Lately I've been thinking."

She rested her elbow on the table, her chin in her hand. "About what?"

"Naw. It's just a dumb thought."

"Oh come on. I bet you've never had a dumb thought."

"I'm not used to talking about some things, but sometimes I think it's not real smart to hang on to a dream. There's too much ahead that can take it away."

"You're too young to be pessimistic, Buck. It's important to dream, otherwise you have no future to look forward to and maybe no way to understand what's going on now. Those are good things for a writer to know."

She smiled at him and he wished his stomach would stop feeling like an icy lake with rocks being tossed into it.

"How about you, Pauline?" He took a drink of beer. "You must dream about something."

She didn't answer right away and he wished he hadn't pried. Then she spoke. "I've always wanted to be a painter."

"Ray told me how you taught him to sketch when he was a kid."

"He did, did he?" She leaned back and her hair fell over the back of the chair and he ached for wanting to touch it, but she sat up quickly, almost self-consciously. He wanted everything to stop. To go back to the moment he'd first seen her hanging clothes. He didn't want to say what he was about to, but he did.

"I ran into Ray's father at Wheaton & French." He pushed the beer bottle around in small circles. She watched him silently. "He asked if I'd seen Ray and I said no. Asked me to tell Ray that his old man's looking for him."

Late-summer moths, dry and dusty, beat against the screen door.

"Mind if I get some water?" he asked.

She walked to the sink and poured a glass, setting it on the table in front of him, and sitting down again to watch him.

Why had he started this? "He asked me if I knew a Pauline Moon." He gulped the water. This would be the time to use his inhalator, but he didn't want to.

She hadn't moved, but still watched him. The screen door banged lightly in the wind, like a thin invitation for escape.

"He told me that he'd bought a pearl necklace for you and it had disappeared. He started asking me if I knew where Ray might be, like maybe he thought Ray had something to do with taking it."

"And," she said very slowly. "You know where it is? This pearl necklace?"

He nodded. "Pauline, I'm real sorry I brought any of this up. Fact is, Ray should be telling you all of this."

"Then why are you telling me?"

His stomach dropped. He felt dizzy and stupid and didn't know why he was telling her except he was afraid for her. Thunder rolled deep in the mountains. He didn't want Perez to hurt Pauline again; that was all he cared about. That and wanting to see Pauline every day for the rest of his life.

"Ray took the necklace. I don't think he meant to keep it, but his old man saw it in Ray's jacket pocket and took a knife to him. That's where the blood in the trailer came from. Ray still had the jewelry box with him when he hid out in the Seminary. Lorrie spotted the box and figured it was for her."

"So, you're telling me that Lorrie Rathburn is wearing a pearl necklace Arturo Perez meant to give to me."

Buck glumly nodded.

"And you're telling me that Ray was hiding out in Lorrie's room at the Seminary."

He nodded again.

"And you are also telling me that Arturo Perez, whom you scarcely know, told you all this? About buying the necklace for me?" She took another long drink of beer. "Why would he do that, Buck? Tell you all this?"

It had never occurred to him to wonder about that.

"Probably because he didn't know where Ray was and he knows me 'n' Ray hang out together." He groaned inwardly. Now he'd have to tell Ray about his father meeting him at Wheaton & French.

As if reading his mind, Pauline said, "Does Ray know about this conversation?"

Buck shook his head. "Haven't had a chance. There's something else."

She looked disbelievingly at him.

"The situation triggered a bad asthma attack at the drugstore. He followed me out and asked if I could give him a lift to the bus stop, but after a few blocks I was in such bad shape I had to ask him to drive me to the emergency room."

Buck paused, almost imagining he was writing a story, it sounded so unbelievable. "He saved my life, Pauline. I would have collapsed, maybe crashed my car, if he hadn't helped me. After he took me to the ER, he just disappeared." He grew quiet, then said, "I should have thanked him."

She left the beer on the table and he followed her as she walked into the front room. Like the kitchen, it was another large room, sparsely furnished with a couch in front of a wide picture window. A chair and a trunk with a quilt folded on top were next to a stone fireplace.

"The fact is, Pauline, I worry about you and I want to see you again and nothing's likely to change that. Guess I thought if you knew about Perez telling me all this, you'd be safer, but now I'm not even sure about that."

"You don't need to worry about me where Arturo is concerned." She touched his arm lightly and led him onto the porch. "You need to tell Ray what Arturo said. His father can be unpredictable."

She started across the lawn toward his car. "And it might be wise to tell Lorrie not to wear the necklace in public."

She looked into the distance, avoiding looking too closely at Buck. "You shouldn't be thinking about me either. I know you're smart enough to see the problems of seeing me again."

"I wish you wouldn't think that way. There's no way I'm not going to worry about you. Besides, I'm getting to know you better every day." He smiled.

She crossed her arms and shook her head, but she was smiling.

He stepped off the curb, then back up. He stood as close to her as he dared, then moved closer.

"Okay if I come by? Make sure everything's okay?"

She looked up the deserted street toward the Bluffs and he was afraid she was thinking of something else and didn't hear him.

"I'm not sure that's such a good idea."

His heart sank. "Don't mean to be personal, but mind saying why it would be a bad idea?"

She looked across at the foothills, and then down at the grass they stood on.

"Well maybe it's not a bad idea exactly. I guess that's not quite what I meant." She tilted her head and looked up at him.

"Besides, that is a personal question."

"Sorry." He put his hands in the pockets of his jeans and rocked back and forth on the heels of his boots. "Then how's about I come by tomorrow?"

She laughed lightly. "Tomorrow?"

"'Bout six be okay?"

"Six! In the morning?"

"Breakfast."

She laughed and took a step back from the curb. "Do you behave this way with all girls you first meet?"

"What way?" He took a step toward her, remembering her arm around him on Mesa Road, her head on his shoulder when they danced. "Sorry if I seem pushy, but I get hungry early, and that cheese sandwich was the best I've ever had."

"Oh, for heaven's sake." She laughed. "Well, maybe wait a day or two."

He stepped off the curb again. "Reckon I'll go see Ray now. Thanks again." He walked as slowly as he could, counting the steps until he heard her call him.

"I suppose if you want to come by tomorrow it's okay. But make it closer to eight."

"Yes ma'am." He turned. "But you might check at six just to be sure I'm not frozen. Gets cold up here."

By the time he got into his car, she had gone inside.

* * *

It was not yet dusk, and late-afternoon light filtered through the thin curtains in the dining room. The breeze coming through the half-open window lifted the edge of a curtain and it felt good. He grabbed a handful of popcorn from the bowl on the table and sat on the piano bench. Just as he was about to call Ray, the phone rang.

"Honestly, Buck, I've been calling the *Gazette* and your house all morning. Where have you been?" Lorrie said.

A hint of irritation came through his voice. "Maybe I don't want people to know where I am."

Silence. "Well, I'm sorry. I wasn't trying to be snoopy."

He took a swallow of Coke and waited for her to say why she'd called.

"We made a date last week to have pizza at Giuseppe's tonight. Maybe even see a movie after."

He'd forgotten. "I'm pretty done in, Lorrie. Thought I'd take it easy. Besides, isn't the Retreat still going on?"

"Well, maybe just pizza then?"

Something particular was on Lorrie's mind?

There was a pause and Buck considered how quickly situations were piling up around him. Pizza sounded good, but being with Lorrie sounded complicated.

"No."

He pictured her clasping and unclasping her hands the way she did when she was trying to distract people.

"You left the Seminary so fast I didn't have time to see if we were still going out tonight."

If he'd already made a date with her it would be better to keep it than set her wondering. "Just pizza, okay?"

"Okay. Pick me up at the Seminary?"

He groaned at the idea of taking her back after dinner. "You staying up there tonight?"

"You don't need to make this sound like such an ordeal."

He agreed to meet her at the Seminary and left a note on the kitchen table saying he was having dinner with Lorrie and would be home later. He gathered his book bag and notebook and headed to Wheaton & French.

* * *

Outside, the sky had turned slate gray and thunder rolled across the mountains as he parked in front of Wheaton & French. He saw Horace Wheaton hovering near some college girls who were debating what color rouge or face powder to buy.

"Hey, Mr. Wheaton," Buck said. "Art Packer wanted me to talk to you about something missing?"

"He told me you might be coming along." He led Buck back to a small area near the pharmacy and sat behind a table cluttered with papers. Buck sat on a folding chair opposite. "Actually, Buck, you were here when the disappearance happened."

Buck averted his eyes, concentrating on opening his notebook. "How's that, Mr. Wheaton?"

"The day you and Lorraine Rathburn were here. You might remember I couldn't find a little compact I'd been showing her?"

So far there was nothing accusing in his tone. "Now that you mention it, I do remember it. You haven't spotted it yet?"

Mr. Wheaton shook his head. "I don't think it's enough to fuss over. It wasn't expensive, but it made me think that over the last few months, other little things have gone missing. One of those nice handheld mirrors, a little glass bottle. Like I say, nothing expensive, but it troubles me."

"Yes sir. I can see that." He made useless scribbles on his notepad, remembering the small, cut-glass bottle he'd seen in Lorrie's room.

"I'll be honest"—Horace Wheaton smiled and leaned forward—"I think Art's a little hard up for news if he figures there's a story in this."

"Did you talk to the police?"

Mr. Wheaton shook his head.

"You want us to write a little something in the paper? Maybe you can describe the item?"

He shook his head again. "I don't think so. If it happens again, I might want something said."

*   *   *

At the Seminary he parked out of sight of the main doors, cracked the window, and let the high mountain air fill his lungs. He slid down and rested his head against the seat back, until tapping on the passenger window broke his reverie. He leaned over and opened the door for Lorrie.

"Honestly, Buck. You could have parked closer. It's all muddy here." She slammed the car door, pulled a cloth from her purse and started cleaning barely visible smudges on her leg. "I might as well have been invisible. What were you thinking about?"

"Nothing." He pulled down Seminary Drive and headed toward town.

"Why don't you take Mesa Road?" She smoothed her skirt.

"Why would I do that?"

Lorrie leaned forward and turned the radio on. "I wondered if we could go to Ruby's instead."

"Why would you want to go there?"

"I like the music."

He looked at her from the corner of his eye. "Never knew you to like country bands."

"Maybe there's a lot you don't know about me."

He didn't say anything.

"All the kids from the Retreat will be at Giuseppe's and I'm tired of them. They're so noisy." She curled her legs on the seat, shifting closer to Buck. He saw that she was wearing the pearls.

They reached the center of town and Buck pulled into a space next to the park.

"I just feel like going someplace different. I liked Ruby's the other night."

You liked Ray the other night. "It won't be open early like this, Lorrie. We can go another time."

"Where do you and Ray go when you just want to talk?"

"Generally we talk in the car." He wondered what was on her mind. "We can sit in the park there, if you want."

"No."

He looked at the familiar corner, at the way it was a part of his life that he'd taken for granted. The park, the high school, Wheaton & French. Behind them the impressive stone entrance to the Twin Towers Hotel rising against the backdrop of the mountains. In all of this he could think of no place they could just sit and talk.

"Have you seen Ray yet?" she asked.

"No."

"Where is he? Is he back at the trailer?"

"He's staying with a friend."

"A friend? What does that mean? Is he staying with you?" She pressed him for more information that he didn't want to give.

"Lorrie, I have an idea. Let's go to the Village Inn and have a burger. We can talk better there."

"Why won't you tell me where Ray is staying?"

"Because I don't think he wants everybody to know."

She looked at him. "Since when am I everybody, Buck? Remember, I helped both of you?" Her voice cracked. "You know, don't you?"

"He's staying with Lyle Samuels at his house." It was easier to give in to her.

"Well, that's funny. Why's he staying with the art teacher?"

"Don't know."

She watched him. "You must have some idea."

"No, Lorrie. I have no idea."

He felt the pressure of the compact in his pocket, together with the knowledge that Ray had stolen the necklace intended for Pauline, that Lorrie now wore.

She looked out the side window and when she spoke, he heard the catch in her voice. "Maybe could I go with you? When you see Ray, I mean?"

"I'm not sure just when I'm going by, but I'll tell him you want to see him, Lorrie." He started the car.

"Oh, that's okay. Now that I think about it, Giuseppe's sounds fine."

In the end, then, they went to Giuseppe's, where Lorrie glowed in the attention. She took the best table by the window, and smiled at the college boys looking at the cute little blonde who had nabbed their table.

"The Fine Arts Players are holding auditions for a production of *Picnic* in September," she said. "Maurice Salis is the director. It would mean so much for me to get a part in that play. I just bet he knows all kinds of people in Hollywood who could help me."

"Maybe you best take one thing at a time. Seems a bit early to be planning on Hollywood."

"Don't you think I'd be perfect for the part of Madge?" She ran her fingers through her hair and smiled at a college boy who'd been watching her.

"I don't know anything about the play," Buck grumbled, and wanted to leave. The waitress came to their table.

"The works," he said, giving the order. "Any chance I could have a beer?"

"Any chance you're eighteen?"

He didn't answer, but when she came back she brought a beer for him and a Coke for Lorrie.

"Didn't you see the movie? Honestly, Buck. The part Kim Novak played."

He hadn't seen the movie and he wasn't sorry.

"I'd never play the part of Millie. Twice in the first two minutes of the play she says 'ornery bastard,' but she's nothing but a tomboy." She stared out the window. "No," she said quietly. "I'd never take that part."

She talked about the play and the audition and Buck thought how, of all the girls he knew at Mountain States High, he didn't know one who would come right out and say she wanted to be an actress. He remembered seeing the envelope from Pasadena Playhouse in her room and realized she had no intention of hanging around Eagle Springs. He wondered if Ray knew.

She asked him to take her home, not back to the Seminary, and was quiet until he pulled to the curb in front of her house.

"Will you tell Ray I'd like to talk to him, Buck? Please? Ask him to meet me at Wheaton & French tomorrow morning at ten o'clock?"

"Sure."

"I'd feel so much better if you'd ask him. Maybe Mr. Samuels wouldn't approve of a girl calling a boy." And then she was gone, her skirt swaying in the night breeze.

CHAPTER ELEVEN

Buck drove to Lyle Samuels's house later that day. It was dusk, and Ray sat on the porch steps. Moths fluttered around the yellow porch light, its beam of light spreading across the grass.

Ray walked to the car and slid into the passenger side. "Hey."

"Hey." Buck pulled from the curb, turned at the corner, and headed back to town. "Village Inn?"

"Coop movie showing at the Chief," Ray said.

"Frontier Classic Western Movie Week," Buck said. "*High Noon*. Seen the damn thing twice already."

Ray laughed. "You're a good ole cowboy." He lit a cigarette. "Welcome sight to see you."

"Sorry about not calling sooner. Did you get your bike?"

"Yeah. Lyle helped me get it. Dang thing don't run, though."

"It's just good you got it before Eagle Springs PD spotted it."

"The Chief Theatre," Buck said as they settled into seats in the back row. "Once used for the ritual sacrifice of virgins, has now fallen into such a sorry state that if you leave your feet on the floor, rats'll eat your shoes."

Ray slumped down in the seat next to him. "Sounds like the makings of one of those romance novels I spotted in Lorrie's room."

The Movietone *News* came on just as Theresa Gonzales and Rosa Santos came in. They paused when they saw Ray, and then sat across the aisle. Rosa was a pretty girl, dark and slim. Buck knew Ray had gone out with her. Theresa was another story. A gang member, she was rough-looking and mean. She lit a cigarette and slid down in the seat, and Buck remembered Lorrie telling him that Theresa scared her. How she talked about the gang she was in and that she'd lost her virginity to be a member.

"You picked a great day to come to the movies," Buck mumbled.

"Ignore them," Ray said.

"I mean to. Don't have to tell me that."

When the movie ended, they didn't wait for the houselights to flicker on and left before the others.

Outside, it had started to rain and they stood under the marquee, watching the big drops hit the sidewalk.

"I'm goddamn sick of this movie." Buck grumbled and kicked at the sidewalk.

Theresa and Rosa came out and stood across from the boys, looking at the rain.

"Want a cup of coffee?" Buck asked. Ray shook his head, and they hurried to Buck's car.

"Any reason Lorrie would be afraid of Theresa?"

"How would I know? You think just because I'm a Mexican I'm supposed to know about every other Mexican in this town?"

"Never knew you to be so touchy. I was just asking because you used to date Rosa Santos and she hangs out with Theresa. Thought you might have an idea."

"I do," Ray sounded sullen. "Ask Rosa."

They were quiet on the drive home, in some way their silence echoing the stillness of the town. Buck pulled to the curb in front of Lyle's house. The studio light was still on.

"Lyle works all the time. Guy doesn't seem to sleep."

Buck opened his window. The rain had stopped and the air felt cool and nice.

"Want to come in? Maybe sit on the porch?"

Buck shook his head. "Must be nice living with your art teacher."

Ray shrugged. "My old man would knock me around pretty good if I went home, and I looked beat-up enough. Isn't really anyplace else to stay."

Buck looked out the side window. "Guess I best tell you that your old man caught up with me in Wheaton & French yesterday. Started grilling me on your whereabouts."

"Damn. What'd you say?"

"What do you think I said? Nothing." Buck waited. "Then he started on about the pearls."

Ray grew so quiet that Buck thought he was holding his breath. "How is it that your old man's buying a pearl necklace for Pauline?"

"Figure that's for Pauline to tell you."

"I'm asking you, damn it!"

Ray opened the car door. "Getting all stiff here, Buck. That's about all I got to say anyway."

"Hold on." Buck got out and followed Ray to the porch. They sat on the porch step. The compact he'd taken from Lorrie felt heavy in his pocket.

"Boys? That you?" Lyle turned on the porch light and stood in the doorway.

"Yessir," Ray said. "We're just finishing up a conversation."

"Damp out there. How about finishing it inside?"

"Be there in a sec," Ray said.

Lyle didn't move. "If I can help, let me know."

"Thanks, Mr. Samuels," Buck said. "I'll be leaving in a minute." Lyle went back inside.

"Why did he take you in?"

Ray shrugged.

"Because Pauline asked him?" Buck prodded.

"Well, that's obvious, ain't it?"

"She decided on asking him pretty fast. Why is that?"

"He's a friend of hers. Besides, he helped me with my painting and thinks he could get me into the Art Institute in

Denver. Far as that goes, he'd probably let you move in if you needed to. He's that kind of guy. Believe we've talked enough here, Buck. What say we meet up tomorrow?"

Buck didn't move. "You ever see your old man hit Pauline?" He felt queasy asking the question.

"No."

"But you saw her looking beat-up?"

Ray looked away, his expression set. "No. If I would have, I'd have done something."

"Such as?"

"Such as beat up my old man." His voice was angry. "But you can see my chances there. Ain't we already had this conversation? If you want to know more about Pauline and my old man, why'nt you ask her? I'll tell you one thing. She wouldn't take the pearls even if we got them back from Lorrie."

"Why's that?"

"The way I see it, he bought those pearls to make up for something, and then she told him to leave her alone. He must've got to her before you saw her at Wheaton & French. I'll tell you, though, if my old man sees Lorrie wearing those pearls, no telling what he'll do." Ray's voice was serious. "After he gets me for swiping them."

Buck looked at the lights coming on in the houses on this nice, respectable street.

"What else?" Ray said.

Buck stood up. "I had a bad asthma attack the day your dad spotted me in Wheaton & French. Real bad," he said softly. "I agreed to drop him off at the bus stop near the hospital."

"Hospital?"

"Yeah. Mr. French could tell I was in trouble and he was going to call my folks or drive me to the ER if I didn't."

"You were that sick?"

Buck nodded. "It's been getting worse lately." He pulled out the inhalator. "They gave me this at the hospital. It's easier to carry around, so if I feel an attack coming on, I have something on me."

"Sorry to hear that, Buck. How's this figure with my dad?"

"I said I'd take him to the hospital where he could get a bus, but I only drove a block before I collapsed." He took a deep breath and sat next to his friend. "The thing is, Ray, your dad saved my life. He drove me to the ER and helped me in. He was gone by the time I left." He paused. "I told Pauline," he added.

Ray's expression was confused and angry. "Did you tell her about running into my old man? About the necklace, and that Lorrie has it now?"

Buck moved toward his car. He felt more tired than he could ever remember feeling. He couldn't form his thoughts into words. "I should've let you tell her. I should've come here first instead of seeing Pauline. I'm sorry."

"I wouldn't have told her, you damn fool. The less she knows, the safer she'll be."

Buck felt his stomach turn.

"I told you if you went for Pauline you'd be buying into a mess of trouble. Now I have to figure out how to get the necklace away from Lorrie."

"Maybe you can do it tomorrow. She asked me to give you a message. She wants you to meet her tomorrow at Wheaton & French. Ten o'clock."

"What for?"

"Well, Raymundo, that's something you'll have to ask her, isn't it?"

The compact weighed as heavy in his pocket as the pearl necklace did in his mind, and he unsnapped his pocket.

"While you're at it, give her this." He dropped the compact in Ray's hands and turned down the path toward his car.

"What's this?" Ray yelled, but Buck had already pulled away from the curb.

* * *

In his room, Buck pulled out his journal and put it at the back of a shelf, out of sight so he couldn't see it. He hated writing. It didn't help him through a single thing. The wasted hours spent writing about Eagle Springs, about the mountains, and rivers and creeks and Indian massacres; about the Valley of Miracles—all of it meaningless. He'd failed. That wasn't writing. *I could talk to the wall*, he thought, *and get as much figured out.*

He looked at the books scattered about his room and remembered the way they had once lifted his spirits, made him think about things he'd never thought of before. Had he read anything about a woman beaten? About a man so drunk he'd tried to kill his own son? Had he missed that? Were there lessons there on how he could be with the woman he loved when probably everything and everyone was against it, or how lonely and afraid he felt when he knew that what he needed was something he might never be able to have? He lay down on top of his covers with his clothes on, falling into a restless sleep as the moon dropped below the mountains and the town lay in darkness.

CHAPTER TWELVE

The next morning was hot and the mountains looked bold. Buck tried not to see this as a premonition, just as he sloughed off the dry wind that continued to coil down the canyons and snake down streets and alleys, bringing restlessness and unpredictability with it.

He headed downtown, stopping at a light just as he saw Ray cross the intersection and head toward Wheaton & French. Buck moved his hand to the car horn. One small blast and he could stop Ray from going in and giving the compact to Lorrie in the drugstore, where she'd stolen it. If Horace Wheaton saw Ray with the compact, he'd think Ray took it.

I wish I hadn't told Ray she wanted to see him, or given him the compact. It's none of my business.

He waited, unsure whether to go in, but what would be accomplished if he did? It would only delay the inevitable. Meanwhile, there was a stolen compact and a stolen pearl necklace to consider.

He shifted gears and drove to the *Gazette*. Inside, it was quiet and there was no sign of Art. Buck sat at his desk in the corner and leaned back in the chair, feet on his desk. He couldn't stop thinking about Ray. He took a tablet of foolscap and began to write, notes at first and mostly about how every moment of Ray's life was a struggle: his father, his feelings for Lorrie, his vague hopes to be a successful painter.

"Seems like I'm all he can count on, and I'm not even very reliable," he wrote.

I'm going to need a plan, and it needs to be big. Not just about protecting Pauline, but making things straight with Ray and Lorrie.

For the next hour, he scribbled notes on plans, including he and Ray running off to Denver on their own, and thinking that had the makings of a great story, when the back door flew open and Ray stood silhouetted in the doorway.

Buck put down the pen and pushed the tablet aside. "What're you doing here, Ray?"

"Need to talk to you. Now. It's about Lorrie." Ray's voice was flat. Buck heard the hurt in it.

Buck followed Ray out the door, locking it behind him. They hurried down the busy sidewalk toward the park, oblivious to the attention they drew from those who watched a white boy hurrying behind a dark, sullen Mexican boy.

"What the hell you trying to do, Buck?" They'd reached the edge of the park. Ray clenched and unclenched his fists. His eyes were dark with anger.

"What say we sit somewhere?" Buck took short painful gasps of air, his chest feeling like a lead ball had settled there.

Ray sat on the nearest bench set back from the path. "What's the idea of asking me to give that compact to Lorrie?"

"What happened?"

"What do you think happened, you damn fool? I gave it to her, and in a split second, Wheaton was ready to call the cops on me for stealing it. That what you planned on, Buck? They'll nail a Mexican right away? Well, guess what?" He stood and paced the grass behind the bench. "Lorrie looked up and says *she* took it. You mind telling me what the Sam Hill is going on?"

Buck leaned forward, hands clasped between his legs. His breath was a rattle deep inside, and he almost wished he'd have an attack so bad he'd have to go to ER again. He heard Ray light a cigarette, stop pacing, then start again.

"Where's Lorrie now?" Buck asked.

"What difference does that make?"

"Did she know I gave you the compact?"

A young woman crossing through the park glanced at them and hurried on.

"No. Why'd you do it?" Ray's voice cracked.

"Ray, you don't know the whole story."

"That so? Well, you're the storyteller, you tell me." He stood in front of Buck, his body tense, and Buck imagined feeling his friend's fist jamming against his face. Instead, Ray sat next to him on the bench, doubled over, his hands limp between his knees.

Buck waited in the way that helplessness stretches time and sense out of all proportion. He didn't have a good answer.

"Ray," he began. "It's true that Lorrie took the compact. I saw her swipe it, and later I saw it in her bathroom when I went back to get you. I don't know why, but I picked it up. Maybe I intended to give it to Mr. Wheaton, tell him I found it. But before I did, I gave it to you."

"Why did you give it to me?" Ray looked stunned by these facts. "You could've figured I'd get in trouble."

"No," Buck said quietly. "I didn't figure that." He lied.

"Shows what the hell you know about Mexicans in this town."

"I was mad because of Pauline. I was jealous because you knew her and knew all about her what I wanted to know and you weren't going to tell me. So I thought, Okay. I know something about Lorrie too and here's the compact and you can find out about Lorrie on your own."

Ray stared across the park toward the high school. "So you figured to have me arrested for petty theft to get back at me because you all of a sudden want Pauline?"

"No. I thought that if you gave it to Lorrie, she'd admit that she took it in the first place, and return the damn thing to Mr. Wheaton then and there."

Ray sat back and looked at Buck, a half smile playing around his mouth. "Well, she did admit it, I guess." He looked around the park. "Ever consider you might have just let her keep the damn thing?"

"I'm real sorry, Ray. You're my buddy. Lorrie is my friend. I'll try and straighten out the business with the compact with Mr. Wheaton at least." He started toward Wheaton & French, leaving Ray standing by the park bench.

There was no sign of Lorrie inside, and Buck breathed a sigh of relief. Mr. Wheaton and Mr. French were in conversation at the back when Buck went in. Laverne was behind the fountain and moved to the corner when Buck came in.

"This is getting good." She smacked her chewing gum.

"Shut up, Laverne." Buck walked toward Mr. Wheaton.

"Hello, Buck." Wheaton sounded surprised.

"Mr. Wheaton, I understand there's been a little mix-up about a compact. Fact is, I was going to give Lorrie something in honor of her being Rodeo Queen and all, and I asked her to pick out something she liked and I'd get it for her. I was waiting for her at the fountain and saw her looking at the compact, so I figured that's what she wanted. When she sat with me at the fountain, though, she didn't mention it so I forgot about it and figured she changed her mind. You asked us about it, but she was pretty clear she didn't know where the compact was. Later I was at the Seminary doing a story on the Retreat and saw it in her room. I figured she'd forgotten about it."

He was amazed at how easy and logical this story seemed to be coming out. Lorrie would see that he'd taken the blame and then she and Ray could be together.

"I took it back then without telling her and intended to come in and pay for it, then give it back to Lorrie."

The older man stared as though trying to link this twisted scenario to what had seemed a simple case of young people acting up. He motioned Buck to sit down. "That doesn't sound like you, Buck. When you were here doing a follow-up for the paper, were you covering up?"

Buck had forgotten about that. He made his face a mask. "Sorry. I was, but not intentionally."

"I see." Wheaton was quiet, looking at the college girls testing perfumes. "So you never did give it to her?"

"No sir. I meant to return it, but instead I asked my buddy, Ray, to give it to her." Mr. Wheaton looked puzzled. "Because he was meeting her today. I planned to pay for it today," Buck added.

"I see. The Mexican boy with Lorraine was your friend?"

"Mine and Lorrie's. Yessir." Buck didn't like Horace Wheaton's hesitation. He took a deep breath. He could understand Ray's point now; this was about more than a compact.

"Buck, I don't know what's going on with you and Lorrie, but you need to sit and talk with your folks. You see, Lorrie told me *you* took it."

Buck's mouth dropped open in shock.

Mr. Wheaton continued, "She didn't want to say anything in front of the boy who was with her, who as far as I can tell is innocent of any wrongdoing here."

Buck sat, stunned at Lorrie's lie. Had she lied to protect Ray? Protect herself? Why hadn't he seen this coming?

"Reckon I best pay for it," Buck said. "I don't get paid on a regular salary, but I'll make good on it, Mr. Wheaton." He stood, and Wheaton stood as well.

"Buck," he patted his shoulder and left his hand there, "I don't think for one minute that you stole that compact."

"Say what?" He looked at Wheaton.

"I just don't think you could do it, then talk to me about it like you did. I don't know what happened, but Lorrie returned the compact and as far as I'm concerned it's over with." Wheaton stood and patted Buck's shoulder. "Have a talk with your folks and your friends, Buck. Just be sure you're standing up for the right person."

Buck left in a haze of confusion and hurt. One summer afternoon, a young girl had stolen a useless, fancy object, perhaps out of boredom or daring, and that selfish act had brought about lies that he seemed powerless to correct. Caught in the middle was Ray, his trust in two people who he cared about broken.

Buck headed toward the park, but there was no sign of Ray. Buck was desperate. His foolishness, his failure to think before acting, had hurt his friend. Dry leaves scraped down the sidewalk. He walked through the park, and circled the block by the Chief Theatre. He looked in the Village Inn even though there'd be no chance Ray would be there. He looked down the grassy slope above the river but Ray was nowhere. Exhausted, he went into the library and sat at his special table under the window. The next morning when he could see Pauline seemed years away.

The quiet of the library calmed him. Not only had Lorrie stolen the compact in the beginning, in the end she had lied about him. Anger over her actions quickly replaced the pain he'd felt for hurting Ray. He needed to talk to her in private, so he headed to the newspaper. The office was empty and Buck's satchel lay on his desk where he'd left it when he'd hurried out with Ray. He sat at his desk and stared at the phone. What would he say to Lorrie? The lies had already been said, so what good would it do to confront her? He called her at home. He was about to hang up when Lorrie's voice came on the line.

"It's me. Buck." Silence. Did he hear a slight gasp? "You by any chance know where Ray is?" He tried to sound terse and indifferent.

"No." She was silent. "He was a little upset when we left the drugstore."

Did she know that Ray had come looking for him? That Buck knew what she'd done? "Why'd you do it, Lorrie?" He blurted it out. "Lying to Wheaton about me taking that compact?"

"Well, you did take it. You took it out of my room."

"That's why you lied? To get back at me?"

"Oh, what's all the fuss, anyway? I gave it back like you wanted me to."

His heart was pounding. She had no sense of how her actions had affected either himself or Ray. "No need. I talked to Wheaton."

"When?"

"After Ray told me all that happened at the drugstore." Now he heard a gasp. "Yeah," he went on. "Ray was mad at me, so I went over and told another lie to Wheaton. Said I meant to buy it for you but walked out with it instead; that's how come I had it." He waited. "I tried to make it seem like an accident."

Lorrie was saying something but he wasn't listening. "Buck?" Her voice was insistent.

"Yeah?"

"I asked you if Ray was mad at me."

His head ached. He realized he hadn't eaten, and was feeling weak. Lorrie kept repeating his name, and he wanted to say that he hoped Ray was mad at her, and ask her if it mattered that she'd made him out to be a thief and a liar, but it would be wasted.

"You'll have to ask him, Lorrie." He hung up, picked up his book bag and walked out, unsure where to go, certain only that friendships had been forever changed.

CHAPTER THIRTEEN

The next morning was chilly. The sun hadn't risen above the high range, and the distant sky wasn't yet fully light. He felt as if he were stranded in a foreign place, and not simply on the northernmost edge of town. He drove to the Bluffs and pulled into the driveway of Pauline's house.

Everything was quiet. The shades in the front window were drawn and the hanging flower baskets on the porch swayed slightly. He sat in his car and looked at the neat and silent house, at her pickup parked at the side, before getting out and closing the car door quietly. He knocked lightly on the front door. Silence. He walked around the house and onto the back porch.

"Pauline?" He knocked on the screen door. "Pauline?" He bent down and called through the half-open kitchen window.

"What?" came a whisper in his ear.

"God Almighty!" He jumped, banging his head on a rafter in the low roof.

Pauline stood behind him, holding two bags of groceries. She smiled.

"Jesus, Pauline. You scared the hell out of me."

"Such language from a well-bred young man. Besides, I told you eight o'clock."

"I said six. Actually, I'm late."

"Well, you're in time to help me with these groceries." She handed the two sacks to him and opened the door. "I need to take them to Sam."

"You always go shopping at the crack of dawn?" He put the sacks on the counter.

"Have you eaten?"

"Nope."

She looked at him, came close and touched his face. "What's wrong? Has something happened?"

He put his arms around her, and she put her arms around his neck, and he buried his face in her hair and when he pulled back and kissed her, she kissed him back before moving away.

She stored some groceries in the refrigerator and left others in the bag, poured them each a cup of coffee and fixed breakfast. They didn't talk and he watched her, happy when she looked at him, at first seriously, but then with a smile. He took in the easy morning and her beauty, his troubles forgotten for the moment.

"You're quiet this morning." She put down two plates of scrambled eggs, toast, and bacon.

He began to eat and the food tasted good, but the previous day's events made eating feel forced.

"What is it, Buck?" Pauline watched him. "Something's bothering you, I can tell."

He took a drink of coffee. "Dry wind always kicks up my asthma, that's all. I forgot about you going to Sam's."

"Once a week. I should see him more." She hesitated. "If you're not busy you can come with me."

"That'd be swell. I'll check in for assignments at the paper later but to tell you the truth, since I'm an intern I don't get many assignments."

She washed the few dishes and put them in a rack to dry, and moved to the living room, where she opened the windows. The curtains blew gently into the room, and she sat on the couch. He sat next to her, his hand brushing her hair as he rested his arm on the top of the couch behind her.

"Looks like your lawn needs mowing. Be happy to do it for you."

"No, thanks. I let the grass grow long on purpose. I like the way it smells flying back at me when I mow the lawn."

He nodded. "Maybe I can paint your house?"

"Don't worry, Buck. You can come back."

She touched his face and left her hand there on his cheek, and he leaned forward and kissed her. The morning quiet and calm surrounded them, and he put his arm around her shoulders, drawing her to him. She hesitated only a moment before moving into his embrace.

He kept his arm around her shoulders even as she moved back. Before she could speak, he laid his fingers gently over her lips, fearful she might say, "This is all wrong." But she kissed his fingers, held his hand and sat back, resting her head on his arm. He knew she would say it, though. It was just a matter of time.

He noticed a painting against the far wall.

"Mind if I have a look-see?"

"Of course not." She got up and moved it to the fireplace mantel for better light. "It's a portrait of Sam." She sat down again.

"What made you paint him like this?" Buck asked.

"Earth colors suit Sam: his age, his history, his mystery. The way he's grounded to an inner life."

The old Indian's eyes were heavy-lidded and deeply lined, but there was a core of bright blue in the center.

"What do you think?"

"I'm thinking I wish I could write the way you paint."

"Maybe you can describe it?"

He studied it. "His hands make me think of chunks of earth just sitting there on his knees."

"That's a good description. Sam is full of stories. A circling hawk is a blessing: a sign of protection, but a hawk circling through falling snow is a warning that one is falling into circumstances beyond their control. A halo around a harvest moon can signify birth." She shrugged. "Sam thinks I don't pay attention to these old stories. They are all he believes in, but I do feel them as part of my soul, part of the sound of my own chanting."

Buck leaned forward, hands clasped between his knees. His breath was easy. He wanted to write stories about all she was telling him, but how would he ever understand what those stories meant? Would Pauline be part of them? Would he?

"Once," she said, "I watched a hawk circle above the canyon. I imagined him as old and dusty, his wings embracing the sky. The sky turned into a vision of color and light, and light leaked through the fringed edges of the hawk's wings. He began to descend, but the wind caught him and swooped him up and out of my sight."

"Wish I'd see something grand like that."

"You will. But I want you to remember something; will you?"

"Pauline, I'll remember anything you say."

"Remember the hawk, and that it is always better to land than to circle endlessly."

She walked back into the kitchen, and he followed, watching while she began to check the grocery sacks.

"Help me get these into the truck, please?"

He picked up the two sacks of groceries. "My pleasure."

She turned at the door. "You look better now. I'm glad."

She took the Sand Creek cutoff south. By now the sun had warmed the air and they drove with the windows open. Pauline's hair blew around her face. They drove in silence and Buck thought how he should write down the things she said so he could use them in a story.

"Sam came to Santa Fe after my parents died," she said. "He'd promised his brother, my father, that if anything happened he'd take care of me. When my parents died, Sam came down from Colorado and got me."

"Was that long ago?"

"A few years."

"It's hard to imagine a little girl dealing with something like that," he said. The foothills had settled into a pattern of shadow and sunlight. "How'd they die?"

She turned toward the trailer park, the truck raising dust from the unpaved road.

"A car accident. We lived on a reservation near Santa Fe. They were coming back late at night. My father was drunk and slammed his truck into a propane tank next to a roadside restaurant. It exploded and they were killed instantly." She waited a moment before going on. "Luckily the restaurant was empty."

They drove in silence before she spoke again.

"The whole way to Colorado I bet Sam said ten words, and they were mostly in Navajo, so I didn't understand him. Later he told me he was chanting my parents' souls to a safe place. That's when I started to think about changing my name."

Buck remembered Sam had called out a name a few nights ago, and he'd forgotten it.

"My mother named me Misae."

"Damn. That's swell. What's it mean?"

"White Sun."

Clouds were accumulating toward the east. "Why'd you choose Pauline Moon?"

"I used to look at the moon and feel part of it in a way I wasn't part of anything else." She smiled at him. "Pauline just came to me. Isn't that silly?"

"Nothing about you is silly." He put his arm along the back of the seat and felt her hair brushing against his hand.

Her pickup held to the rough road and before long she pulled into the space next to Sam's trailer. She turned off the motor and they sat in the truck. Outside, grasshoppers leapt through the heat, and an angry-looking cat swung at them listlessly.

The Perez trailer looked deserted. Perez's black Dodge was nowhere in sight, and Buck breathed a sigh of relief.

"Everything seems quiet here," he said.

She watched him. "Is there something wrong between you and Ray? Is that why you're so preoccupied?"

The wind blew through the cab of the truck. Even Sam's trailer looked deserted except for the milk crate he used as a stool.

"There was a mix-up, you might say. A . . . misunderstanding."

She waited.

"Pauline, you reckon we could take care of Sam now? I'll tell you later?"

She hesitated. "All right. But I need to know, Buck."

She pulled the sacks of groceries from the truck bed and handed them to him, and grabbed another sack and headed up three steps to the front door.

"What've you got in here?" He followed her into the trailer.

"Tomatoes," she said. "Sam loves tomatoes cold and sliced thin with only salt and pepper, or in a sandwich with mayonnaise and bologna. Other supplies to keep him going for a week or so." Buck stepped into the small room while she held the door.

Sam sat upright in an old rocking chair. He wore the same worn plaid shirt buttoned at his neck and wrists, with dusty boots and faded jeans that Buck had seen before. Sam stared at the grainy images flickering on the small television screen.

"He watches soap operas all day long," she said. "Until they end and Huntley-Brinkley news comes on."

"He watches them all day?" He smiled at the idea of the old man filled with history and myth watching soap operas all day. He put the grocery sacks on the narrow kitchen counter.

"Sam." She leaned down and spoke in the old man's ear. "This is my friend Buck. You saw him the other day, remember?"

He stood in front of Sam. The old man's eyes, watery as a newborn bird's, looked at Buck and back to the television.

"Come help me." She touched Buck's arm. He unpacked one sack and she stored the groceries in the small cupboard: a tin of coffee, a box of Rice Krispies, a jar of hot peppers, Kraft Macaroni and Cheese, and a large loaf of Wonder bread.

"It's the only bread Sam wants, mostly because he likes poking at the circles on the wrapping," Pauline said. "I'll just be a minute if you don't mind waiting."

"Nope. I'll wait all day." There was no clear place to sit except a small, beat-up couch against the wall, where he could sit and watch Pauline fixing Sam a sandwich. She washed a tomato and sliced it, layering thin slices on a piece of bread and then adding baloney and a hot pepper and another piece of bread.

Sam ate as she straightened the small trailer, lifting a film of dust from the one table. She swept the bedroom, kitchen, and living room while Buck washed the dishes.

As The World Turns had started and Sam held up his empty plate.

"Do you want another sandwich?" He nodded. She fixed him a second tomato sandwich and put a Coke on the table beside him. He raised his head; his blue eyes had teared over so she put two eye drops into each eye.

His white hair hung narrow and braided down his back. "I need to brush out your hair, Sam."

She stroked his forehead and touched his hands folded on his lap, and Buck wondered how many times she'd drawn him this way? Quiet, his hands gnarled like tree roots, knuckles swollen with arthritis, eyes looking out at nothing.

She didn't brush out his hair, but instead moved back to the kitchen and Buck followed. She opened beers for both of them. "I should take him to live with me."

"Be just as hard to take care of him at your place, wouldn't it?" The beer tasted good.

"Not really. It would save me driving out here every week."

He glanced at the Perez trailer.

They watched television until the news came on and Pauline flicked off the set. She finished her care of the old man and Buck waited on the small porch. Children were playing hopscotch near the clutch of evergreen trees at the end of the road, and he suddenly wondered if the blood had faded from the stairs and the door handle, and where, he thought, was Perez and what would he think if he saw Buck with Pauline? He stepped back inside the trailer.

"Stay inside, Sam, Don't go over to Perez's trailer, even if you happen to see Ray." The old man turned his attention back to the television. "I love you." She kissed his cheek. "I'll be back."

She stepped out and closed the door. "I forgot to wash his face. I'll just be a minute." She got out and Buck waited nervously, anxious that Perez would suddenly drive down the incline and find them there.

They were quiet on the way home. Pauline took a shorter route and soon they pulled into her driveway.

"Why did you tell Sam not to go over to the Perez trailer?"

She stared ahead at her small yard. "No reason in particular."

"You have reason to think Perez would harm Sam?"

"Of course not. Besides, Sam doesn't move one foot from that trailer." She got out of the truck. "Thanks for helping me today."

He got out. "Pauline, you're right about me being preoccupied 'n' all." He leaned back against the side of the truck and pulled her gently toward him.

"Is it about you and Ray?"

He nodded. "Maybe I can stay and talk about it some?"

She leaned into his arms, held him. "Maybe another time. I think you need to see Ray."

"You're real hard to leave, Pauline." He kissed her quickly, then again and slower.

"Buck, I'm older than you, and . . ."

He tilted his head and looked at her seriously. She kept her arms around his neck and they stood silently, Buck leaning against the truck, Pauline's head on his shoulder while he stroked her hair and held her.

CHAPTER FOURTEEN

Eagle Springs eased toward autumn reluctantly. Dry leaves scattered across the changing lawns that, once green, now faded to brown.

Buck told his parents he was working on stories and doing research for Art Packer to account for the time he wasn't at home. He hadn't talked to Ray since they'd argued in the park. They'd gone a spell without talking before, but this time was different. He'd reach for the phone to call Ray, but held back, unsure what to say.

He tried to please Pauline in little ways. One time he asked if she wanted to go to a movie, but she said no. He thought it might be because of the gossip it would bring, but she said the movies were so unreal they bored her. They drove through the foothills, and lay in tall grass at the base of the Front Range. A bee stung her shoulder and he worried all day that she'd have a reaction. Back at her house, he insisted on applying a cold compress even though there was no swelling. He watched over her to be sure she was all right until she convinced him she was fine.

All this time there was no sign of Perez. Buck was grateful for the older man's help, but the danger he represented never left Buck's mind. He checked the police blotter at the newspaper for news of any trouble, but it was just the usual roundups of juvenile delinquents.

* * *

He was working on a story at the newspaper office one morning when Lorrie called. "Hi, Buck. Do you have a minute to talk?"

"Not really. I'm a little busy."

"I called your house but your mother said you've been working a lot lately." She waited but Buck didn't respond. "That's why I'm calling you at the paper."

He didn't know what to say, so he waited. "What's on your mind?" he said finally.

"Well, I wanted to explain about the mix-up over the compact and I want to do it in person."

"Mix-up! You told Wheaton I stole that damn thing."

"Compact," she interrupted.

"Whatever. Besides we've already had this talk. Taking it in the first place was a dumb thing to do, Lorrie, but dragging everybody else in was mean."

He heard a gasp and the faint jingle of her charm bracelet.

"It's not fair to call me mean or accuse me of dragging everyone else in. Weren't you the one who brought Ray into the whole thing when you gave him the compact? Besides, I gave it back. Isn't that what you wanted?"

He didn't know what to say. He didn't want to talk about the compact or Ray, but Lorrie was right. He was as much to blame as anyone.

"Maybe we can talk later, but I can't go for pizza now. I'll call you."

He hung up, grabbed his hat, and left for Pauline's.

Driving there, the idea of how to make things right with Lorrie and Ray wasn't on his mind. He hadn't called Pauline, so she didn't know he was coming. What if she wasn't home, or home but busy? What if Ruby was there, or worse—what if Pauline didn't want to see him?

He pulled to a stop in front of her house and waited. He didn't want her to think he was some kid with a crush. He knew it was more than that, he could feel it inside. But what was it really? Love? Concern for her safety? Was it the physical longing he felt for her, even when he wasn't with her, that tightened his breathing and made his hands shake?

He gave two puffs of his inhalator to steady his breathing, got out, took the three stairs onto the porch and rang the buzzer. The house was still. Then Pauline was there, wearing a thin, white cotton shift, and her hair pulled to the side where it fell over one shoulder. He stared at her like a fool, took a deep breath, and hoped he wouldn't wheeze.

"Thought I'd see if you could spare a cup of coffee." He kicked at the wooden floor planks.

She hesitated and looked at him for a moment. "Sure." She stepped back and held the screen door open. "After you help me make the bed."

He followed her as she crossed the living room and went into the bedroom, entering the room just as she finished tucking the sheet under the mattress.

"Here." She unfurled the top sheet and it billowed above the bed and Buck grabbed it and raised it high again and it billowed again and they both laughed. The sheets were spicy with the scent of evergreen.

They finished and Buck sat on the edge of the bed and Pauline sat next to him. She leaned over and kissed him lightly on the mouth.

"I wasn't expecting you. This is a nice surprise."

They kissed again, fuller and more deeply, and he lay back on the bed, his arms around her, pulling her gently down with him until he was surrounded by the scent of evergreen and lavender that rose from her hair as it fell forward. He didn't want her to know this was his first time, or that he wasn't sure about anything except his desire for her.

He sat and pulled off his boots, then his clothes. He watched her slip out of the white shift and lay beside him. Her skin was the color of cinnamon, and he kissed her and he knew she knew everything he felt, but he couldn't speak because she kept touching him, and kissing him, and then she moved on top of him and he felt his breath leave him but he could still breathe and it felt like he was holding her in a dance again but the only music was a rushing in his ears, and the cry of her name coming from him.

The light against the wall turned rose-colored as she pulled the sheet over them. They slept, her head on his chest and his arm around her until she rose and slipped on the white shift, her body a lean shape beneath the sheer material.

"I'm not exactly ready to get up, Pauline."

"I'll meet you in the kitchen." She smiled, leaned over and kissed him, moving away before he could pull her to him again. "I make great muffins."

He groaned and buried his face in her pillow, breathing in her scent. He heard her in the kitchen making a late breakfast, and reluctantly he dressed. That was when he noticed small flowered packets, sachets, scattered across the top of the dresser, and one on the nightstand.

He picked up a bright-yellow cotton one tied at the top with a narrow strip of leather. It smelled of spice, nutmeg maybe, and it felt good to hold in the palm of his hand. He went into the kitchen tossing it in the air and catching it.

"What are all these little things lying around the bedroom?" He came up behind her and wrapped his arms around her waist.

"Sachets I made when I was a young girl. I keep them because they remind me that I don't need them anymore; that I can have them just because I like them."

She turned in his arms and kissed him. Maybe it was his imagination, but she seemed suddenly distracted. He wanted to ask her if everything was okay, to know she wasn't sorry. He sat at the table and pushed the sachet in a circle.

"Why did you need them when you were young?"

"I grew up in a house that smelled of whiskey and cigarettes in the living room and the smell of beans in the kitchen. I made dozens of these sachets and put them everywhere in my room. I imagined they would keep the smells away."

She poured dough into a muffin tin and put it in the oven.

"What's inside?"

"Blueberries."

"No." He laughed. "What's inside the sachets?"

She laughed and put two cups of coffee on the table and sat down. "Lavender, marigold, geranium, rose, carnation. No flower was safe. I'd prowl the dirt alleys of the reservation picking dried flowers, weeds, anything."

She took the yellow sachet from him. "This one has spices from my mother's kitchen." She held it to his nose and he sneezed.

"Did they work at keeping all the bad stuff out?"

"I like to believe they did."

"I don't have anything to protect me," he said. "But maybe I've never needed protection the way you did."

"You have your writing and your ideas to protect you. Believe in that and know it will always be there for you."

They ate and he said he'd clean up. He was nervous to do something.

"That's okay. I'll do them later. I have to get ready for work now." She took his hand and led him to the front door.

"Okay if I come by Ruby's tonight?"

"I'd rather you didn't." She stepped outside and stood on the porch. "Buck, I think it's best if you don't come to the Cantina, and please don't ask me why." She touched his face.

"Okay if I come by here tonight, after you get home?" He wrapped his fingers around the sachet he'd put in his pocket. Was it possible she'd felt nothing? That she didn't want to see him again?

"I've done a selfish thing here, Buck. You won't understand, I know."

"I understand. I just don't agree. I don't think love is selfish and I don't think what other people say is worth thinking about."

"One of the things I love about you is your naïveté, but it worries me as well."

They walked to his car, where he stopped and put his arms around her. "What are the other things you love about me?"

Pauline shaded her eyes from the sun. "Your kindness." She touched his cheek. "You're the kindest person I've ever known." She kissed him and stayed in his embrace for a moment before turning and walking back to the house. When she turned, the wind caught her hair and blew it back from her face and Buck thought she was the most beautiful woman he would ever see.

*   *   *

At the library, he took his favorite table beneath a window that wouldn't close so the fragrance and sound of the river came through. A book of poetry by e.e. cummings was on the table and he copied a few lines from a poem by cummings into his journal.

"96"
i like my body when it is with your
body. It is so quite new a thing.

He read some Hemingway and made more notes:

Pauline. A Love Story.
We had breakfast. Pauline made blueberry muffins. All I could do was look at her. I wanted to go back to the bedroom and make love all afternoon but she said no. She said, "It's not because I don't love you."

He wanted to be with her all the time. Live with her in her house near the Bluffs and begin life with her.

He drew a line through the heading. It wasn't a story. He had no idea how to write a story at all, let alone his own.

I can write about how breathing is like sucking air through a straw, but I don't know the words to describe how I feel about Pauline. I know we wouldn't be able to go to the movies without getting stared at, not just because of the difference in race, but because I'm younger than she is.

He couldn't say it clearly; the thought was dim but there. The story of the judgments they would face in their own town.

* * *

That night his sleep was restless. He gave up on sleep, crept out and eased his car down the alley and headed to Lyle's house. It was late, but Lyle and Ray were used to late hours. Lights from neighboring houses were the only signs of life. The well-kept street remained as flawless at night as it was during the day.

The studio light at the rear was on, but not the porch light Lyle usually kept on. Suddenly the studio light flickered on and off. Buck felt an inexplicable uneasiness. Once on the porch, he pushed at the front door that Lyle usually kept unlocked. It was locked. He stepped off the porch and onto the soft, damp grass. He buttoned his jean jacket, jammed his hands in his pockets, and walked around the house to the back. A half-filled bottle of beer sat at the top of the back stairs. He heard slow, romantic music drifting through a crack in the studio window—not what Ray would listen to. Again a light flicked on, then off. Something wasn't right.

Buck moved around the back steps to the side. Through the window he saw Ray silhouetted in the doorway of the studio. Lorrie came out of a bathroom and kissed Ray before turning toward the living room. As she moved, Buck saw she was barefoot and wore one of Ray's paint-splotched shirts.

He stepped back. He should leave. He shouldn't be watching this, whatever it was. He looked down at his boots as though willing them to walk back to the car. What if Perez were to watch him and Pauline just as he was now watching Ray and Lorrie? He took quick, short breaths and felt for his inhalator. It wasn't there.

He watched as Lorrie moved down the dark hall and through the living room, turning a light on, looking at magazines, lamps, ceramic figurines, running her fingers over the backs of chairs and Ray following, slowly, turning the lights back off as though they were part of some odd ritual that he didn't understand. *But what if Lyle walks in? How did this happen? Have they been together since the day in her room at the Seminary? All that time I was looking for Ray on Mesa Road, almost killing myself in the process, had he been making love to Lorrie?*

They came back down the hall, Ray still following Lorrie and turning off the last light she'd left on, before they went into the studio. The door was open, and through the window Buck saw Lorrie settle on a couch draped with a blue cover. She took off Ray's shirt and, nude, assumed a pose on her left side with her arm curving along her hip. Her right leg was angled slightly at the knee but she'd made no attempt to cover the blonde brush of hair at her crotch. Her breasts were small, the nipples pink.

Buck stared at the completeness of the scene, their familiarity and ease with each other, the shared experience he was witnessing.

He braced himself against the side of the house. He was shaking. In an instant he seemed to understand everything and nothing. He crossed the grass, started the car, and circled the block, back down the narrow alley, car lights off. The bottle of beer still sat on the stoop.

*   *   *

The next day, Buck went with Pauline on her weekly visit to Sam. He felt good with her there, even though the old Indian seemed unaware of his presence. While Pauline worked inside, he cleared the ground around the trailer. He thought he saw Perez's black Dodge idling on the road above, and jumped back. A second later the car eased down the gravel road and rounded a curve, out of sight. Buck couldn't escape the feeling he had been watched, or the fact that Pauline's truck was visible from the road.

He hadn't told Pauline what he'd seen at Lyle Samuels's house, but he had to call Ray to find out about Perez, and for once he wasn't eager to talk to his friend. Not because of Ray's involvement with Lorrie, but because of the guilt, bordering on shame, he felt over spying on them.

"Sorry I haven't called," Buck said when he called Lyle's house.

"'S'kay. I could've called you." An awkward silence followed. "Sorry I got so riled in the park that day, Buck."

"Not your fault. I feel real bad about giving you that damn thing. If I wouldn't have done that, nothing would have happened. How are you feeling?"

"Okay."

"Don't mind my saying, you sound down in the dumps."

Ray chuckled. "Don't mean to. I'm really doing okay."

"Thought I'd swing by and we could go to the Village Inn for burgers."

"Sounds good."

* * *

They settled into a booth near the back. The restaurant wasn't crowded and they relaxed until Buck asked Ray about Lorrie. "You planning on making it clear you're going out with Lorrie when we're back in school?"

"What kind of a question is that?"

"No need to get riled. Just that walking down the halls hand in hand might stir up some trouble." He took a bite of his hamburger. "For you."

Ray ate without answering.

"You hear from your old man?" Buck asked. "Seen him around?"

Ray shook his head. "Sometimes he takes off to work on some ranch. For all I know he could be back in Texas or New Mexico. If he's here, I figure he'd be living at the trailer. Why?"

Buck shrugged. "I worry about Pauline. I go to Sam's with her, and the other day I thought I saw your old man's car on the high road."

Ray stiffened. "Think he saw you? Or Pauline?"

"Don't know, but Pauline's truck was in plain sight."

"Wish she wouldn't go out there all the time." Ray tried to motion to the waitress for more coffee but she ignored him. "You and Pauline together now?"

Buck nodded. "I'm trying to watch out for her. I spend as much time there as I can. I wish she'd stop working at Ruby's, but she won't."

"You mind smiling at that hag and see if you can get us some more coffee?"

Buck gave a little wave and the waitress came over. "My friend here would like some coffee," he said with a twinge of anger in his voice. She glared at Buck and poured coffee for Ray. "None for me," Buck said.

They both chuckled. "Guess we can cross this place off along with Wheaton & French," Ray said.

Buck shook his head. "Just leave her a nice tip." They laughed again.

"How's everything going with Lorrie?" He felt self-conscious asking. Even if Ray didn't know he'd seen them, seen the painting, he knew.

Ray's voice sounded tired. "Okay. I'm doing a painting of her." He looked at Buck. "Don't know if you'd approve."

"That doesn't matter. Do you like it?"

Ray nodded. "Lorrie wants me to paint the pearls in." He lit a cigarette and Buck shook his head.

"You going to?"

"Hell no. No sense in advertising that she has them." He

blew smoke toward the ceiling. "She's auditioning for a play at the Fine Arts Center. Talks about it all the damn time."

Buck chuckled and his friend looked at him. "Get used to it, Ray. That's all she ever talked about around me, too."

"Some play called *Picnic*. Says she's going to try for the lead and the director has promised to help her in summer stock in Denver."

They left and headed toward Buck's car.

"Guess I'm happy for you and Pauline," Ray said before Buck could say anything. "But if my old man's back and hanging around, you best be real careful."

Buck watched Ray walk away, still without a clear plan on how to protect Pauline.

CHAPTER FIFTEEN

Buck was digging up the hard, rutted ground in the backyard of Pauline's house for her to plant spring bulbs, when he had the idea he'd build a fence.

"I'll start with the front and work around," he told her.

"Do you know how to build a fence?"

"Sure. I watched my dad build the one in our backyard." The truth was, he had no idea how to build a fence. He'd probably have to ask his dad how to do it.

"I don't need a fence," she said. "I don't even really like the idea of a fence. Besides, there's a lot to think about. How will you pay for it?"

He found some guides on how much wood he would need, what kind of wood, and how much it would cost. It looked impossible to do on his own, and it was true he had no way to buy as much wood as he would need, unless his father could help him get it at a low price. There wasn't much chance he'd help Buck out with this project.

He didn't bring it up again, and a few days later Ruby came by and the three of them sat at the kitchen table and drank beer and ate the tamales she made. If Ruby objected to, or worried about, their relationship, she never let on.

"What about your plan to build a fence?" Pauline asked during dinner.

"Fence?" Ruby said. "Buck, you intended to build a fence here?"

He remained silent, embarrassed that he had no plan.

"I might have to talk to my dad about it since he's a carpenter. Guess that plan is on hold."

"That's better anyway," Pauline said.

He went to the market once a week with Pauline when she bought supplies for Sam. They shopped at a midsize store on the northeast side of town and not very crowded, yet the few women who were there glared at them. Buck heard the whispers and he hated them.

He went with her to Sam's and taught the old man how to play solitaire, but each visit made Buck increasingly nervous. Before they left, he'd take a quick look around for the black Dodge.

"You still think about Sam living with you?" He tried to sound nonchalant.

"Why would I be thinking about that?"

"Well, maybe not with you, but closer." He couldn't bring himself to say he worried about her being where Perez might show up.

"Sam's all right. If anything, it would be worse to have him with me."

"How so?"

They were driving back from Sam's and she started across the intersection. "Has something happened to make you think about this again?"

"I thought I saw Ray's old man the other day. Up on the road just sitting in his car. He's mean-spirited, Pauline. I worry about you being so close to him when you're at Sam's."

"Don't forget he saved your life."

"He was sober then. Drunk, there's no telling."

They drove toward Kiowa Park. "Arturo wouldn't hurt Sam." She concentrated on the street ahead. "He can be dangerous, but I know how to manage him." She put on her dark glasses and tapped her fingers against the steering wheel in rhythm to the tune on the radio, waiting for the light to change.

He wasn't convinced, but he knew better than to push her.

They passed a group of high school kids, some he recognized, clustered together, laughing. The girls carried shopping bags from Gray Rose Clothing, and the boys had notebooks and binders under their arms. Buck realized the school year would begin next week. He hadn't even thought about it. He looked at the kids and felt he didn't belong. It was not a reluctance to return to school, he liked it and had always done well. But he couldn't escape feeling that the knowledge he wanted, he could get on his own. He'd tried to talk about it to Pauline.

"One year," she'd said. "It's your senior year. Don't be foolish."

"Plenty of people make it fine without graduating from high school. Besides, life experience is better for a writer anyway."

"Writers?" she said. "Name a writer who's made good without a high school education. If you don't finish school, Buck, I'll never forgive myself. Believe me, you don't want to drop out."

Her meaning was clear. If she blamed herself, she wouldn't go on seeing him.

That afternoon they made love and he promised he'd finish school. Lying in her arms, he wondered what he'd do after that. What promise would he have to make to keep her with him?

To spend time with Pauline, Buck told his parents he was working on a project for the paper, but he knew they didn't believe him. His mother had a thin smile on her lips and his father avoided looking at him. Buck tried to make excuses to himself. If it weren't for Pauline, he would be at the library, or movies or any of the excuses he used to use. But they could see he'd changed, even if they didn't know what had happened. When school ended, he'd hurry to Pauline's house.

* * *

He was at her kitchen table working on a story for his English class when he decided to go to Ruby's and surprise

Pauline. Even if she was angry, he reasoned, it couldn't last forever.

He drove through the foothills and the narrow, dark streets of Three Corners. A scattering of lights in the hills hinted at life, maybe a crusty old miner waiting to make a fortune. The tourist shops and restaurants lining the main street were closed, but a quick turn could lead to a wood-floor bar with a jukebox and variety of patrons.

Buck turned on Canyon Road and down the grade leading to the parking lot at Ruby's. Just as the first time he'd come here with Lorrie, cars and pickups were parked at all angles, and the garish neon sign flashed into the night. He inched the Chevy into a space near stand of evergreens, off to the side.

Inside, the bar had its familiar haze of smoke. The usual crowd of college kids sat in the booths along the wall, and cowboys took every stool except one at the far end of the bar. There was no sign of Pauline.

He took the vacant stool at the far end. "Hey, Ruby."

Her eyes narrowed. She never judged him, and in her presence, Buck felt her tender energy. Tonight, though, she looked serious. "Pauline left me with the impression she didn't want you to come up here."

"I'll just have a beer, if that's okay."

She returned quickly and put a bottle of beer on the bar. "I don't like doing this, Buck," Ruby said.

He took a long swallow. "Don't worry, Ruby."

He was about to ask where Pauline was when he saw her at the end of the bar, ready to place an order. A man sat close to where she stood, and he must have asked her to dance, but she shook her head. He persisted. She served drinks to a few tables, came back, and he asked again. Buck saw her mouth form the words, "Just one."

They moved easily onto the dance floor and Buck could tell they'd danced together before. That's when he saw she was dancing with Arturo Perez. He said something to Pauline and pulled her close. She didn't smile and moved back.

Buck felt sick.

Ruby appeared at the bar in front of him. "Might be just as good if you left."

"Why is that, Ruby?"

"Perez could take you out in about one swing, flat. If he's sober, that is."

"Maybe I should buy him a round or two."

He realized how little control he had over what was happening, or what might happen. He had to get out of the stuffy bar. He eased around the tables, keeping clear of Pauline's line of vision, and pushed out the door. The air was heady with the scent of evergreen brushing down from the mountains and he breathed deeply, and headed for his car.

Once behind the wheel, he pumped his inhalator and patted his shirt pocket. No pill. He rested his head on the seat back, taking deep breaths to calm himself. He couldn't drive away, not until he knew Pauline was all right. He cracked open the window and breathed in the high mountain air while he watched the door of the bar. He wanted Pauline to come out, walk over to his car and slide in, bringing all her mystery and richness with her. She'd lean over and kiss him and her mouth would taste smoky and hot.

But each time the door opened, another college kid stumbled out, his hand down the front of some girl's blouse. Buck's stomach churned, thinking about Pauline dancing with Perez. Was this why she'd told him not to come here?

He rolled down the window. Light streamed across the gravel as the door to Ruby's opened and Perez stepped out, Pauline not far behind. Buck took quick, short breaths while gripping the steering wheel.

Pauline seemed to be trying to calm Perez, but in one second Buck saw the man's arm swing wide and his hand smack against Pauline's face. The sound was sharp and echoed through the high air. She staggered back.

Before he had time to think, Buck was out of the car and running toward Perez.

"Get away from her, damn you." Buck shoved his hands against Perez's chest and he stumbled backwards, arms flailing for balance.

"Buck?" Pauline stood with her hand to her cheek. "What are you doing here?"

Perez came at Buck with a wide swing, but Buck pushed against his chest again and this time, he went down.

"Come on, Pauline." Buck turned toward her.

From the corner of his eye, he saw Perez struggle to his feet and lunge toward him. Buck took a wild swing, losing his balance and landing on his rear, with his back against the building. Perez came at him, dark and grunting. In the flashing neon lights of the bar, Buck saw the look on his face. It was a look that said he meant to win this fight.

Buck crawled to his feet. He had virtually no air in his lungs and was gasping, functioning on adrenaline only. The older man was surprisingly agile in spite of his size and drunkenness. He circled, easy on his feet, his arms spread wide, and his eyes on Buck.

It was the first fight Buck had ever been in. What had been instinct up to this point was now apprehension. He stayed on his feet, unsteady, his legs and arms spread wide, more or less as he'd seen it done in Western movies, waiting for his opponent to come at him again. He felt a stream of blood trailing from his ear and heard the rasp that was his breathing. If he didn't knock out Perez soon, he'd die from an asthma attack.

"Son of a bitch." Buck ran at him, ramming him in the stomach. Perez fell to his knees, panting.

"You little punk!" Perez's voice was low and threatening. "Who the hell do you think you are?" He got to his feet and moved fast. Buck saw his fist just before it connected with his jaw. He heard a tooth crack, and the metallic taste of blood rose in his mouth.

"Stop it," Pauline cried. "Buck, come inside, please."

She reached for him and he turned toward her, for no reason except to see the light in her eyes, when he heard the quick click behind him. As Pauline screamed his name, he felt the thin sharp edge of the knife ripping his shirt as it sliced front to back across his side. He went down.

Thunder rolled across the mountains and rain started to beat a rhythm on the cars. He started gagging, but nothing happened and he wondered why he was lying in the mud.

Three cowboys ran from the restaurant and half dragged, half carried him into the bar. A couple of college guys tried to grab Perez, but before they could, he made it to his car, grinding the gears as his car lurched up the driveway.

Inside, Buck slumped against the leather back of the booth. The fear he'd contained inside now built in his chest and his breathing was ragged and strained. He couldn't go to ER now; they'd call the police for sure. Ruby put a glass of water on the table and he couldn't drink it because his breathing was so shallow.

"Do you have your inhalator?" Pauline asked.

"Car."

She ran to the car and picked it off the passenger seat, hurrying back to the bar. She put her hand on the back of his neck to calm him, and he pumped the medicine. The wheezing and the panic of the attack eased enough that he could drink more water. Ruby asked Pauline about calling a doctor, and pressed a clean, damp, dish towel against the knife wound while Pauline held her hand against his neck and her touch drained the fear out of him, and calmed his breathing. Her face was so close to his.

He leaned toward her with a weak smile. "You okay?" he said.

"I'm fine. That was foolish to do." She cleaned his mouth and took a look at his teeth. "Looks like you'll need a trip to the dentist."

He tried to reach for her and she gave him a light kiss.

Ruby insisted on calling an ambulance, but Buck said no.

"He's right, Ruby. Can you imagine the questions? Besides, it isn't a good idea for any of us to report Perez to the police. Buck has settled down a little. I'll drive his car and take care of him at my house. He'll have his car to get home."

"If Perez is hanging around and follows you, you could wind up with a lot more trouble than you have now."

"He knows better than to come after me now. Too many people saw what happened. Maybe you can bring my truck in later, or tomorrow?"

Together they got Buck to his car. "Pauline, it's time you called the police on Perez. If you don't, I will," Ruby said.

"Let me help Buck first."

Once in the car, she drove north toward the Bluffs and her house.

"Do you feel sick?"

"Little. Not bad." He looked at her profile and could tell she was worried. Was she afraid? Should she even be seen with him? Would this bring more trouble to her?

"This isn't the first time he's hit you, is it?" Buck said.

"No."

"Pauline—"

"Thank you for trusting me to drive your car," she interrupted.

"That's okay. Figure you can handle that beat-up old truck, you can drive a first-rate automobile like this."

She slapped his arm lightly. "Oh no," she said when he winced. "Did I hurt you?"

"Nope."

Eagle Springs lay dark and shuttered. His parents would be sleeping, maybe even thinking he was safe in his room and not half beat-up and headed to the house of a woman he wanted in his life but was helpless to protect from Perez's wrath.

Pauline pulled into the rough drive and eased close to the back porch. They both looked around; he half expected Perez to stagger out of the darkness.

"Come in and let me clean you up before you go home."

They sat at the kitchen table.

"You were a fool to take on someone like Perez. He's big and strong and mean."

"Beat the heck out of him, didn't I?" He managed a weak smile. His ear hurt.

"Take off your shirt, please?" She washed and cleansed the scratches on his face and iced the bruises. "What were you doing there, anyway?"

"Wanted to surprise you."

"You couldn't think of a better way?"

"Pauline." His voice sounded far away and he shook his head to clear it. "Why in the hell do you let him hang around? Why were you dancing with him?"

"Stand, please." He stood while she wrapped some gauze around the knife wound. "You really should see about that. It looks superficial, but don't let it get infected. Go lie on the couch." She motioned toward the living room. "I'm going to make us something to eat."

"Don't feel much like eating." He rose unsteadily and put on his shirt, leaving it half-buttoned. She turned on a floor lamp near the fireplace.

She scrambled eggs and made coffee, while Buck sat on the long couch facing the fireplace, his legs stretched in front of him. Pauline brought out a tray with the food and coffee. They ate in silence at first, and then she told him that she thought she'd finally settled everything with Perez.

"I told him I was moving on with my life and that he needed to move on as well. He . . ." She paused. "He was sober when I told him and almost seemed to accept it. At least I'd hoped he had. Tonight he tried to talk me into seeing him again and I said no. He was drunk and mean. I shouldn't have followed him out of the bar. I told him to leave me alone, that's why he hit me."

She rose and took the plates back to the kitchen, and Buck wondered what she meant by moving on with her life.

"I thought I'd settled everything." She sat next to him again.

"You gotta tell the police, Pauline. He's not going to leave you alone." He started coughing. "What'd you mean about moving on with your life?"

"You have to go home, Buck. We can talk about all this later. Can you drive now?"

He nodded. He knew enough to accept they wouldn't talk of this again.

She waited before speaking. "I'll be all right. We need to go slowly here, be careful. Not just because of Perez, but because of your parents. And the town," she added after a pause. She touched his cheek lightly "What will you tell your folks about this black eye?"

He shrugged. "What do we have to be careful of, Pauline? I'm in love with you. I want to be with you and whatever my parents or Ray or Eagle Springs or anybody says doesn't matter."

She brought a wide purple shawl from the top of the chest and wrapped it around herself and led him to the door. "Right now all that matters is your healing. Your eye doesn't look too bad, but please see about that cut."

He held her, wanting above all else to stay with her, have her hold him, and wake with her in his arms the next morning.

* * *

He slept an uneasy sleep in his own bed. He dreamed he'd made love with Pauline and lived with her in her house. When he woke, he felt the burn where the knife had sliced him, and the pressure of the dressing Pauline had wrapped around him. He studied his face in the bathroom mirror. One cheek was bruised and slightly swollen, but his eye wasn't as bad as he'd feared.

He folded his torn shirt and put it in a sack to throw in the trash. He washed and put on fresh clothes. By the time he went through the back door of his house, his father was at work and his mother had gone shopping.

CHAPTER SIXTEEN

Pauline insisted he go to his classes and see his parents, but when he tried, the dinners at home were silent and uncomfortable. Inevitably he'd say he had to go to the library or to the paper and he'd be home late, when instead he went to Pauline's. His parents seemed to have accepted that he had his own life now, but how it had happened they didn't know. There was no more talk of being a writer. Even if he'd wanted to bring up the subject, he was too involved with Pauline to put his mind to writing.

He told himself he was in limbo, a state of uncertainty that left him feeling as though he stood at the center of a wide circle, unable to touch the edges of his life.

He was leaving the campus one day when Lorrie called out to him.

"I need to ask you a favor, Buck."

He hadn't seen her since the night he'd spied on her and Ray. She didn't look good. "You sick, Lorrie?"

"I just have that flu that's going around."

They walked to his car, and he held the door open while she got in.

"Maybe a cola will make you feel better?"

"No. I'm feeling better each day. Opening night of *Picnic* is next Thursday. I wondered if you'd take me?"

Something was going on. "I figured Ray would do that."

"Honestly, Buck. Can you see Ray picking me up at my house?" She pulled a short wool jacket around herself. "If you don't want to, I'll just see if Arlene can take me."

"Lorrie, you always were one to jump to conclusions. I'm kind of preoccupied these days."

"I noticed. I hardly ever see you. I figured you were working harder at the paper."

He looked out the side window, then back at Lorrie. "Okay. I'll pick you up."

"You'll stay to see the play too, won't you? I've worked hard on the part, even if it isn't Madge, the lead role."

"Sorry you didn't get the part you wanted but you'll be good, Lorrie."

She kissed his cheek and he could see dark circles under her eyes and her usually bright skin looked ashen.

"Thank you, Buck."

"Lorrie," he held her arm lightly, "how's about I drive you to a doctor first?"

"No. Stop worrying about how I look. Besides, the makeup I wear in the play will hide these circles."

She crossed into the park, and before driving away Buck decided he'd see if Ray was still in the school. He hadn't mentioned anything about Lorrie and now Buck wondered if he knew she seemed sick.

Only distant conversations from the teachers' offices hummed behind closed doors. He headed to Lyle Samuels's office on the chance Ray might be there, but halfway down the hall, he saw Theresa Gonzales leaning against the lockers.

He remembered the last time he'd seen her when he was at the movies with Ray. How she looked dark and sullen, and he could understand why Lorrie was afraid of Theresa. He stopped in the middle of the hall.

She moved forward. "Say, white boy."

He took a quick sidestep.

"Your attendance is worse than us spics. You're giving us a bad name."

He hated her.

"Your little white girlfriend has taken up with Ray Perez." She was close to him now. She smelled of sweat and tobacco.

He stopped. She moved to the wall nearest him, bracing her hip against one of the lockers, watching him, her eyes hard and black.

He didn't say anything.

"I told her girls around here with names like Rosa Sanchez, Inez Rodriquez, Agnes Montoya had their eyes on Raymundo Perez for a long time."

Buck didn't move. She moved toward him, pausing when she was right in front of him, so close he almost gagged.

"Funny about the time I told her she shouldn't mess with Ray Perez. The way it scared her, thinking we might gang up on her or something. I saw her in the girls' restroom."

Buck looked away. He wanted to move but couldn't.

"Imagine puking like that early in the morning. I told her she should see the nurse." She lit a cigarette, against the rules. "She told me to go to hell." She blew a line of smoke toward the ceiling. "Imagine that. Preacher's daughter talking that way."

Buck waited. "Something on your mind, Theresa?"

"Maybe yes, maybe no."

"If you don't have anything on your mind," Buck said as tersely as he could, "I'll move on now."

"Now ain't that funny," she hissed. "That's just what Lorrie said. But then, she also said she had the flu. You know, that nine-month flu that hangs around and then everything's all right."

Buck felt his stomach drop. Theresa leaned toward him. He held his breath.

"I gave her the name of somebody," she whispered in his ear. She stepped back. "You say hello to Raymundo Perez the next time you see him."

She walked back down the hall, her footsteps echoing heavy and slow and the smell of cigarette hanging about the place where she'd stood. Buck walked back the way he'd come in, through the front door and across the fading late-autumn lawn to his car.

He buttoned his sheepskin jacket against the cold that had suddenly moved across the eastern plains. He was shaken, not only because of Theresa's confrontation, but also by Lorrie's appearance. He needed to talk to her. If she was pregnant and Theresa had given her someone's name, it had to be a backstreet doctor.

He started his car and drove home, trying to put the pieces together. He wouldn't be surprised if Lorrie was pregnant, especially after seeing them through the window at Lyle's, but did Ray know? He called him at Lyle's. "Need to see you, Ray. Think we can meet up later?"

"Sounds serious. Is Pauline okay?"

"Isn't about Pauline."

"Some reason you can't tell me now?"

"I'm not keen on telling you anything at all. If you can't make it, just forget it."

"Hold on. Where do you want to meet?"

"You name it."

"The Fine Arts Theatre around six. We can get in through the stage door and talk in a dressing room."

"That's the best place you can come up with?"

Ray was quiet for a moment. "You seem downright cantankerous, Buck. If you can think of a better place, call me. Otherwise I'll meet you at the stage door at six."

* * *

The Fine Arts Theatre was dark and almost eerie, surrounded by the wooded slopes of the college grounds. Buck parked near the deserted back lot leading to the stage door entrance. Ray waited under the dim light, stomping his feet and slapping his arms to stay warm. His motorcycle was next to the door.

"Damn cold for this time of year," Ray said. "This better be good." They pushed through the door and walked down a short hallway.

"How is it you know your way around here?" Buck said.

"Been here a few times with Lorrie. I'd wait for her now and then in the green room but Salis, the director, doesn't take kindly to me hanging around."

He pushed open a door and the dry, musky odor of material drifted out.

Buck coughed and took out his inhalator. "Great pick, Ray. If this isn't the dumbest damn thing you've done yet."

"Nope," Ray said. "I've done dumber." He flipped a light switch, revealing racks of costumes. One wall was lined with purple, green, and red velvet gowns trimmed with gold brocade, satin ribbons, or sequins. There were racks of gray-and-white-checked women's suits and cream-colored blouses. Extravagant hats clustered on a high shelf, and rows of shoes filled the back wall. Ray pulled out two folding chairs and they sat.

"My old man showed up, Buck. He didn't see me, but I've seen him hanging around here. I told Lorrie to quit wearing those damn pearls and I must've scared her enough because she stopped." He leaned his forearms on his legs and looked at the floor, then back at Buck. "Might be a good idea to keep Pauline away from Sam's place."

"I don't know how to make that happen. Sam can't get along without her." He thought for a minute. "Maybe I could take supplies to him, but I sure can't do everything else for him that she does. I go out there with her every week though, and I haven't seen your old man hanging around the trailer park since I thought I spied his car on the road above Sam's trailer a while back."

"He'll come after everyone he thinks is my friend." Ray's voice sounded tired and worried.

"If you or Pauline don't call the cops on him pretty damn soon, I'm going to. All we do is worry about when your old man's going to show up."

Ray looked swallowed up by the musty darkness.

"Sorry, Ray. Reckon it's easy for me to say." Buck walked down the narrow aisle, riffling through the costumes. "Lyle knows he's back?"

"Yeah. He said he'd try to keep an eye on Pauline now 'n' then."

Buck stiffened and spun around. "Say again? Lyle's keeping an eye on Pauline?"

"Now and then, I said. They've been friends a long time. He's as worried about her as we are."

Buck walked back toward Ray. "You think he's as worried about Pauline as I am? Think again." He slapped at a costume.

"He's not too happy with me, though. He knows about Lorrie, us having sex and all. Said he could lose his job for contributing to my delinquency. Told me not to get her pregnant or I'd have to marry her for sure."

Buck sat down and leaned forward, feeling the weight in his chest. He coughed hard. He had to get out of this room.

I have to tell him about Lorrie now.

"Lorrie wants us to come to opening night," Ray said. "Figures it'd be easier if you picked her up, then you and me can meet up here for the play."

"She already asked me and I said I would. But I don't like it, especially if Perez's running around and I have to leave Pauline alone."

"You can cut out before the play's over." Ray started to light a cigarette, looked around the room at the old material, and decided not to. "There's something else," he said. "There's a girl—Marsha. She's the lead in the play. She . . . poses nude for art classes at the college. She wants to pose for me."

Buck leaned back in the chair, stretching his legs in front of him.

"I love Lorrie, Buck. I have from the first time I saw her. Remember those little sketches I did of her when we sat in the park? I still have them. Back then, when drawing was about all I had, it was one way I could keep her close to me. I almost believed we could be together, so when it happened, I felt like I had to ruin it all before someone else did. Then she told me she's going to California soon as the school year ends, to the Pasadena Playhouse. She wants me to come with her." There was a look of helplessness in his eyes. "How can I do that, Buck? Run off with Lorrie to California?"

"What'd you tell her?"

"Nothing." He stood and paced a slow circle in front of the chair and sat down.

"You seem a little nervous."

"I guess I had too much to drink one night." He paused, concentrating on the floor. "The next thing I know I'm in bed with Marsha."

Buck stared, not sure if what he'd heard correctly.

"Just like that? Nothing leading up to it?"

Ray looked at the floor and Buck stood, pacing in front of where Ray sat. Should he tell him now about Lorrie?

"You think getting involved with Marsha was a way you'd keep yourself from going to California with Lorrie? Maybe you've been so preoccupied you haven't noticed Lorrie?"

Ray's head shot up. "What the hell you talking about?"

Buck bent down, his face close to Ray's.

"I'm not going to help you two-time Lorrie, and I'm not going to cover for you and Marsha what's-her-name. You keep watch on Lorrie and your old man, and you tell Lyle to stay the hell away from Pauline. I can protect her just fine."

He pushed open the door and left, too bitter and angry to tell him Lorrie was pregnant and that in all likelihood Theresa Gonzales had given her the name of an abortionist. All that remained was the sound of his boots echoing down the long hall and the old, dead smells.

*   *   *

Buck couldn't leave things this way with Ray, but he didn't want to meddle again. After the hard feelings about the compact, the lies and confusion, he didn't want to get involved in Ray and Lorrie's issues again. Three days after his meeting with Ray in the little theatre, he drove to Pauline's. It was early evening and Ray was sitting on the porch talking to Pauline. Buck hesitated before walking up the path toward them.

"I'll let you two talk," Pauline said. "When you're through come on in for dinner."

"Mind telling me what was on your mind about Lorrie the other night?" Ray said as soon as Pauline had gone in.

"Not really my place to." He sat on the wicker chair across from where Ray sat.

"It was your place the other night, until you got mad and walked out."

Buck hesitated and looked at his friend. "I'm thinking Lorrie might be pregnant. I saw her last week and she looked like hell. She said it was the flu."

Ray stared, disbelieving, at Buck.

"Later that day I saw Theresa Gonzales. She told me she'd given Lorrie the name of a doctor."

Ray stood and moved to the porch rail, his shoulders showing his tension. "You haven't asked her, have you?"

"What do you think? That's not exactly something Lorrie and me would talk about."

Pauline came out and stood on the porch. She'd brushed her hair and glossed her lips a pale mauve and she wore a long dark skirt and white blouse. The purple shawl rested lightly around her shoulders.

"You two about ready for dinner?"

They started toward the door when Buck turned to Ray. "I

don't imagine you want Pauline knowing about Lorrie's situation?"

Ray nodded. "Does Lorrie know you're telling me?"

"No, she doesn't," Buck said. "Don't worry. We'll figure out something." He patted his friend on the back. "C'mon, Let's wash up. We're having some of Ruby's tamales for dinner."

CHAPTER SEVENTEEN

The week passed slowly, fall giving way to an early winter. Buck stood in the dim living room and Lillian Rathburn sat on the edge of the couch coolly sipping a drink.

"This is a big night for Lorrie." There was a slight slur in her speech. "Personally I don't think she should go on."

Buck shifted on his feet. *She knows. Lorrie could be in real trouble now.*

"She's been ill. Throwing up almost every morning and doesn't have an appetite." She glanced at him over the rim of her glass. "Why don't you sit down, Buck?" She patted the couch where she sat.

He remained standing. "Sorry to hear that. I imagine everything will be okay tonight."

"I'm not sick, Mother." Lorrie came into the room. "It's the flu going around school."

Mrs. Rathburn looked at her daughter, then at Buck. "Did you get the flu, Buck?"

"No ma'am."

Lorrie pulled him to the door. "See you at the theatre, Mother."

Buck drove in silence before he said how pale Lorrie looked.

"I'm fine. Besides, I wear makeup in the play." She looked out the window. "Will you write about my performance, Buck? For the paper?"

He pulled into the lot behind the theatre and stopped the car. "Sure. You'll be great. Don't worry about anything."

She didn't get out right away, and they watched the other cast members, laughing and going in through the stage door.

"Lorrie, I saw Theresa Gonzales at school. I was there late, and she was just hanging out in the hall. The thing is, she said she'd seen you sick in the girls' restroom." He stopped. How could he bring up the pregnancy? "She said she gave you the name of a doctor."

Lorrie was quiet, still looking out the side window. "She's lying." Her voice was small and quiet and she rubbed her hands nervously. "Honestly, Buck." She shifted but didn't move to get out of the car. "You'd believe someone like Theresa Gonzales, who hangs out with gang members? Besides, what kind of a doctor would she tell me to see?"

"There's stories about back-alley doctors north of town who are willing to perform abortions," Buck said.

"You think I'm pregnant and that Theresa gave me the name of one, those doctors who do abortions?" Her voice cracked. "Well, don't worry about me."

More cast members, laughing and excited, were going in the stage door entrance.

"I am pregnant." Her voice was very small. "Don't tell Ray." She touched his arm. "Don't worry. I won't do anything stupid." She kissed his cheek and got out. As he watched her walk alone to the stage door he thought he could have waited for a better time to bring all this up.

He realized he hadn't eaten since early morning, so he drove to the Village Inn and ordered a hamburger and coffee. He took out his pocket notebook, but felt stripped of words. He had to put together a review of the play by five o'clock tomorrow afternoon, but as usual he didn't know how to write about Lorrie, and again he couldn't connect the girl he saw and thought he knew, with what she did and said.

Outside, light flakes began to drift through the glow of a streetlight.

"Ever see snow this early?" The waitress sounded indifferent and put his order on the table.

"Nope. Can't recall I have."

The restaurant wasn't crowded. A family of four came in and distracted him briefly. He wanted desperately to see Pauline, but she was working, and looking at the snow, he didn't want her driving home alone.

Once outside, he hesitated. He didn't want to go to the play. He headed toward Canyon Road and Ruby's, but turned around. Then he started toward Lyle's, but in the end, he drove back to the theatre.

There was no sign of Ray outside or in the lobby. Act One had already started when Buck eased through the door and took a seat in the last row. Lorrie and a good-looking college guy were onstage. He heard a longing in Lorrie's voice, even saw it in her posture, and he realized with surprise that she was good. *Who knows? Maybe her dreams are possible after all.*

During intermission he looked for Ray in the lobby, but didn't see him. He stepped outside and stood on the wide marble porch near one of the pillars. The Fine Arts Theatre was set into a grove of tall pines midway down a gently curving hill. Tonight the high trees bent in the wind and a thin coat of snow rested on the dry lawns. It would be a long winter.

From behind the dark strands of a weeping willow, he spotted a spark glowing steady. A cigarette. A shape emerged and moved toward Buck, stopping short of the brightly lit theatre entrance. It was Ray. Buck walked toward him.

"Hey. How's the play?" Ray said.

"Okay, I guess. Character named Hal makes me think of you. Rides a motorcycle so he can get far enough away that nobody could touch him."

"Lorrie good?"

"Yeah. Real good."

People had begun filing back to the auditorium.

"She was counting on you seeing her tonight. She thinks she's your girl, Ray. Doesn't seem to me that this Marsha is worth hurting Lorrie."

"I know." He nodded. "I don't want to hurt her. I just keep feeling she's too good for me."

"You're making excuses. I don't think you really believe that. Do what you want about the play, but you better talk to Lorrie." He started toward the theatre and turned around. "I don't figure she'll feel like pizza after the play. I'm going to see Lorrie after the play and then leave to get to Pauline's. I don't want her driving down from the mountains in this weather."

"Why won't Lorrie want to go for pizza with us?"

Buck kicked at the ground. "Like I said, you better see her soon as you can."

Lorrie received a standing ovation. People said how much talent the minister's daughter had to play the part of a rowdy, bookish girl so effectively.

Before he headed backstage to congratulate Lorrie, he waited just outside the stage door hoping Ray would show up. He'd been there only a few seconds when the door opened.

"You must be freezing." It was Marsha from the play. "Step inside." Her voice was husky and an earthy fragrance rose from her skin.

"No, thanks."

She stayed in the open doorway. "Did you like the play?"

"Yep."

"Yep." She smiled. "Don't want to commit yourself?"

"No, it was great." He could feel her allure. She had auburn hair that had been up in the play, but now fell around her face.

"And your girlfriend? Everyone says a star was born here tonight." She lit a cigarette. "You think Lorrie can be a star?"

Buck shuffled. "Maybe."

She looked around, and he wondered if she was looking for

Ray. He wanted to tell her Ray was gone. Had hit the road. Anything.

She touched her ring finger to the edge of her mouth. "Lorrie hasn't felt well for the last couple of weeks." She stepped aside so he could get in. "Why don't you go say hello to her?"

Lorrie sat at a long dressing table. The other girls laughed while they got ready for a cast party. Lorrie looked up when Buck came in. She'd been crying.

"You were great, Lorrie."

"Where's Ray?" She looked over Buck's shoulder.

"We need to talk." He rested his hand on her shoulder. She was clammy. Even the theatrical makeup didn't hide her pallor.

"Isn't Ray with you? I'm not sure I can have pizza tonight." Her voice cracked.

Mrs. Rathburn came in the door, followed by the director, Maurice Salis.

"You need to see a good doctor, Lorrie," Buck whispered.

"Don't bring that up again." Her eyes were suddenly sharp, pierced with fear, and her words snapped from her mouth.

Her mother headed toward them.

"My star," Salis cooed, and Lorrie stood while he embraced her and kissed both cheeks.

Buck left and walked down the hall and pushed through the stage door. There was no sign of Marsha, or of Ray. It was snowing harder, and he tried to shake the ominous feeling that had started to grow in his mind. He pumped the inhalator to ease the strain aggravated by the cold temperature and stress building in his chest.

His car stalled a couple of times before he got it started, and he turned north, toward the Bluffs and Pauline's house. The streets were quieter than usual, even for Eagle Springs. Only lights in the windows of houses shone dimly through the curtain of snow.

*   *   *

Snow-covered, the Bluffs had an otherworldly glow. Buck pulled to the curb in front of Pauline's house. It was dark. Instinctively, he looked around for Perez's black Dodge, but there were no cars on the street.

There was no sign of Pauline's truck in the driveway. Buck thought she wasn't back from work yet, and the idea of her driving down from the mountain town in bad weather bothered him. His watch showed eleven o'clock. He didn't want to drive to Ruby's and maybe miss her.

He was jittery. The moon had finally given up and slipped behind a heavy cloud. He looked up and down the street, but his was the only car on the block. He felt oddly unguarded, defenseless, and even foolish.

"She should be home." The sound of his own voice startled him.

Without turning on the headlights he started the engine and eased the car along the rutted dirt driveway toward the back porch. He hit the brakes so suddenly he was thrown forward against the steering wheel. Pauline's truck sat dead in front of him, parked at the end of the driveway. He hadn't even seen it.

He got out and took the stairs to the back porch fast. The kitchen light was on.

Why the hell didn't I come back here? Walk around the house at least?

He peered through the window. No sign of her. "Pauline?" Silence. His chest tightened and he took short gasps of cold air.

He stepped inside the kitchen where she'd taken care of his cuts and bruises after the fight with Perez; where he'd written and talked about books; where she'd made sketches of him. Where they'd eaten blueberry muffins after making love. The room was in shambles. One kitchen chair lay against the far wall, another lay overturned near the table. Apples scattered across the floor, the bowl in shards.

"Oh Jesus God." He was suddenly drenched in sweat. "Pauline?" He called into the silent house. "Pauline, where are you?"

He moved slowly into the living room, unsure if someone might be hiding in a dark corner. His heart pounded and his breath was a heavy wheeze.

A beam of light came from the bedroom. He could never have seen this from outside.

Pauline lay semiconscious on the bathroom floor. Her nightgown was torn and bloody. The odor of whiskey and cigarettes hung about her. Her left eye was swollen almost shut and her right cheek was scratched. A deep purple bruise rose on her left temple. She must have been grabbed hard because fingerprints were slightly visible on her forearms. Her hair hung in tangled strands to her shoulders.

Buck heard his voice saying over and over, "Oh God, oh God, oh God," as he lifted her carefully and carried her to the bed. The house was freezing. He covered her with the quilt. *The Sun Also Rises* was face up on the bed, open to the page she must have been reading.

She'd been here all along. While he sat in his car, she was here all along. When had this happened?

"Pauline?" he whispered. "Pauline, I'm going to call for an ambulance."

She murmured, "No." He bent to hear her whisper. "Lyle."

He felt neither anger nor jealousy, but ran to the kitchen and dialed Lyle. He answered on the third ring.

"Lyle, this is Buck. Get over to Pauline's. Now. I'm going to call the police and ambulance."

"Buck? What—?"

"Get over to Pauline's now."

He hung up, and then dialed the operator. "We need an ambulance and police right away at the Bluffs." He gave the address. His voice was a squeak.

He gulped water from the faucet in the adjacent bathroom. He was losing energy and bent over to cough up the congestion. By the time Lyle rushed in minutes later, Buck had moved back to the bedroom and was on his hands and knees beside the bed gasping for air, clutching his inhalator.

"Sweet Jesus." Lyle took in the scene. "Can you stand?" He put an arm around Buck and helped him up quickly. He turned to Pauline. The wounds and bruises were still fresh. "Did you call the police?" Lyle asked.

Buck nodded and stepped back to the bathroom for more water from the faucet before dampening a cloth. In the sink was a tooth she must have spit out; he picked it up and put it in his shirt pocket, snapping the pocket shut and moved back to sit on the edge of the bed. He gently began wiping the blood from her face. Her eyes flickered in and out of consciousness.

"Perez?" Buck asked.

"I can't think of anyone else who would do this," Lyle answered.

The low moan of a siren died out and Lyle walked to the front door. Buck heard voices, and then two men wearing white jackets came into the bedroom carrying a stretcher. A police officer followed them.

"You the one who called for an ambulance and police?" one of the ambulance attendants said.

Buck nodded, helplessly watching as they lifted Pauline onto the stretcher.

"You got a serious wheeze there, son," one ambulance driver said.

"Asthma."

"Come on out, I'll give you a shot of oxygen." As they moved into the living room, Buck followed them.

"You need to stay here, son," the detective said. "We have to talk to you."

"They have to get her to the hospital right away, Buck," Lyle said. "Use your inhalator, let's help the police out, and we can go together. Pauline's in good hands now."

The police officer followed them into the kitchen and stood in the doorway watching them.

Buck was shaking. He lowered his head to the table. He was still wheezing.

"I need an aspirin," he whispered, pulling on the inhalator. Lyle brought the pill to him.

By two in the morning, the police had finished their search of the area and inside the house. They found faint footprints in the snow. Pauline was most likely attacked in the kitchen because of the condition of the room and also because they found a knife near the door, where it most likely had been kicked. Traces of blood clung to the blade and there were blood spatters on the floor.

"I'm gonna puke." Buck ran to the bathroom. When he came back he sat and folded his arms on the table, and rested his head.

"Looks like she put up a hell of a fight," the officer said. "How'd you come to be here, son?"

"I was waiting for her to come home from work." *If he calls me "son" one more time, I'm going to slug him.*

"She expecting you?"

"No." He paused. "I don't know. She might have been."

A chair scraped across the floor and the second officer sat down near the door.

"So she's a friend of yours?"

"She's a friend of both of ours, Officer," Lyle said.

The officer seemed to weigh the comment. "You're the art teacher at the high school?"

Lyle nodded. The silence buzzed around them and the room was becoming unbearably cold.

"You used to visiting the victim late like this, son?"

Buck cleared his throat and looked at the officer's pale, fleshy face, his indifferent expression.

"My name is Buck." He waited to be sure the officer took this information in. "I was worried about her." He felt the slight pressure of Lyle's hand on his arm.

"That so? Why's that?"

"The truth is, Officer," Lyle lied, "I asked Buck to make sure Pauline had made it back from work okay."

The officer looked at Lyle, then Buck.

"Where does she work?"

"Ruby's Cantina."

"Um hmm." The officer's voice changed and his expression was now smug. "The place in the foothills?"

Lyle nodded.

"Any chance somebody might have followed her back home? Maybe somebody she knows from working there?"

"I'm gonna be sick again." Buck felt weak. His body and head ached, but he wasn't sick. He heard Lyle's steady voice and the officer's monotone. He sat on the edge of Pauline's bed and ran his fingers over the pillow and dried smears of blood. He strained to feel the warmth of her body, but everything was cold. He picked up the Hemingway book. Two sentences were underlined.

After supper, he read, *we went upstairs and smoked and read in bed to keep warm. Once in the night I woke and heard the wind blowing. It felt good to be warm and in bed.*

The front door closed. He put the book down when Lyle came in.

"He might come back with more questions, but I'm pretty sure he knows you're the good guy here."

Buck nodded.

"I told him about Perez, that he might have been stalking her. They're putting out an All-Points Bulletin."

"Looking for him?" Buck's voice was shot through with anger. "Arrest him, you mean?"

"If they can. Don't get ahead of yourself. My bet is that he's on his way to Texas, then to Mexico."

"Son of a bitch." Buck stood. "I need to get to the hospital."

"Have you eaten anything?" Lyle said. "You look weak as hell."

"I ate." He walked slowly to the door on unsteady legs.

"You're not driving like that. We'll go in my car."

The streets were impossibly empty, the night still improbably silent. While they drove, Buck tried to sort out what might have happened. Had he fallen asleep and Perez had done all this just a few feet away? Had she screamed? Was she there bloody and beaten and alone, and all the time he could have saved her?

The emergency waiting room seemed part inside and part outside at the same time. The walls were the same gray crenellated concrete blocks as the monochromatic exterior of the hospital. High, wide windows revealed the scrawny limbs of trees bent under the snow that was now falling heavily. An irritable child was throwing wooden toys on the linoleum floor while his mother looked tired and indifferent.

Chairs upholstered in royal-blue material lined the walls, and more were arranged in a square in the center of the room. Lyle checked in at the registration desk. Buck stumbled toward the locked doors leading to ER. Lyle grabbed his arm.

"You can't go back there, Buck."

Buck stared at Lyle uncomprehendingly and pushed at the door. A guard behind the window told him to move.

"This boy has severe asthma and the stress of these events has worsened his condition." Lyle had his arm around Buck's shoulders. "Is there any chance a doctor can see him briefly?"

The woman behind the registration desk looked dispassionately at Lyle and Buck.

"We only have one doctor on call tonight and he's with the woman who was just brought in." She seemed uncertain on how to handle this double emergency.

Lyle sat next to Buck, who had slumped forward, hands dangling between his legs, his shoulders heaving with the effort to breathe.

A nurse came out and called the young mother and her son, and put a Styrofoam cup of coffee on a table next to the chair for Buck.

"Maybe caffeine can help until someone can see you. What medication do you usually take?"

"Theophylline."

"Have you taken any today?"

He shook his head.

"It sounds pretty bad. All you take is a pill?"

He shook his inhalator. "Almost out."

She retreated behind the doors. He sipped the coffee while Lyle rested his hand on Buck's back, and within seconds the nurse returned with a pill and a cup of water.

"I'll see if the doctor can issue you an inhalator but you'll have to pay for it."

"I want to see Pauline." He swallowed the pill. The nurse looked blank. "The girl you just brought in here. I want to see her now."

"The doctors are with her. They'll let you know when you can see her. She's sedated and probably wouldn't know anyone."

"She'd know me." He sank weakly against the back of the chair. "Ray," Buck said suddenly. "He doesn't know."

"Before I came here I scribbled a quick note to him that there'd been trouble at Pauline's and to come here."

As if on cue, a cold blast of winter air came through the door and Ray entered. "What the hell's going on?"

Buck turned away. Lyle stood and put his arm around Ray's shoulders, but he pulled back.

"Were you there, Buck?"

"No, goddamn it. I was at the stupid play watching your girlfriend prance around while Pauline was getting beat up by your old man." His fists were clenched as he moved toward Ray.

"If you two don't settle down, I'm going to make you leave." Lyle led Ray to a chair and sat between them. "Listen to me. We all love Pauline. Each one of us equally. Pauline knows that and she's going to need our love, not your bitterness and anger. We didn't do this to her."

"Yes, we did," Buck said. "I kept asking her to call the police and report Perez." He turned to Ray. "I asked why you hadn't called when you knew your old man was hitting her. Not a damn one of us did anything to help her." He looked at Lyle, his bitterness spilling over. "Ray said you were keeping an eye on her. Where were you tonight? How long have you seen her knocked around by Perez and done nothing?"

His breathing had finally eased but he slumped over. There was nothing any of them could say.

A doctor, young and serious-looking, came out of the emergency room. They all stood as one, looking at his expression with dread.

"Anyone here next of kin?"

"We're all her friends," Lyle said. "Her next of kin is her uncle, an old Indian, Sam Lightfoot. He wouldn't be much help."

"Still, he should know," the doctor said. His voice sounded weary.

"I want to see her," Buck said.

"And you are?"

Lyle moved toward the doctor. "I'm Lyle Samuels. I teach at the high school. We're all her friends. This is Buck Malone. He found Pauline . . . Miss Moon."

The doctor looked at Buck. "The ambulance attendant said someone had asthma. Is that you?"

Buck nodded.

"I have an order in to refill your inhalator and I'm also prescribing a low dose of prednisone. You can pick them up before you leave."

He watched Buck as if assessing the impact the incident might have had on him. Too tired to argue, Buck sat down.

"She's sedated and will be out for the next several hours. All of you need to get some rest before seeing her."

"How bad is she?" Ray's voice was low.

The doctor looked tired. He sighed and glanced at Lyle. "You want it all?" Lyle nodded. "All right, but then all of you sit down and keep calm."

Buck and Lyle watched the doctor. Ray buried his face in his hands.

"She was raped and beaten pretty viciously, probably because she fought back. Her hands and knuckles are bruised, and one finger broken. Trouble is, her fighting probably enraged her attacker more. Her left eye may have a detached retina, but we need to examine that later. She lost a tooth."

Buck felt his pocket where he'd put the tooth.

"There don't appear to be any broken bones other than the finger, but X-rays will tell us more. She has defense wounds on her hands, and some cuts on her legs that are minor. The police indicated there was a knife found on the floor?"

Ray's head shot up. Lyle nodded.

"She's lucky to be alive," the doctor said. "Whoever attacked her did so out of rage."

Ray moaned softly and Buck stared at the floor. Lyle gazed stone-faced at the wall.

"You can take care of these boys?" The doctor looked at Lyle, who nodded. "I'll get something to calm everyone down," the doctor said and returned with three small yellow pills.

"I'm not going anywhere," Buck said quietly. "And I'm not taking any pill. I'll be calm and behave myself, but I'm going to be here when she wakes up."

"I ain't moving either," said Ray.

"There's a cafeteria in the basement," the doctor said, turning back toward the emergency room door. "You might give each other a break and get something to eat. I assume you're staying too, Mr. Samuels?"

Lyle nodded and sat between the two boys. When the doctor looked back, Lyle had an arm around each boy's shoulder.

Lyle and Ray decided to go the cafeteria, and Buck stretched out on a long couch against the wall, his feet propped up on the arm, the pointed toes of his boots jutting toward the ceiling. He heard the dull hum of the fluorescent lights above him and put his arm over his eyes to cut the artificial glare, but all he could see was Pauline, alone and afraid, fighting for her life.

The outside door swung open, letting in a blast of cold air. Startled, Buck sat up. His father stood in the doorway with a policeman.

"This your boy, sir?"

Charles Malone nodded.

"Dad." He was stunned to find his father here. How did he know where to find him? Had Lyle called him?

"Where're your friends, son?" the officer asked.

"Cafeteria."

"I'll leave you two while I go talk to them. Be glad to give you both a ride home soon's I'm through."

"Officer?" Buck said. "If you've got something to add about what happened, I need to know too."

"Nothing new. You have a little talk with your dad here."

Buck sat on the edge of the couch and studied his boots. His father took the chair opposite him. "Who's hurt? The officer said it was a friend of yours."

"Yeah. Hard to explain right now."

"Why would that be hard to explain? We hardly see you anymore. Tonight with the bad weather, your mother was afraid you'd been in an accident."

Buck started coughing and bent over to control it. The nurse looked up from behind the reception desk. Buck pumped the inhalator, and rested his head on the back of the couch.

"How long have you been coughing like that?"

"Just a little bit tonight. The snow and cold aggravated it." He waited until he felt calmer, his chest less painful. "I'm here because my friend, Pauline, is hurt."

"I don't know any friend of yours named Pauline."

What you don't know about me, Dad, would take too much time to explain. He closed his eyes and wanted the hum of the lights to sink into him. "It's not important. You shouldn't have come here. I'll be home directly. Soon as I know Pauline's okay."

"Why didn't you call?"

"Things happened pretty fast."

"Fast? It's three in the morning, Buck. I wonder how you'd explain the expression on your mother's face when I left her tonight, or the embarrassment I felt having to call the Rathburns."

"What? Why'd you call them?"

"Because Lorrie's your girlfriend, isn't she? We hoped she'd have an idea where you might be."

"Oh." Buck stood, jammed his hands in his pockets and walked toward the emergency room door. He gave a tentative push. He looked to the door leading to the hall and the cafeteria, hoping Ray and Lyle would get back.

The harsh light emphasized his father's thinning hair at the crown and Buck felt a twinge of regret over his inability to confide in his father. The shoulders of his father's overcoat looked damp from the snow outside. His hands were clasped between his knees and his head bowed toward his chest. Buck sat opposite his father, wanting to say something to make a difference, to make his father feel better.

"It doesn't mean I don't love you, Dad."

But nothing was as it had been. This night was not like any other night and whoever he was this morning had been replaced by another person who had to learn to walk in dense shadows that had replaced everything familiar. He wanted to say he was sorry, but he didn't know what to be sorry for.

"What?" His father looked up and Buck saw his face swollen from tiredness.

"Dad, my friend's name is Pauline Moon, and she's more than my friend. I love her, and I'm not leaving here until I see her, and then I'm going to take care of her until she's well. I didn't know how to tell you."

"All this talk about Lorrie being your girl was a lie? A story?"

"Some of it. Lorrie's my friend too, and lots of times I was with her. And Ray Perez. He's my friend too, Dad."

Charles Malone's shoulders fell. He seemed to physically withdraw inside himself. "And your mother and me? We're not important enough to tell us about all this?"

"No, that's not it, Dad. You're my parents." He sighed. "I wanted to tell you, but I figured you wouldn't understand."

"What is it I wouldn't understand?"

"Pauline is, well, she's older than me." He stopped just short of saying she was Indian.

His father looked bewildered. "Older?"

"Couple of years. I'm seventeen, Dad. I'm old enough to choose my friends."

Just then Lyle and Ray came in with the officer. Ray's eyes were dark and angry.

"There's some news," Lyle said. "Detective Skinner reports that Perez was spotted boarding a Greyhound bus headed south, probably Texas."

"Be happy to give you and your son a lift home, Mr. Malone," the officer said.

Buck took a small step toward his father and stopped.

"I'd appreciate a ride, Detective. My son informs me he

can take care of himself now." He looked at Buck. "If you want to pick up your clothes, try and do it when your mother isn't there. You not living there anymore will hit her hard."

"There's no need to say that, Mr. Malone," Lyle said, but Malone was out the door, leaving Buck staring at the bitter world through the slowly closing door.

CHAPTER EIGHTEEN

Leaves lay flattened against the pavement, wet from the recent snow. The streets sat absent of traffic except for an occasional delivery truck. Eagle Springs waited in the cloudy dawn for the day to open. Sodden tree trunks, dank and musty-smelling, added to the gloom of the morning. Buck buttoned his jacket and pulled the collar up.

His jaws ached as he pictured his parents going through their morning ritual, and thought of how hard this morning must be for them. Had he walked away from them, or had his father finally sealed shut the gap between them? They were his parents and he wouldn't let it stay this way, but right now he wouldn't deny his love for Pauline, or his determination to keep her safe.

It was a long walk from the ER to Pauline's house. He cut through the quiet, ordered grounds of the college campus and finally came to the Bluffs. A kid on his bicycle tossed papers onto lawns and porches and Buck fell into the rhythm of the *thunk-thunk* as they landed on porch steps.

He suddenly thought about the police reports. Art would be bound to see them and he would want some kind of article about it. Buck had to get something written so he could keep Pauline's name out of it.

Another block and he was at her house. His car still sat in the driveway behind her truck, but a gray two-door Ford was parked at the curb. His breathing tightened, from exhaustion as much as from asthma. A light was on in the kitchen.

It's nothing. We all just forgot to turn the lights out when we left.

He took the steps on the back porch lightly and peered into the kitchen. Ruby was sitting at the kitchen table, her hand gripping a cup of coffee, the other hand spread flat against the table, staring at the far wall. Buck knocked on the screen door, then pushed it open slowly. The kitchen had been cleaned, chairs uprighted. Shards of the shattered dish were nowhere in sight; the apples now sat in a new bowl in the middle of the table. Ruby shivered a bit in the early morning chill, and pulled a sweater around her. She looked up when Buck came in, her eyes dull and expression numb.

After the sharp morning air the kitchen felt warm and safe, and Buck tightened the muscles in his jaw to keep his emotions calm. He moved to the table and, exhausted, sat and rested his head on his crossed arms. Ruby sat quietly watching him before she put her hand on his shoulder. After some minutes, she asked him if he'd eaten anything in the last few hours and he said no.

"I let her leave early last night," Ruby said as she fixed some breakfast. "Because of the weather. Maybe around eleven. She was nervous. Thought somebody was following her, but then she forgot about it. Perez had stopped coming to the Cantina, and I didn't like it. I figured that was worse than if he showed up, at least then we knew where he was. Before she left I told her I could stay here until things settled down. At least until he left town or got arrested."

She walked to a low cabinet, took out a bottle of brandy and poured some into her coffee and Buck's as well. "She didn't call, so I came down."

An ache hard as stone sat in his chest. "I was here."

"How's that?" She leaned toward him.

"Sitting in my car right out there at the curb." He waved toward the front of the house. "I wanted to pick her up because of the snow'n' all, but she didn't want me to go up there. So I came here, waiting for her to come home."

He lowered his head again, his forehead hitting the table so hard Ruby winced.

"Did you see anything?"

"No. I drove up the driveway to be out of sight and that's when I saw her truck and busted in here."

He wanted to lie on her bed, in the imprint she'd left. "You see the bedroom?" he said. Ruby nodded. "I cleaned it up as best I could. I hope the police don't mind."

He went to the bedroom. Pauline's bed was neat, the Hemingway book still face down but now on the nightstand. Her scent was everywhere.

He returned to the living room and looked out the wide window at the sky, blending into a mixture of blue and gray, the eastern horizon brightening with whatever today held. He went onto the porch.

Ruby joined him. "It's none of your fault. We all knew what Perez was like. I blame myself for not watching out for her better. You got help to her in time, just hold to that thought."

"If we all knew what Perez was like, why the hell didn't we do something?" He turned toward her. "I'm staying here with her. In the house."

"I guess I'd expect you to say that, but don't cut off ties to your folks."

"In all likelihood those ties are already cut."

He went to the *Gazette* office late that night, after Ruby had left, and typed up a report for the next day's edition.

ATTACK IN BLUFFS AREA

Last night a young Indian woman was brutally attacked in her home in the Bluffs area north of town. Her attacker disappeared but police have a description and an All-Points Bulletin has been issued. The woman is in the hospital and is expected to survive her wounds.

He wanted to put in a description of Perez, but the police would never allow that. After all, he hadn't been identified as the attacker. He clipped a note for Art to the brief report and said he'd talk to him with more details.

*   *   *

Pauline was released on the third day following her admittance. She was given pain medication if she needed it, and told to rest and the bruises would heal over time.

At first, she slept almost all day, mostly on the couch. She wouldn't sleep in the bed, not even with Buck beside her. He sat on the other end of the couch, with Pauline's feet in his lap, stroking them. After a week, she felt calmer and said she wanted to sleep in the bed again.

He did the laundry and cleaned the house, and he watched her. Did she want some water? Another pillow? He read to her: stories and poems, nothing too long because even with a short story, he saw her attention wander.

He sat at the kitchen table making useless notes in his journals. After all that had happened, all that he wanted to write about, the words wouldn't come. There was only the vision of violence and Pauline withdrawing into herself.

She didn't want to see anyone. Only Ruby, who came each day, bringing enough food for several dinners: tamales, chicken and beans, fruit. Sometimes she'd stay while Buck drove to Giuseppe's for a pizza and they'd all sit at the table and eat pizza and drink beer. No one talked much. Pauline spoke only in fragments, never giving away how she felt. Ruby told Buck to be patient. "She's been through a lot. Healing in mind and body will take time," she said.

Still, he couldn't deny feeling that their lives were changing forever.

Pauline started wanting to know where he was going and what he was doing. When he left her alone to do grocery shopping, and take supplies to Sam, he had to be back exactly when he said he would, or he'd find her standing on the porch, shivering despite the heavy purple shawl wrapped around her shoulders. She felt that standing on the porch would bring him home.

She seemed to forget the promise he'd made to attend high school, but she did wonder if he could ask his teachers to let him do the lessons at home.

No one mentioned Perez. Ray said he'd kill him if he ever saw him again, but when Perez didn't show up at the trailer or at his usual bars for several weeks, Ray quieted his threats. He continued working in Lyle's studio, where he finished the portrait of Lorrie.

"Lyle submitted it to the Art Institute in Denver. Thinks I have a chance at a scholarship," he told Buck.

"What happened to Marsha, the woman from the play?" Buck asked.

"I stopped it with her, but things aren't the same with Lorrie. I can hardly get to her because of her mother. It would mean a lot if you could call her, Buck. Ask how she's feeling and all."

Before he could put his attention to Lorrie, Pauline said she was going to begin working with Lyle in his studio. "At least some of the time. I used to study with him there. Besides, it will be good for me to be working on something."

They had finished eating and he was cleaning up the dishes. He didn't know what he was supposed to do or say, afraid the slightest thing would tip her over the edge.

"So," she turned to him with a light smile. "You can get back to school now."

His heart sank. She took his face in her hands and kissed him lightly.

"Don't worry. This will be better for both of us. Besides, Christmas break is just a few weeks away. I won't be at the studio every day. After the holidays, I'm going back to work at the Cantina for just a few days."

"I don't want you to do that, Pauline. Seems to me you're doing too much, first studying with Lyle and now back at the Cantina? If it's money you're worried about, I'll work harder at the paper and ask Art if he can hire me instead of this damn intern thing."

She pulled a chair close to him. "This is hard for both of us. I know that. But I have to find my way back to myself and that means connecting with what I know and not running from what I know, even if there's possible danger. Right now, painting and my job at Ruby's will help me. It doesn't mean I don't need you. I just need myself as well."

That night he was restless. He wanted to drive through the winding wasteland of the Bluffs, to get drunk and thrown in jail by Officer West. He had a beer but it tasted sour. Twice he went to the phone to call his folks and didn't.

Pauline was working on sketches at the kitchen table when he went to bed. He was intently reading a small paperback when she came in an hour later.

"What are you reading?" She slipped into bed.

He held it up: *Howl* by Allen Ginsberg.

"That looks unique. May I see it?" He handed her the book and she flipped through it. "I didn't know you were interested in poetry." A magazine photograph of a wild-haired, bespectacled man with an equally wild, scruffy beard fell out and she studied it for a moment or two.

"Miss Kennedy gave it to me. She says it's a new way of writing, a new way of thinking about language that I should know about." He lay back, his hands beneath his head. "*Revolutionary*, she called it."

"What did she mean?" She handed the book back to him and turned on her side, leaning on one arm and watching him.

He waited, collecting the new ideas as they formed. "The way it's written mostly. It reads like prose, even a novel, not like a poem with stanzas and verses." He paused. "It's written the way people talk and think, kind of in spurts."

"Spontaneous?"

"Yeah. Like that. He writes about things that I never thought you could write about, at least in a poem. About people who are frustrated, angry, and not able to get what they want. Even about politics and cities."

She turned and lay on her back, and he wanted to touch her.

"Do you like it?"

He picked it up again. "Yeah. I do."

"That's all that matters then." She leaned over and kissed him lightly before turning on her side and falling asleep.

He read into the night that hummed with night sounds and with Pauline breathing next to him. He tried to imagine his world as Ginsberg might see it, fractured in some way but whole in a new way, and he began to understand what Miss Kennedy had meant by *revolutionary*, just as he was beginning to understand what Pauline had meant when she said he needed to believe in his writing.

"Don't wait for something bad to happen," she'd said, "to prove to yourself how much you need it."

CHAPTER NINETEEN

Buck felt an edginess to Christmas. There had been no sign of Perez and the police accepted that he was most likely gone from Eagle Springs. They stopped watching the bus station and ended their few patrols of the trailer park. The same small, bright lights used for the summer dances were now strung through the bare branches of the acacia trees in Kiowa Park. The vast, elegant facade of the hotel shivered with elaborate lights, and store windows were bright with decorations.

He and Pauline decorated the house with candles, some fat and squat, others tapered and slim. They were in the bedroom, living room, and the kitchen, the whole house embraced by a golden glow. Pauline had started working two or three nights at Ruby's. She gave in and let Buck drop her off and pick her up, and Ruby let her leave early.

On Christmas Eve he had dinner with his parents. They sat in the dining room with the lace tablecloths and green taper candles. He bought a small toolbox for his dad and a shawl for his mother that Pauline had helped him pick out. He talked about school, and said that Art Packer was going to give him a couple of stories to follow up, but there was no mistaking that his life had changed and he was intent on moving on.

When he got home, Pauline was busy in the kitchen, wrapping presents for Sam. Buck opened them each a beer and sat on a chair, watching. She put some shirts in a box and wrapped it in bright Christmas paper. A new blanket was in a long box. She was intent and silent as she wrapped the gifts.

Christmas Day was gray and cold with the smell of snow in the air. They spent the morning with Sam, who looked mildly interested in presents of new shirts and underwear, and smiled at the new blanket for his narrow bed. He thanked Pauline before turning to stare bleary-eyed at the holiday celebrations on the soap operas.

That Christmas night, Pauline wore a long black skirt and a white blouse with full sleeves. She pulled her hair back and held it with the hand-carved, alabaster comb Buck had given her. She seemed happy and more relaxed than she had in weeks, although there was still no intimacy between them. He would hold her, but any attempts to excite her failed and she would turn away. "Just give me some time," she said.

She handed him a long box with a big ribbon tied on top. "Bread box." He smiled. "You want me to bake bread?"

He lifted the top off and saw a new pair of cowboy boots, soft tan leather with a diamond design etched around the top and down the sides.

He drew in his breath. "Pauline, you shouldn't be getting me anything fancy like this. I'm not going to want to wear them."

But after struggling to fit them on, he walked a crooked little walk around the rooms to break them in. "Ma'am?" He bowed to her where she sat on the couch. "May I have this dance?"

The usual nighttime radio D.J., Sheriff Bob, continued playing popular tunes instead of Christmas carols. Buck held Pauline and they circled the living room, Buck stumbling now and then in the new boots.

"This is my best Christmas ever, Pauline. I'll write about it so our kids can know how great it was."

Just then the phone rang and he went to the kitchen to answer it. It was Ruby, and she wanted to talk to Pauline. He returned to the couch, content to look at the bright Christmas tree, the wrapping paper strewn about. Pauline was talking to Ruby, her shoulders tensed and her voice subdued. Something had happened.

"I understand," she said. "Yes, that would be fine. I'll tell him. No, you don't need to come over. It's going to get stormy."

Pauline hung up and returned to the living room.

"What is it?"

She sat next to him on the couch. "It's Lorrie. She's in the emergency room. She asked some people to take her to

Ruby's, I guess to find Ray. Ruby said it looked like Lorrie was in pretty bad shape. Ray went with her to the ER. He asked Ruby to let us know."

His body tensed. "Was she in a car wreck?"

"No." She hesitated. "Ruby just said she looked in pretty serious condition."

"Oh Christ." He held his head in his hands and began to rock back and forth. He started coughing, the wheeze building inside. Pauline brought water and a pill and put her hand on the back of his neck. He pumped his inhalator and kept his head down until his breathing cleared. "I better go."

"I don't think you should drive. Let me take you."

"I'm okay." He stood, taking deep breaths but still coughing.

"Please be careful, Buck. Call me so I know you're all right."

* * *

The minute he pushed through the emergency room doors, he saw Ray. He sat in a chair propped against the wall, his head tipped back. His eyes were closed and his mouth slightly open, almost as if he were sleeping. It was the same room where they'd waited the night Pauline was attacked.

Buck walked quickly to his friend. Ray looked up, his face gaunt and strained, his eyes red. "Hey, Buck."

Buck pulled a chair next to him. "Hey. How's Lorrie?"

Ray leaned forward, his arms wrapped about his thin frame. "They ain't sure she'll make it. She about bled to death on the way here." He covered his face. "The hospital called her folks."

Ray's shirt and jeans were stained with blood. He mumbled something.

"Say what?" Buck said.

"She had an abortion, Buck." Ray's voice was just above a whisper. "She was bleeding all over the place. Never saw so much blood. And kind of out of her mind, kept on and on about the pearls and babies and a dry cleaners."

"You mean in the ambulance? She was bleeding in the ambulance?"

"Hell no. Theresa Gonzales and her no-good boyfriend, Jesse, brought her to Ruby's. She was bleeding all over the backseat."

"What the hell you talking about, Ray? What's this about a dry cleaner? Did she have the abortion there?" He put his hand on Ray's back and felt him trembling.

"I don't know. Theresa was yelling at her to shut up and Jesse was tearing down the mountain and I'm trying to hold her still. Lorrie was mumbling and soon as the emergency doctors got her out of the car, Jesse and Theresa took off."

"Ray, we have to call the cops and tell them to find this guy. Did Lorrie say anything when you were with her in the car?"

"She was in bad shape —"

"Think! What did she say about a dry cleaner?"

The only sound was the buzz of the fluorescent lights.

"She said they told her she didn't have enough money. She gave a lady the pearls as part payment."

"A lady? You mean a woman did this to her?"

Ray shook his head. "Something about a man behind a screen, and the smell like a dry-cleaning place."

"Did she say what part of town they were in?"

Ray shook his head.

"Think," he said again. "Did she give some clue?"

"I am thinking. She said the man put a cloth over her nose and mouth. Next thing she knew she was laying on a couch. She said she was all wet." His body shook. "The doctor said it was from the bleeding."

Buck sank back in the chair. If Theresa had been part of the abortion plan, she'd be hard to find now, knowing Lorrie's condition.

"It's all my fault, Buck. Now look what's happened."

Buck was about to say it wasn't all Ray's fault when the door flew open and Lillian Rathburn stood in the freezing blast of air. Lorrie's father stood behind her.

"Just what did happen?" Lillian strode toward Ray and stood above him. Buck saw pure hatred in her eyes. "You little son of a bitch!" She slapped Ray so hard it echoed through the empty room. Ray didn't lower his head.

Buck jumped up. "No need to do that, Mrs. Rathburn." He saw the imprint of her slap on Ray's cheek.

"Get out of my way, Buck Malone. You two are a real pair. Buddies. You living with an Indian woman who was raped by this pervert's father."

"Lillian!" Robert Rathburn moved toward his wife.

"What!" she yelled at her husband. Her eyes were a hard, icy blue and her face almost twisted with anger. In all his life, Buck had never seen such rage. "Listen, all of you. If my daughter lives, she's never setting foot in this one-horse town again." She bent low and glared at Ray. "You come near my daughter again, I'll kill you and enjoy the hell my husband is right now praying to keep me out of."

Buck had to get Ray out of here, or at least away from Lillian Rathburn. Mr. Rathburn was listening with no expression. Buck touched Ray's shoulder. "Come on, Ray. Let's go."

Ray didn't move, as if he wanted to receive the verbal blows of Lillian's anger.

"Come on," Buck said again, and moved them toward the door. He pushed it open quickly, the blast of cold air slapping them with a jolt. Ray turned, as if to speak to the parents who stood waiting for word of their daughter. He half started toward them but Buck stopped him.

"There's nothing to say, Ray," Buck said. "Maybe another time." But even he knew there would never be another time when either of them could speak of this night to anyone. What would they say, and to whom would they say it?

They walked around to the front of the hospital, where Buck had parked. Ray had no jacket, and Buck put his around his friend's shoulders. They were as silent as the night around them, their footsteps barely making a sound on the snow-dusted sidewalk. They got into the car but Buck didn't start it right away; he was trying to make sense of all that had happened.

Ray slumped, looking out the front window. "It's all gone, Buck. All of it. Nothing matters anymore. Not Lorrie, or my painting, or trying to fit in, or even trying to get somewhere."

Buck didn't want to believe that it was all over for Ray. If something was gone from Ray, something was gone from him as well. It had been disappearing for weeks now. He just couldn't admit it. He coughed hard.

"Got your inhalator?"

Buck nodded, grabbed it from his shirt pocket and gave two puffs.

A hole opened up inside of him. Any time, any day, he could be sitting somewhere just as Ray was sitting next to him now, knowing it was all lost. He started the car and drove to Lyle's.

"White Christmas." Ray looked at the winter yard covered with snow.

"Looks like it."

"Tell Pauline I'm okay?"

"You shouldn't be alone tonight. Let me wait with you until Lyle comes home."

The space between them filled with questions and no answers.

Ray took a drag on his cigarette, rolled down the window, and tossed it out.

"Lorrie'll be all right," Buck said, stopping at the curb and shutting off the motor.

In the eerie half-light, he saw Ray's crooked smile as he opened the door.

"I'll see you tomorrow, Buck."

He watched helplessly as Ray climbed the porch stairs and disappeared inside.

"Damn." He hit his hands against the steering wheel. "Damn."

He waited until the living room light went on, followed a few minutes later by the studio light. He stayed in the car, holding the events of this night inside, staring at the light and wondering at the pain that lay ahead, as if pain was all he had on this bitter December night.

He didn't go to Pauline's right away. He drove north, then west, into the surreal and ancient formations of red rock, some jutting away from the Front Range while others tilted toward the earth. The full moon turned the rocks into sensational shapes, intimidating but strangely comforting, and he stayed there, perhaps wishing he had nowhere else to go. He stopped the car, got out, and walked the silent landscape, ghostly with the snow, and then sat on a craggy outcrop of rock until the moon moved and the space became black and cold and frightening and he turned back toward Pauline's.

CHAPTER TWENTY

Pauline spent more afternoons in Lyle's studio. Buck tried not to want to go there, to spy through the window as he had on Ray and Lorrie. A sense of failure began to build deep inside him. He hadn't protected Pauline. He'd failed Ray and Lorrie. He tried to take his mind off his pain by reading Ginsberg and other writers, the ones calling themselves "Beat." He studied photographs of them in cafés and bars in Greenwich Village, and in front of a famous bookstore, City Lights, in San Francisco's North Beach. The more he read, the more he wanted to write, but he didn't know what story he needed to write.

He held Pauline at night even though they hadn't made love since the attack. He knew she was painting something blue because her fingers were smudged with blue paint. One morning, as he watched her sleep, he saw a streak of yellow behind her ear and imagined her scratching there with the tip of the brush without realizing it. Each night he came to look for new colors to try and guess what she was working on.

His life slid further away with each passing day. He'd made one choice, to love Pauline, and now that had changed. He had to sort through the alternatives the same way he tried to guess what Pauline was painting from splotches of color left on her skin.

The day Ray finally called was cold. Buck felt an unaccountable apprehension when he heard Ray's voice.

"Hey," Ray said.

"Hey." He heard country music in the background. "Where are you?"

"Horseshoe Tavern."

He looked at the clock. Eleven in the morning. "Kind of early for that, isn't it?"

After a pause, Ray said, "Guess I won't ask if you want to meet up with me, then. I ain't exactly in the mood for the corner drugstore."

"You drunk?"

"Not yet."

The Horseshoe Tavern was a run-down saloon east of town. It dated back from the gold-mining days, when miners and even Indians spent long, empty hours there. Not much had changed. The floor was scuffed, unpolished wood, and a jukebox played country tunes but no one really listened. The few Indians who straggled in were left alone to sleep in corners.

Ray was racking the balls when Buck came in. "Hey, Buck."

"This what you've been doing?" Buck motioned to the pool table.

"Now 'n' then."

"You painting?"

Ray took a swig from the beer bottle. "You writing?"

The weight of each second slid down Buck's arms. "I heard Lorrie left town," he said. "Moved to Denver. Did you see her before she left?"

"From a distance, you might say." Ray paused to concentrate on the break. "Thought it best to avoid being murdered by a pastor's wife." He moved around the pool table. "I hid out at the Union Station in Denver, watching her get on the California Zephyr headed toward Los Angeles." He tossed the cigarette down and ground it out on the floor. "She looked—" He hesitated. "She looked fine."

"Wish you would've called me. At least I could have been there with you."

"Thought about it, but I wasn't sure I'd even go until the last minute."

Buck looked around the dismal room. "Hear you're not living at Lyle's anymore." The beer he swallowed was so bitter he had to check the label. "Where you been staying?"

"At the trailer. My old man's long gone, and if he came back I figure he knows I'd kill him flat out."

A shiver ran down Buck's spine.

"Grab a cue," Ray said.

"I'm no good at that." But he picked a cue stick anyway.

"Just follow the rules," Ray said.

Buck made a sloppy attempt to guide a ball into the pocket and failed. "Sure," he said.

"How are things between you and Pauline?"

"She paints at Lyle's during the day and works at Ruby's at night."

They finished the game and walked outside, the day having darkened from the winter sky. Ray's bike sat covered in snow.

"Sorry to hear you're having troubles, Buck. I thought if anybody could make it work, you could."

He watched Ray walk to his motorcycle. "You going to drive that thing in this weather?"

"I got up here okay. Besides, I put chains on."

They hesitated, awkward and wordless.

"I forgot to ask why you wanted to see me?" Buck said.

Ray pulled the collar of his jacket up against the snow and cold. "Wanted to tell you I've joined the Army. Leaving from Fort Carson tomorrow for basic training at Fort Ord in California."

"Tomorrow? Some reason you're telling me hours before?"

"Happened fast. Don't get on me now. I plan to finish high school and get my diploma, get trained for some kind of a job, maybe have a chance to make something of myself."

"In the Army?" Buck was surprised.

Ray nodded. "GI Bill. If there was a chance your asthma would clear up, you could join up with me. Be one way we could see the world like we used to talk about."

Buck kicked at the side of the building, remembering nights when they'd talked about the future, their lives. How he'd thought they'd always be together, if not forever, at least until their lives were settled. Now Ray was going to California, and he was left in Eagle Springs: uncertain of his life with Pauline, estranged from his family, and on the verge of being expelled from school.

"You wouldn't last a minute in the military, Buck," Ray tried to joke. "Stick to writing, I'll take care of the Army." He tried to sound upbeat, but Buck was still dejected.

Ray's voice cracked. "I'll write and let you know where I am."

"Why'd you decide to do this? If it's because of Lorrie and your old man . . ."

Ray stepped away from his bike. "Well hell yes, Buck. It's because of all of that."

"What about your painting? The scholarship?"

"Guess I forgot to tell you. Lyle sent my portrait of Lorrie to the Art Institute for the scholarship but it was rejected. *Promising* they called it, but no scholarship."

Buck looked down at his new boots collecting snow.

"Take care of yourself." Ray got on his bike. "You'll always be my buddy. I could always count on you." He paused. "Sorry I brought down so much trouble."

"You didn't bring any more trouble than any of us, Ray. If you're using that as a reason for signing up, it's not right."

Ray looked west, toward Eagle Springs and released the kickstand. "Take care of Pauline, Buck. If anyone can work things out, it's you."

He turned the bike and eased it down the slope before gunning the motor and taking off. Buck listened until the sound of the motorcycle faded in the distance, until his eyes teared up from staring into the windy, white emptiness, until he had no reason to stand in the small, barren plot of land and went to his car, and drove it down the mountain toward town.

*   *   *

In February, Sam had a stroke. Pauline found him lying on the floor of the trailer, a grainy test pattern rolling on the television screen. He lay face up, arms folded across his chest as if he'd just lain down to take a nap and decided the floor was a good place to stay.

She called Buck from a nearby clinic because the hospital wouldn't treat an Indian. She called Lyle too. Buck was at the clinic when Lyle came in.

"They don't have the facilities to treat him here," she said.

"Let Buck and me talk to them, Pauline," Lyle said.

"It's no good. At least they've agreed to transport him to a clinic in Denver."

"Let me go with you," Buck said. "In the transport, I mean."

"No, Buck. Just watch the house for a couple of days and call Ruby for me. I'll be at a motel near the hospital. I'll call with the details."

Then she was gone.

*   *   *

Buck didn't return to school after the holiday break. He spent hours in the library reading, or writing at Pauline's kitchen table. At first short stories, but he was too preoccupied to see if they flowed together, or if he was writing one long story. Later he began to make notes for a novel, but the story and characters blended into his own experiences and he couldn't separate fact from fiction.

Some nights he missed Ray and Lorrie as much as he missed Pauline. He stayed in the *Gazette* office until after midnight, ate at the Village Inn because it was the only place that stayed open late, and when he left and looked at the ridge of mountains silhouetted black against the predawn sky and felt the mountain air coiling around him, he knew he needed to write about Eagle Springs, too.

After a month, Pauline hadn't come back. Ruby said it might be time for him to move back in with his parents, but he said he couldn't do that. He was angry she'd even suggest it.

Even though he hadn't moved out of Pauline's house, he slept nights in his car, covered with Pauline's quilt; other times he slept in the *Gazette* office. One night he pulled to the curb in front of her house and the lights were on. He raced up the porch steps and into the living room. "Pauline!"

Ruby came out of the kitchen. "Sorry, Buck. It's just me. Pauline asked me to see how you're doing."

He shrugged. "I haven't heard from her, but she calls you. What's going on?"

"Can't push that girl."

The pungent odor of chili came from the kitchen. He sat at the table and Ruby put a steaming bowl in front of him. "You look skinnier than ever, if that's possible," she said.

He ate the chili and she brought him another bowl and a bottle of beer for each of them.

"You're a damn good cook, Ruby."

She sat next to him. "I have a proposition for you, Buck. I'd like you to come and help me out at the Cantina. I'll pay you. And you can stay here as room and board."

"Nope."

"Pretty quick response."

"No offense, Ruby, but your place is filled with memories of Pauline and that so-and-so, Perez. I have enough trouble just staying in Eagle Springs after all that's happened. I've decided to rent a room at the YMCA until I figure out what I want to do."

"Why don't you go to your parents? Even if you only sleep there."

He pushed the bottle of beer around in a small circle on the table. He thought his answer would sound silly, but when he said it, it just sounded sad.

"I'm not a kid anymore, Ruby, and that's all they'd see me as. Their son, still needing them. Maybe it's wrong, but I don't want to need them, and that's the truth."

She poured some whiskey in two glasses, put one in front

of him, and pulled a small white envelope out of her shirt pocket. She pushed it toward him. Buck recognized Ray's scrawl.

"Came this morning. He wasn't sure where you might be, so he sent it to me." She moved to the sink and began cleaning up.

Hey Buck. Nope this ain't no joke. Thought I'd see the world and the first place they send me is California. Doing basic at Ford Ord and then bound for Hawaii. It's not bad. Army's helping me with my education & I'm eating good and look fit as all get out. Strong enough to beat the hell out of my old man should I ever come up against that bastard again. I migrate to S.F. every now & then, and hang out at North Beach with all those abnormal, confused writers you're so fond of. I made the unforgivable mistake & said "Frisco," that brought down more cussing which came so fast and loud that all I heard was "go back to L.A." Anyway, that North Beach looks like the place for you, Buck. Here's wishing you good luck & it's probably for the best your asthma kept you out of the Army. Tell Pauline & Ruby I'm doing fine. Your friend, Ray Perez
PS: We had some good old times, didn't we Buck?

CHAPTER TWENTY-ONE

The graceful, sloping lawns surrounding Denver's State Capitol building were a brilliant bright green. Daffodils sprung up yellow and delicate, but if history held true, a spring snow would soon bury them.

Buck followed the directions Ruby had given him to Pauline's apartment. It was on a quiet, tree-lined street on the top floor of what was once one of Denver's grand mansions, a three-story, red-brick building with a deep porch and wide lawn. Pauline lived in a studio apartment on the top floor.

Buck parked in front, took a box from the trunk, and climbed the stairs.

It had been four months since he'd seen Pauline. Before he left her house he'd packed the quilt, the portrait of Sam, and a small box filled with a few remaining sachets. All he took for himself were some line drawings she had made of him writing at the kitchen table or sleeping.

He felt strangely calm when he knocked on the door, until the door opened and Pauline stood there in a bright, sun-filled room.

"Buck." That was all. Just his name. He put down the box and stepped into her arms and it was like coming home.

They sat at a tiny table in the small kitchen overlooking the street and talked.

"How's Sam?"

"Better. The clinic has managed to keep him alive but I can't really afford to keep him in a home."

She opened two beers and they went into the small living room and sat on the couch—it must open into a bed because there was no sign of one in the small studio. The room was neat and spare, just as the house had been. Some painted canvases were propped against one wall.

He leaned back, his head against the back of the couch, and tried to find his way in this space.

"Is your asthma better?"

He patted his shirt pocket where the inhalator made a slight bulge. "I still need this, but it seems to be tapering off. Still no chance I could join the Army, though."

"Would you have?"

He shrugged. "Never know now."

"I'll have to have Sam with me, at least until I can save some money to have him in a rest home."

"Here? How is Sam going to fit in here?"

"I'm going to move again."

He felt his heart pounding. He walked to the window that overlooked the quiet street, the sloping lawn, and the elm trees bordering the street as far as he could see. He wanted to be with her. Here in this small, neat space on the top floor of an old mansion. "Where are you moving?"

"I'm getting an apartment a bit closer to the Art Institute with a small room for Sam until I find a nursing home to care for him. Lyle helped me get a part-time teaching job at the institute, so that will help."

He nodded. "Thought you might like these." He put the box on the couch next to her.

She ran her hands over the quilt and propped the painting against a small table.

"Thank you, Buck."

"Your painting is working out for you then?"

"Working out enough to get a part-time teaching job, but doubtful I'll be able to show or sell much."

He thought about Ray losing out on a scholarship, and Pauline maybe unable to move along with her painting, and the unfinished story he'd packed in his suitcase.

"Please sit beside me." She patted the cushion next to her on the small sofa, but he sat on the chair opposite, leaning forward, with his hands clasped between his knees.

"Funny you should say you're moving. I'm moving on myself."

He handed Ray's letter to her.

She read it once and then again. "I'm glad he's okay."

"So I'm taking Ray's advice and checking out San Francisco. Maybe find a place in North Beach and hang out with other writers. I'm selling my car at one of those used car lots out on Colfax Boulevard. That'll hold me until I get a job."

"You loved that car, Buck."

"Yeah. Well, I loved a lot of things."

"Your parents know, of course?" Pauline said after a long moment of silence.

"Told them." He walked to the paintings stacked against the wall. "Guess they figured there's not much they could say to stop me."

She lowered her head and her hair fell around her face the way it had that first time he'd seen her in Wheaton & French, and the way it did when they'd made love. It all felt so long ago that he wondered if he remembered correctly.

"This is all my fault," she whispered.

The room had darkened. Dusk or a storm. He heard distant thunder. He should be going, but he didn't move.

"It's not anybody's fault, Pauline. Or maybe it's everybody's. Point is, nothing is going to change if I hang around."

She rose and turned on a lamp. "When are you leaving?"

"No sense waiting. Lorrie's already in Los Angeles, Ray's going around the world thanks to the Army." He moved to the couch. "Taking a Greyhound bus tomorrow."

She lowered her head and said in almost a whisper, "So soon."

"You wouldn't happen to have anything stronger than beer around, would you?" he said.

She poured two whiskeys and sat next to him.

"How's Lyle?" he said.

"He teaches one semester a year at the institute. He's here for the spring term but returns to Mountain States in the fall. He'd love to see you, Buck."

He shook his head.

"Do you still see your English teacher? I forget her name."

"Miss Kennedy. Nope, but I still read the writers she recommended. Reckon the first place I'll head for is City Lights Bookstore in North Beach."

"I'm glad you're following your dream, Buck. I'm sorry you had to lose so much, but I'm glad." She touched his arm. "Will you do something for me?"

He nodded solemnly.

"Write when you're in San Francisco. Don't brood and think about Eagle Springs and all that happened. I've read enough of your stories to know you have a good, clear voice." He looked at her and she leaned toward him, kissing him lightly before moving back.

"Guess I'm not sure what I'll write about, but it's more than likely I won't forget what's happened here." The familiar wheeze rose in his chest. He got up and reached for the inhalator in his jacket and pumped the medicine. "Have you heard or seen anything of Perez? Before Ray left I asked him, but he thought there was no way his old man would show up in Eagle Springs."

She shook her head. "I haven't heard anything about him. He won't find me here, though. You're through with that, Buck."

He knew he'd never be through with it. He told her he'd send his address and phone number right away; that if she ever needed him he'd come back. He stayed that night. Pauline made up the sofa bed, covered them with the quilt, and they lay in each other's arms as the shadows cast by the streetlight filtered through the limbs of the trees. They didn't make love. Before the sun crested the distant mountains and while the sky was still navy blue, and before the traffic started to life on the street beneath her window, he dressed quietly, took slow steps down the carpeted stairway, out the front door and across the front porch. He waited before getting in the car, wanting to look up at the window, but in the end he drove away without turning back.

At the Greyhound station he bought a one-way ticket to San Francisco. He stashed his suitcase in a locker, then drove out to East Colfax to a used car lot and sold his car, and walked back to the bus station. He looked at the mountains, farther away here than in Eagle Springs, and how the snow on the high peaks shimmered in the bright morning sun, and he wondered if he should leave after all.

Downtown, pretty girls hurried down Seventeenth Street on their way to work, their high heels clicking on the sidewalk as if they were dancing, and young men in suits and carrying briefcases looked at them.

He had breakfast at a small restaurant, but didn't eat much. He felt his journal in his satchel, his pen in his shirt pocket. He had nothing to write.

A WAY WE NEVER WERE

CHAPTER TWENTY-TWO

At a store in Cheyenne, Buck bought a postcard of a cowboy riding toward purple-hued mountains, a Mickey Spillane novel, and Steinbeck's *East of Eden*. As he was leaving he saw the name of an author he'd heard about, Jack Kerouac, and he bought his novel *On the Road*.

The bus driver hadn't returned from his break yet, so Buck waited at the edge of the highway. The sun was hot against his back, the air dry, and he looked back at the road they'd just travelled. It wasn't too late. He could exchange his ticket for a one-way back to Denver. He'd help Pauline with Sam; he'd write and she could paint. He kicked at the dirt and looked at the highway stretching ahead. California seemed farther away than he'd imagined.

Across the highway a diner, stark and dingy in the morning sun, sat a few yards away from a dilapidated, single-level frame motel. Both looked uninviting. A young man came out of the diner and a girl followed him. She wore a waitress uniform and her shoes were white with thick soles. She was small, with short, dark hair. Buck couldn't help watching them. The man looked slightly older than Buck. His hair was dark and fell over his forehead when he bent to kiss the girl.

She rose to her toes, put her arms around his neck and pressed herself to him, and Buck felt a longing so strong he felt dizzy. The man stepped back and picked up the suitcase he'd set down on the ground. The girl buried her face in her hands; he whispered something in her ear, paused, then turned and crossed the highway.

The driver walked from the café to the bus and got behind the wheel. He was checking the map and timetable when Buck got on and went back to his seat. Buck stuck the postcard in the window and took the Spillane out of his bag. Outside, the girl hadn't moved. She stood with her feet close together and arms folded across her chest, and she looked impossibly young and small.

"This seat taken?" The man who'd said good-bye to the girl stood in the aisle.

"Nope." Buck picked up his journal from the seat, and the man tossed his suitcase in the overhead rack.

Outside, the girl raised her hand in a tentative gesture and Buck wanted to wave back. He was watching her when the man next to him said, "Excuse me," and stretched toward the window and waved. The girl jumped for happiness and waved wildly, her arms flailing back and forth like a semaphore while the bus lurched into gear and eased out onto the highway toward the plains and deserts of the great American West.

Buck tried to glue the image of the girl standing in the dust, watching the bus pull away, to the back of his eyes; to remember her in that desperate moment of love and longing. He hoped someday he'd write about it.

Tonight, he thought, *she'll cry all night and probably tomorrow. She'll watch buses come and go, east and west, for days and weeks.*

The young man next to him slept while Buck read. By the time they reached the lunch stop, he'd finished *I, the Jury*. Outside, the air was sharp and bright. In the diner, he headed toward a stool at the end of the fountain.

"Hey, man." The man who'd sat next to him on the bus now leaned against the back of one of the booths. "Welcome to join me here. Those stools don't look too comfortable."

"Thanks." Buck slid into the booth across the table and grabbed a menu.

"Boys?" The waitress came with two mugs of steaming coffee. Her face was weathered and her skin looked thin, as though the dry air had scraped across it, but she had nice eyes.

Buck ordered bacon, sausage, and eggs with a side of toast, and the man ordered a stack of pancakes and side of bacon.

"Francis Johnson. Folks call me Frankie."

"Hey. Buck Malone. No, thanks," he said when Frankie offered him a cigarette.

"First trip?"

Buck nodded. "You?"

Frankie shook his head. "Travelled all across the great U.S. of A. courtesy of Greyhound bus."

"Bet you've got some stories to tell." Buck thought about the girl left at the last stop.

The two ate in silence and after Buck finished, he headed to the restroom to splash water on his face. Outside, waiting for the driver to return, he looked at clouds of filmy, copper-tinged dust rising in the distance and he thought how a rise of dust like that at home could mean a Chinook. Here, the mountains took up half the sky and towered higher than the range of Rockies surrounding Eagle Springs. They were farther away, as if waiting for a town to come to them.

Frankie stood nearby, lingering over a cigarette. "Looks like a whole lot of nothing, doesn't it?"

Buck shrugged. "I come from a town that sits close on the Front Range of the Rockies. Reckon I got used to mountains."

"Come on, boys." The driver climbed on the bus.

"Want the window?" Buck said.

"You mind? I'll probably just sleep."

"'S'kay."

Frankie dozed off as soon as the bus started, and Buck reached for his journal, but the motion of the bus lulled him to sleep as well. As they crossed the border into Nevada, Buck woke, stood, and stretched his legs, hanging on to the overhead rack for balance. He looked out the window at the

Nevada desert rolling out to the horizon and for the first time, he felt something stir inside him.

Heading west. Across America to California and the Pacific Ocean. He eased into the seat again. A father and son—the boy looked about five or six—sat across the narrow aisle. Their hair was shiny and black and lay flat against their heads, and their skin was the color of honey. The boy's eyes were dark and shaped like almonds, and when he bounced his legs against the seat, a purple sock slipped down his thin ankle, and the father leaned over and pulled it back up. The boy sat close to his father, cradled against him, and now and then the father whispered something in the boy's ear that made him smile. If he put his thumb in his mouth, the father removed it with a soft reprimand. The boy was looking at a Dick Tracy comic book.

Buck opened his journal and wrote. *The father looks almost delicate. His hair is flat against his head & his ears are small & neat, as though he could hear sounds of the sea. His brown suit doesn't fit & his wrists, thin, jut out from worn cuffs. His fingers are long. He wears a jade band on the ring finger.*

"Japs," Frankie whispered.

Buck remembered the first time he'd heard Ray called a "spic." How ugly the word sounded, just as *Jap* did now.

"Hope we don't have trouble. I came up from L.A. to San Francisco once on the train and all hell broke loose. Some drunk in the club car yelling at a Jap that he'd killed his son." Frankie shook his head. "Personally, it's none of my business.

Live and let live, I say." He lit a cigarette. "You a Jap hater?" He blew smoke upward.

Buck shook his head. "Don't know much about them."

"Where you from?"

"Colorado. Small town, Eagle Springs. Pretty town with a river running through it. It's not too easy on folks who are different, though."

"How so?"

"Plenty of Mexicans live there, but even so, they stand out. My buddy, Ray, had his share of troubles. He joined the Army. Stationed at a place called Fort Ord."

"You didn't join up with him?"

"Asthma," he said.

"Just as well," Frankie said. "The military sure isn't for everyone." He closed his eyes again.

Frankie's most striking feature was his long, slim fingers, now moving almost imperceptibly against his thighs, his head moving in time with his fingers to some inner rhythm. "You like jazz, man?" Frankie said, as though reading Buck's mind.

"Can't say as I've ever heard it. Back home, we listened mostly to rock 'n' roll. Ray liked Elvis a lot."

Frankie laughed and slapped his knee. "Elvis isn't called 'The King' for nothing. I learned about blues from that man's music. But jazz is the scene in San Francisco. That's why I'm going back. I play jazz piano."

"Oh," Buck said. "That's what . . ." He pointed to Frankie's hands.

"Yeah," Frankie said. "Music's in here, man." He tapped his head, then his heart. "Did the jazz scene in L.A. for a while, but it jumps more in San Francisco."

"Winnemucca," the bus driver called. "Hour and a half stop."

"Great," Frankie said. "Stretch those long legs of yours, man."

*   *   *

Frankie won playing the slots and against his better judgment, Buck gave it a try. Before long they had twenty dollars and some change.

"Tell you what," Frankie said. "We'll use this money to treat us to a nice dinner our first night in San Francisco. Joe's on Broadway for spaghetti and meatballs; Vesuvio's for Irish coffee. And wait until you see City Lights Bookstore."

"I know," Buck said. "First place I'm going."

Back on the bus, he wrote the names in his journal, wondering if any place could be as wonderful as San Francisco sounded.

*   *   *

Close to six in the evening, the bus pulled into the station in San Francisco. A gray, fog-laden drizzle blurred the traffic snaking down the hills and across broad Market Street. Buck hauled his suitcase off the bus and followed Frankie, but just inside the door, he stopped in amazement. The waiting room seemed to be filled with shapes he assumed were human beings, lumped under coats and blankets that smelled of wet wool and canvas. A steamy haze condensed around these motionless mounds.

Frankie chuckled. "Your idol, Jack Kerouac, called San Francisco 'a cold, gray city.' " He lit a cigarette and chuckled again. "He had that right." Frankie headed toward the door. Buck stood in the middle of the room.

"Let me guess," Frankie walked back. "You haven't got a place to stay, right?"

"Figured I'd go to the YMCA."

"Dumb kid. Come all the way to California on your own with no place to stay." He grabbed Buck's arm. "Come on."

He piled their suitcases into a cab. "The Coronet," he said to the driver. "Powell and Bush. It's a residence hotel," he said to Buck. "I know the owners and I know they happen to have a vacancy." He poked Buck in the ribs. "They don't know it yet, but yours truly is moving out. It's a good place. Two meals daily except weekends."

The cab navigated impossibly steep hills. Cable car tracks glistened, reflecting the bright lights of the city, and their steady hum beneath the street created a noisy rhythm to the bustle around him. A giant gold star revolved slowly in the mist atop the Sir Francis Drake Hotel. Buck felt the city's energy with confused emotions: wonder, excitement, and apprehension. It felt as if he'd landed on a different planet. There was so much to take in, so many distractions, what made him think he'd be able to write in this exciting city?

"Here we are, pal." Frankie paid the driver. "Your new home."

Buck looked at the narrow, beige building just off Powell Street.

"There." Frankie pointed to a bay window on the second-floor front. "That'll be your room."

* * *

Enough characters to fill a novel inhabited the hotel. The eldest resident, Mrs. Branson, an eighty-year-old woman, liked to crowd as many young people as she could into her tiny room to watch political debates on a small television set. At meal times in the dining room, four or five men always sat together essentially ignoring the rest of the crowd. A career woman, attractive and smart, and a young girl who took classes at the Extension Center around the corner, sat with him at dinner, but in the end, he avoided all of them. He'd anticipated excitement, discovery of new people and ideas; yet once here, all he wanted was to be alone.

He called his mother and assured her he was fine. "I have a good place to live." He paused. "I hope to land a job in a local bookstore."

* * *

He came to like the transient feel to his life. He could write whenever and wherever he wanted: sitting in the lobby, or in a corner of the dining room, or in cafés or restaurants. It was a city that loved artists. He wrote a small piece based on what Mrs. Branson told him about her coming to San Francisco from Nebraska with a young lawyer husband who had dreams of being a politician. He was shot and killed during the riots over Harry Bridges, an immigrant longshoreman from Australia accused of being a Communist. It wasn't much, but a local magazine accepted it and paid him twenty-five dollars. If he was careful, together with what money left from the *Gazette*, he could still explore the city.

He wanted to call Pauline but didn't have her phone number in Denver. He started to call Lyle, hung up and then started to call Ruby, but hung up again. He ate in coffee shops and restaurants around Union Square rather than in the dining room, sinking deeper and deeper into an isolation that he hadn't anticipated. The anonymity he thought he wanted turned quickly to quicksand.

He walked the city. In rain or sun, at the crack of dawn, or in the dead of night. He walked through the Produce District at four in the morning when it was alive with the shouts of men off-loading crates of vegetables and fruit. He tracked the route of the old Barbary Coast along the Embarcadero, and drank in run-down bars at night and no one questioned his age.

He climbed the highest hills, some so steep the sidewalk became a set of stairs, and he'd stop, gasping, at the top, and pump his inhalator. He walked up the curving road to Coit Tower and spent the day huddled inside because of a cold rain and wind, and he developed a cough and congestion for weeks before seeing a doctor. He'd been without any medication for almost a month and he found a doctor who gave him a prescription.

"If this doesn't work," the doctor said, "I'm going to perscribe prednisone."

He wrote about what he saw and planned to work his writings into a short-story collection. One story began with a walk through the garish painted gate on Grant Avenue leading to Chinatown. Chinese characters in neon swirls of fuchsia and lime pointed to restaurants at the end of a dark, narrow alley, and he felt a twinge because it all reminded him of Ruby's. Ducks heavy with glaze that made them look shellacked were stacked in windows. Aluminum trays, dull and scratched from overuse, were heaped with wonton, egg rolls, pot stickers, sweet-and-sour pork, while all around him, language was a clutter of sound with no meaning.

Into his second month, he turned down the short alley between Vesuvio and City Lights, and emerged on the brash, brilliant corner of Broadway and Columbus in North Beach. The idea came to him that San Francisco was an endless narration of its own, enticing enough to blot out his own story.

At City Lights, it was hard to fathom he was finally at his literary destination. He sat in the basement at a round table with a bowl of apples in the center, writing until they closed, often long after midnight, and then walked down the alley again, and through a deserted and dark Chinatown until he reached the residence hotel.

The City exuded solitude and he liked it because he had room to think about what had happened in Colorado and how to find a way into his writing.

Standing at the edge of the Pacific Ocean, at the western edge of the continent with the deserts and mountains and plains of America behind him, he was amazed to feel nothing special. Just a clear, uncluttered horizon, an even meeting of water and land, the blue Pacific mirroring a cloudless sky. And it was enough.

One day he didn't take the long streetcar ride to the ocean, but instead walked to Civic Center and the main library. The steep streets of Nob Hill descended into a dreary world of low-class hotels, shabby apartment buildings, and a collection of run-down bars and restaurants. City Hall, surrounded by government buildings, had a kind of pathetic elegance, crowning the center of this destitute neighborhood with the main library settled in its shadow.

Inside, the library was unlike anything he might have imagined. It was huge compared to the small granite building built on the high bank of the Eagle River. Inside, a marble staircase populated with the homeless, some sleeping, others asking for money, led to the first floor. A mixture of cheap wine and even cheaper bourbon hung over the place. He turned back, instead taking comfort in the two or three paperbacks stashed in his satchel.

He walked down the long, even stretch of Market Street to the Ferry Building, taking in everything in a search to understand what he wanted to write about, but writing about

San Francisco felt like a meaningless exercise. He might not know what he had to write about, but he knew the words weren't there yet.

The next night he was in the basement of City Lights reading. It was late when the store manager, Jake, came halfway down the stairs.

"Hey you, cowboy. Want a job?"

Buck stared.

"Just had somebody quit. Figure you spend most of your time here, might as well get paid for it. If you don't want to, say no."

"No," Buck said. "I mean, hell yes I want the job."

"Shelving stock, moving inventory around for better sales, that kind of thing. Maybe some selling."

"Does it include a discount on books?" Buck asked.

"Yeah. For you I guess I can swing that."

A week later, Frankie knocked on his door. "Man, I'm glad to see you," Buck said. "I didn't know how to find you and I wanted to let you know I got a job at City Lights."

Frankie slumped in a chair near the window and lit a cigarette. "That's damn good news, Buck. Now you have someplace to put your novel." They both laughed.

"Where you been hiding?" Buck asked.

"Lining up gigs. Don't tell me you missed me."

Buck *had* missed him, or maybe it was the idea of Frankie he'd missed.

"Something wrong with the food here?" Frankie said. "Look like you're not eating too good."

Buck shrugged.

Frankie eyed a stack of lined yellow paper on the corner of the table, held down by a battered copy of *East of Eden*. "What's all this?" He set aside the book and riffled through the loose yellow pages.

"Just scribbling."

"Uh-huh." He put the book back. "Scribbling toward something? Like a book?"

"You have some particular reason for stopping by?"

"Yep. Shine those fancy boots of yours. Time you saw Frankie's San Francisco."

It was the beginning of an end to his rootlessness, to hoping this city would give up a story to him, and he had to admit he welcomed Frankie's companionship.

Frankie made good on the spaghetti dinner at Joe's on Broadway and threw in two bottles of red wine along with it. They walked along Upper Green, the street heady with the fragrance of Italian coffee and the acrid smell of paint from the art stores. Folk music drifted from the coffee houses they passed along the way; someone called to Frankie from Caffe Trieste and they went in, joining a happy crowd gathered around a table near the window. They drank more wine and espresso while the windows steamed over and fog looped around the corners and rolled down the hills, and Buck decided then that San Francisco was a state of mind even if he wasn't sure what that meant.

They left Trieste and a block later, Frankie led him down Broadway, where the streets widened, toward a blue neon sign,

Jazz, flickering in the mist. "Come on," Frankie said. "Time for you to join the human race again."

They went into a bar tucked at the end of a narrow alley. A Tiffany lamp hung from the ceiling above the bar, and red votives with candles inside sat on the tables scattered around a piano. A separate room, dark and deserted except for more tables, suggested room for an overflow crowd.

Georgia, a tiny woman behind the bar, scooted from one end to the other so fast that Buck thought she must have been wearing roller skates. She made him think of Ruby and for the first time since leaving, he missed Eagle Springs. Frankie ordered two drinks and motioned Buck to a table near the piano where a woman sat alone. She had long, lovely legs and she was very beautiful.

"Buck, this is Linda. She's a friend of mine. A fan of my piano playing, you could say." He put the drinks on the table.

"Hey." Buck was having trouble focusing from all the wine, but Linda shifted ever so slightly and he saw her face in the light. Her hair was dark and pulled back, flat against her head, which emphasized her eyes. They were the palest blue Buck had ever seen, and her skin was pale too, and her mouth perfectly shaped by red lipstick. She wore a white dress and a gold necklace around her slim throat that caught the light. What looked like a fur stole was draped across the back of her chair.

"Buck." She smiled and held out her hand. "Glad to meet you. Frankie told me about you." Her hand was cool and her fingers were long and the nails were painted the same red as her lips.

"Do tell." Buck realized he'd been staring at her, and he wished desperately that he didn't feel as if he were about to slide right off the chair. "Pleasumeetyou."

Two musicians came in and Frankie jumped up. "Back in a flash." He walked toward them.

Buck felt numb. Either he'd been alone so long that he had no idea how to communicate, or he was drunk beyond all hope.

Linda said, "Frankie tells me you're going to be famous." She lit a cigarette. "What kind of famous are you going to be?"

"Writer."

"Oh." She flicked the ash from her cigarette into the ashtray. "That kind of famous. Well, you're in the right place."

"Howshtat?"

"Just a few blocks up, North Beach. There are enough writers to stretch from here to . . ." She paused. "Where are you from?"

"Colorado."

"From here to Colorado."

At the moment he couldn't place Colorado.

"I know North Beach," he mumbled. "Work at a bookstore there."

She put the cigarette in the ashtray and rested her chin in her hand as she leaned toward him. "Is Buck your real name?" Her voice was husky and low, and a heavy, musky fragrance rose from her skin. He held his breath.

"Yes ma'am," he said. "Is Linda yours?"

Everything changed that night into something essential, yet hidden. It was the first time he heard jazz—each note resonating like an ache trying to heal; each musician narrating the same story but each as distinctive as the instrument they played.

Most nights he went to the club as soon as his shift at City Lights was over, walking the damp, foggy streets, and if it didn't feel like home, at least it was a way to be in the city that didn't make him feel like an outsider. He'd leave the club in the early morning hours, arriving back at the hotel, tired and bleary-eyed, just as other residents were leaving for work. In his room, he'd sit at the table in front of the window, filling pages of foolscap with his slanted writing until finally he collapsed on his bed, sleeping with his clothes on. Later, when he looked at what he scribbled, there was no story yet.

He arrived early one night and found Frankie eating a hamburger at the bar while Georgia talked low and serious to him.

"Hey." He joined them. "What's going on?"

"Big night tonight," Frankie said. "Some of the jazz crowd from L.A.'s in town."

Georgia was furiously wiping down the clean end of the bar.

"Who are they?" Buck said.

"My guys, man. All the way from Hermosa Beach. You need to stay awake, kid." Frankie stood. "They don't get here until about two, three in the morning. See you later." He waved and was out the door.

"What's that all about?" Buck asked Georgia.

"This L.A. crowd isn't the best thing for Frankie." She was even cleaning the sink.

"Not best for him how?"

"Drinking." She stacked some napkins. "Other stuff."

He needed a break. Outside, pale light from a full moon filtered through a thin layer of fog, and he thought about the moon high above the peaks at home. He'd been so self-preoccupied that he hadn't given much thought to Eagle Springs. Part of him wanted to feel as if it were still part of his life, yet the realization it wasn't came as a relief. It had become a fiction to him, and while he didn't want to admit it, in some way so had everyone there who had once been important to him.

Shortly after midnight, a different crowd began drifting in. The men wore suits and some had colored shirts and fancy neckties. The women wore elegant, low-cut dresses or silk blouses, tight skirts and high heels. The club was transformed from dingy to chic in an instant. Tables around the piano were pushed back and instruments claimed the space: a bass, drums, stands for a saxophone and a clarinet. Even though he'd never seen one, Buck thought it all looked like a symphony.

Exuberant greetings passed between various people, some of whom had driven six hundred miles to a little jazz club in San Francisco. Then Frankie claimed the piano. He played at his peak, stringing chords together, his long fingers skittering across the keys, and the crowd hung on every note. Buck took in the transformation that came over Frankie, the concentration, and the exclusion of everything around him except the music.

Linda arrived at close to one in the morning. She was alone and sat at her usual table. She nodded at Buck.

At the next break, he stepped outside for some fresh air. He was thinking about Frankie's concentration and his own lack of it. By now the fog was thick and low and a light drizzle settled on his shirt and hair. He jammed his hands in his jeans and looked up at Coit Tower, eerie in the mist.

"You're not bored already, are you?" Linda's voice was heavy like the fog and his breath caught in his throat.

"Frankie about ready to start again?" he said.

She didn't answer but instead asked him if he was cold. "You can slip my coat around your shoulders."

"No, thanks."

"How's your writing going?" she asked after a pause.

Nervously, he kicked at the ground. "Okay." He half mumbled the word.

She waited.

"I'm working on a novel, but it's slow going."

She was quiet.

He kicked at the ground again and felt the familiar tightening in his chest. "Guess nobody ever said it would be easy."

"Why do you think that is? That it's slow going?"

He shrugged. "Might have something to do with the fact I don't know a damn thing about writing a novel."

"Oh, I don't think it's that." She lit a cigarette and for a moment he saw her eyes, blue, in the light from the flame of the lighter. "You're bright and talented."

Who was she to ask what was wrong? What made her think he was talented?

"Maybe you're trying to write about the wrong thing?"

He looked at Coit Tower. His heart raced between uncertainty and attraction to this mysterious woman and what she'd just said.

"It's about a character who wanders through a city at various times of the day and night, discovering parts of himself everywhere he goes and with the people he meets, but the parts don't go together."

"That's interesting. A good idea for a novel." Her tone was sincere. "Have you a chapter or two you might let me read?"

They stood a moment more in the deepening fog.

"Well, you think about it," she said. "In the meantime, I'm catering a breakfast for some of the musicians at my apartment when the session ends, assuming it will end. I'd like you to come." She touched his shoulder. "I live up there." She pointed to Coit Tower. "On Telegraph Hill."

She reached in her purse and pulled out a small white card with her address: on Montgomery Street. She pulled her coat around her shoulders. "It's a catered kind of thing. Bloody Marys, gin fizzes, whiskey sours, caviar and scrambled eggs."

"Whoa. I haven't heard of half the stuff you're naming."

Smoke drifted from between her lips like smoke through

a keyhole and became part of the mist around them. Had she moved closer or had he?

"All the more reason to come. More material for your book."

He expected she'd go back inside, but instead she crossed to the curb, and drove off in a white Ford. Only the musky scent of her fragrance lingered where she'd stood.

Inside, the musicians clustered around Frankie at the piano and Buck grabbed a corner table against the wall where he could watch and listen. The atmosphere was electric with concentration, a kind of acknowledgement of the involvement the musicians and audience shared. The music was seamless, sensuous, and moved easily between the individual instruments, Frankie's piano grounding them and setting the tempo. It was the anticipation when the music moved from one instrument to another that stirred some idea in Buck. The way they were bound together by a single rhythm and purpose, yet without each individual moment it would lack meaning.

The moment overwhelmed Buck. He felt both drained and filled up at the same time, surrounded by a crowd quiet and intent on the musicians, and the musicians intent on each other, waiting to find their way back into the song.

It was in that unguarded moment that he felt the presence of Pauline, and of Lorrie and Ray. He closed his eyes. Was it possible that in the end, wherever they might be, they would come together again? Could he touch the story and find them there?

The set ended and Frankie came over.

"You were great, Frankie." Buck tried to shake off the feelings that had moved him. "Never heard you play like that before."

"These are my boys, man. Tonight felt good. Like being home. You're coming to Linda's tonight, right?" He lit a cigarette. "She said she'd ask you. She puts on a great after-jamming bash, and wait until you see her pad." He pursed his lips and kissed his fingers.

"I'll try," Buck said. Half of him wanted to go, but the other half did not. He wanted to think about how to put his feelings into something concrete like Frankie did with his music.

It was almost four in the morning when he left the club and stepped into the damp, still-dark morning. The heavy blast from the foghorn on the Golden Gate Bridge echoed his exhaustion. Coit Tower loomed above, and he half started down the street toward Montgomery, but turned back and walked through the deserted Financial District to Bush and the Cornett Hotel.

"Hey, Pete." He waved to the night manager who was just coming on duty. "Any chance I could get some early breakfast?"

"Comin' up."

He slumped into a chair near the back of the dining room, the echoes of jazz lingering in his consciousness.

CHAPTER TWENTY-THREE

A week later, he came home in the late afternoon to find a special delivery package postmarked San Francisco outside his door. It was heavy, and he dropped it on the bed. The return label read Linda M. Cassidy. He recognized the return address on Montgomery Street as the same he'd seen on her card.

He opened the box and saw a blue carrying case nestled in the packing. He lifted it, set it on the table, unzipped the case, and lifted the top. Inside was a small Olivetti manual typewriter complete with ribbon, and a spare on the side of the case. A ream of paper was on the bottom. He looked for her card, to call and thank her, or maybe send a note but he couldn't find it and he didn't want to ask Frankie. In the end, he did the only thing that seemed right. He began to write.

At the end of two weeks he had several chapters done, but they felt flat. He was trying to write about Frankie and the jazz club, but he didn't know how to write about jazz, or what it felt like to play jazz piano like Frankie. He changed the story to that hot, dry afternoon in Cheyenne, waiting for the bus, and the young girl standing forlorn at the side of the highway.

*   *   *

North Beach was bustling by the time he reached City Lights for his night shift. The lights of the nightclubs and bars on Broadway reflected on the wet pavement. Inside the bookstore, a few customers lingered and a young man sat on the floor reading. Excited voices from downstairs drew Buck to the stairs. He recognized some faces in the small group of young and middle-aged writers that occasionally gathered around the table in heated debates about literature. He heard the familiar names—Ginsberg, Kerouac, Hemingway—and he sat on the stairs, one eye on the door for customers, yet intent on the conversation. So far, they didn't seem to notice him, and even though he wanted to join them, he felt unprepared to discuss literature on their level. Each night, he'd take home one of the books they'd talk about, reading every spare moment and making notes for the time when he could contribute.

They talked about *On The Road* and the difficulty of keeping a story about the hero's journey coherent yet spontaneous, and someone mentioned James Joyce and a sprawling novel called *Ulysses*. At midnight they left the store and crossed the narrow alley to continue the discussion at Vesuvio's. Before he left that night, Buck bought the last copy of *Ulysses*, tucking it carefully in his book bag before he walked the misty and mysterious streets, dizzy with excitement and energy. Was this force and power he felt what it meant to be a writer? Was it part of what he longed for?

He'd been so absorbed in reading and writing he'd forgotten to thank Linda until she called him.

"Hello, Buck. How's the typewriter?"

"Swell. I'm real sorry I haven't called to thank you."

Silence.

"You didn't need to send me a typewriter, though." He paused. "I appreciate it."

"I wanted to do it. I assumed you hadn't called because you've been busy writing."

"Matter of fact, I've managed to get some chapters done. Just drafts, you understand." He heard music in the background.

"Could you come over tonight for dinner?"

He wanted to go but at the same time, he didn't want to. Why had she given him the typewriter to begin with? She hardly knew him. Her invitation to dinner was as mysterious as her gift. Besides, he'd grown to like his solitude and the space it gave him to read and think. He said he'd be there.

"About six thirty. Bring a chapter or two for me to look at."

The day was bright and the hills of San Francisco were stacked in shades of pastel and white like a Mediterranean village. He sat in Washington Square before walking to Linda's apartment on Telegraph Hill, taking in the view of Russian Hill until the early evening hours when the sun drifted west, leaving long shadows behind.

Linda lived at the top of a three-story white apartment building perched at the edge of a rocky outcropping of Telegraph Hill. He stopped at a low cement wall near the bottom and took in the unobstructed view of San Francisco Bay, blue as a precious stone, and thought how, in this city of endless views, he'd looked only at what was up close: things in windows, facades of buildings, ends of narrow alleys. What was he missing?

He sat on the wall. He wanted to leave, to tell her he got lost and couldn't find her apartment. A foghorn sounded a warning. He stood and pressed the buzzer, and the door swung open.

A flight of beige-carpeted stairs led to the flat above, where Linda waited. Her hair was loose and fell about her face, and she wore no makeup except for red lipstick, and her skin was clear and pale. She wore a black blouse and black trousers, and gold earrings, and she looked more beautiful than when he'd seen her at the club.

"Buck." She extended her hand and held his for a moment, and he was glad he'd come.

"Hey," he said.

"Oh good," she said, taking the manila envelope from him.

"I'm so glad you brought something."

She led him into a room where a long window faced San Francisco Bay and a view extending from the Golden Gate Bridge to the Bay Bridge. Another equally long window on the other side of the room gave a view of the Financial District, the city alive with flecks of lights in the buildings. A low glass-and-chrome table sat in front of a fireplace with two sand-colored chairs on either side of the table. The room was sleek and modern, like nothing he'd seen before.

Another woman, tall with short blonde hair that fit her head like a cap, stood when they came in. She wore gray slacks and a white silk blouse.

"Buck," Linda led him into the room. "This is a friend of mine, Maria."

"Hello, Buck." Maria took his hand. "Can I fix you something to drink?"

"I'll get you a beer, Buck." Linda moved quickly into the kitchen behind them.

It wasn't just that the moment was something he'd never experienced, it was something he never could have imagined. The elegant apartment, the sophisticated women, the breathtaking view, and there he stood wheezing slightly and wearing a slightly worn-out pair of cowboy boots.

"It's a beautiful view, isn't it?" Maria stood beside him. She took a sip of a martini. "Linda said you're from Colorado?"

He nodded.

"Do you like San Francisco?"

He nodded.

"You're a writer, is that right? And please don't just nod. So far I'm not sure you can speak." She smiled.

"Yes ma'am. Trying to be."

"Here's your beer, Buck." Linda put the beer on the table by the chairs.

He didn't want to talk about writing. He wanted to grab the envelope and run, down the stairs and back to the bookstore. "The typewriter made things easier for me."

"Easier?"

"Well, easier than scribbling everything in yellow tablets."

"That must be hard to do," Maria said. "Trying to figure out your own work."

Linda disappeared and returned with a tray of hors d'oeuvres: stuffed mushrooms, various cheeses and thin slices of something that looked like ham, and cut slices of French bread.

The two women began talking between themselves, and Buck moved back to the window and looked over the city. He'd never felt as unsure of himself as he did at this moment. He tried to muster some confidence, but his chest was aching with suppressed anxiety and he didn't want to use the inhalator now.

"I have to leave." Maria stood. "I'm glad I finally met you. Good luck with your work. No, that's okay." She motioned to Linda, who had started to walk with her to the stairs. "I'll call you later."

"Come into the kitchen," Linda said to Buck. "I thought we'd eat in."

The kitchen was all white, with bright red footprints painted across the ceiling. He stared.

"From the previous owner. They're fun, don't you think?"

He didn't know what to think. A door to a tiny landing was open and a soft breeze riffled the eucalyptus, raising the smell of menthol. "This is a great apartment," he said. "Lived here long?"

"About a year. I moved from New York. Sort of temporary until I see if I want to stay."

He sat on a stool by the door and felt himself finally beginning to relax. "What'd you do in New York?"

"Art dealer. I have my own gallery there. I came to San Francisco to see if I wanted to try it here."

"Do you? Want to try it here?"

"I'm still thinking about it." She put small dishes of condiments on the table. "I hope you like curry?"

"Can't say as I've ever had it. Smells good though."

She poured a beer for herself and sat across from him at the small table. The first bite Buck took of the mixture of rice, raisins, and bits of lamb, started him coughing.

"Oh no." Linda poured a glass of water for him. "I shouldn't have fixed something so spicy."

"Wow!" Buck laughed. "Wasn't expecting that, but it's good."

They ate in silence and the fog curled around Telegraph Hill.

"What kind of art do you have in your gallery?" He asked while she cleared the table.

"Mostly modern or abstract. Large canvases mostly. I'm not sure there's a market for it here."

"My buddy back home was a painter," Buck said. "He was good. He did a portrait of a friend of ours."

He didn't mention that Pauline was an artist too. That she painted the mountains and Sam, but she was Indian and she didn't have a chance of making a go of it.

Linda asked him if the portrait was good and Buck said yes, but his friend had lost a chance at a scholarship to an art school in Denver.

"Did he stop painting?"

Buck shrugged. "Probably. Joined the Army."

"Let's go into the living room. You can bring the coffee, please."

In the living room, they sat across from each other on the wide sand-colored chairs and she poured brandy into cut-glass drink glasses. Buck said no, but she said to just try it and he did. It burned going down but settled into a glow inside.

"May I?" She picked up the envelope. He nodded, but felt the nervous flutter in his chest. She read it aloud immediately, without reading it over first, and her voice was firm and stronger than he had expected.

The diner was stark and dingy in the dusty morning sun, and a dilapidated single-level frame motel looked hopelessly desperate there at the edge of the highway, as though waiting for the passage of time to transform the obvious absence of desire into life. A young man came out of the diner and a girl, younger than he was, followed him. She wore an ill-fitting waitress uniform and her shoes were white and laced, and she was small with short dark hair. The man bent to kiss her, an edge of hair falling over his forehead, and she pressed herself to him, until he stepped back and picked up the suitcase he'd put next to him on the ground. The girl buried her face in her hands and he whispered something in her ear, paused, then turned and crossed the highway to board the bus. Were it not for the prosaic setting—the highway, deserted except for the bus he was about to get on, the hot dust blowing against the back of his neck as he boarded—any one watching could almost taste the romance of the moment.

"This is good. Your scene is visual, dramatic, and suggests a forbidding future for the young man." She tucked the pages back in the folder. "May I keep these pages to read and return? Are you writing every day?"

"It's okay to keep the pages. I'll pick them up later." He thought he should probably leave, but his legs wouldn't move. "I've been reading a lot, and I try to write some every day."

She rose and turned on the phonograph. A woman's voice, lush and lyrical, was singing jazz, and outside the window the lights of the city were beginning to glow. They sat without speaking. She poured more coffee and more brandy and he didn't say no. He felt tired, and she was taking care of him.

She lit a cigarette and tilted her head back and he watched the smoke drift from between her lips. Her neck was so white.

"I gotta go." But he didn't move.

She took a sip of brandy and hummed to the music, almost as if he weren't there.

He waited and watched, thinking about how long it had been since he'd felt a woman's body next to his. He wanted to stay, to lie in bed with her and see if he could still make love.

He stood and unsteadily walked carefully down the stairs in her apartment and to the front door. Linda was saying something to him. Was it that she wanted to know more about his book? No, she wanted to call a cab.

"'S'kay." He waved gallantly. "Can make it jusfine."

Outside, at the top of the Montgomery Street stairs, he puked. He sat on the cold step waiting for the world to stop spinning and looking up at the lights in Linda's apartment. If he'd been sober would he have stayed, made love with that beautiful, elegant woman?

He weaved down the streets until he reached the Coronet. Inside, the clock above the switchboard read three in the morning. The building was so silent he considered taking off his boots and tiptoeing upstairs to his room so he wouldn't wake anybody. The thought made him giggle, but he kept his boots on and staggered to his room, landing on the narrow bed in a heavy, drunken heap.

CHAPTER TWENTY-FOUR

By July he had almost two hundred pages. He kept them in a cardboard manuscript box that fit in his satchel, waiting for the chance to ask one of the writers at the bookstore to look at them.

It was Jake, the manager, who asked him about it. "You lug that around with you everywhere?"

Buck nodded. "Hoping to find somebody who'll read it."

"Is it the whole thing or just a chapter or two?"

"First two hundred pages or so." Buck started unpacking a box of paperbacks to shelve.

"I'll read it if you want. Maybe show it to some of the regulars here."

Buck just stared at him.

"Don't get excited. I can't guarantee they'll look at it at all. Better pick up those books," he pointed to a stack waiting to be shelved.

Each night he'd come in, hoping for feedback. It seemed forever, but after a week, Jake returned the chapters. "We looked at your pages and agree that you need to be careful not to lose your own voice in your admiration for Kerouac. Don't pattern the journey of your character after Sal in *On The Road*, or even Stephen Daedalus in *Ulysses*," Jake said. "Read widely and learn to fashion your own voice. You're a good writer, and if you keep at it you'll probably produce something of value. It seems to me that you haven't found the story yet that you want to tell. Does the main character wander so much because he's looking for something or someone he lost? Does he want to find the girl he saw left alone at the side of the highway, or is it some other girl?"

Linda continued to read what he wrote and made suggestions. They sat in the living room before the fire, Buck on the floor with his back against the chair. Months later, when he typed "The End," she insisted they celebrate. They ate at Joe's on Broadway and some of the writers from City Lights saw him and crashed the dinner, buying drinks for everyone. For the first time since coming to San Francisco, he felt accepted. His dream was real.

That night he and Linda made love, or tried to. The paleness of her skin, the sheer way it absorbed light and glowed stunned him, but rather than arouse passion, Linda's body brought the memory of Pauline flooding back to him and he sank back on the bed, helpless against what he'd lost.

He told Linda he was sorry and she said it didn't matter; she said she'd always believed he still carried a love for a woman back home. "Maybe she's what you should write about?"

It was Pauline he needed to write about. He knew that, but the words wouldn't come. He wrote her name on lined yellow paper, he typed her name over and over, until he felt he was losing his breath. So he read the manuscript Linda had seen out loud in his room, corrected it, packed it in a mailing box and sent it to a New York publisher. Everyone said not to get his hopes up, but he'd come this far and he wasn't going to stop now.

It was close to midnight when he arrived at the jazz club. He'd never talked about his novel with Frankie, or told him that he was part of the inspiration. Tonight he'd brought a copy of the manuscript with him for Frankie.

The minute he walked in, he knew things weren't right. Music struggled out of the rarely used jukebox in the corner and the air was stuffy with cigarette smoke.

"Hey, Georgia." He sat at the bar. "Thought I'd live it up and have dinner here. Frankie around?"

"Gone. Won't be back, either."

She brought two glasses of Scotch and leaned on the bar facing Buck. Something was bad.

"It happened last night. Frankie had started drinking and it looked like he was smoking dope again too. He was all caught up with his new girlfriend, Marilyn, but he wasn't over Linda. They came in just before I closed. Marilyn was higher than a kite, and Frankie was wacked out on booze and who knows what. I tried to give him coffee, and Whiskey who was back cleaning the kitchen, tried to get him to eat, but he wouldn't have it. He began yelling at Marilyn because she wouldn't marry him. He kept screaming he was going to kill himself and damned if she didn't start screaming at him, to go ahead and kill himself. Next thing we knew, he's out the door waving like God's own fool, and running straight at a sixteen-wheeler barreling down Embarcadero too fast to stop."

Georgia tossed back the shot of Scotch.

"They carted Marilyn away in a straightjacket, screaming for Frankie. The ambulance took Frankie, what was left of him, to the morgue."

Buck crossed his arms on the bar and lowered his head. The ache inside his chest was intense, just like the night he'd found Pauline beaten and raped. He felt his lungs strain, heard his breath rattle, and he started gasping for breath. He sat halfway up and pumped the inhalator, and lowered his head again. He was in trouble and it was only going to get worse.

He squeaked "hospital" to Georgia and hit his chest. She called Whiskey from the kitchen and gave him the keys to her car, and while Buck sat slumped over in the front seat coughing up the phlegm clogging his airways, Whiskey navigated the hills until they pulled into the emergency entrance at St. Francis Hospital.

They monitored him in the ER and put him on a nebulizer. They took X-rays of his lungs just to be sure they were clear. The doctor started him on theophylline, a short course of prednisone, and gave him two rescue inhalators that he could always have with him. He told him to come back in a week. When the doctors asked what had triggered an attack this serious, Buck said he couldn't remember, but he knew it was the memory of Pauline, of making sorry love to Linda, and the death of Frankie.

In the predawn hours, Buck walked through Washington Square. The nearby restaurants were closed and the fog had softened the streetlights to a misty sheen. He caught the fragrance of damp grass and imagined whispered voices of lovers coming from the pools of darkness in the Square. He climbed the steps at Saints Peter and Paul Church, going through the small door at the side that was open at all hours. Inside, it was dense, solemn, and quiet and smelled of dust and old incense, and he thought of the Seminary back in Eagle Springs. When he went back outside he sat on the cold steps and looked at the city. Russian Hill and Nob Hill rose ahead of him, their narrow streets like mountain passes.

He thought about Frankie and how he'd let his story slip away, perhaps thinking he'd always have time to hear about his life. Like Ray, though, Buck had lost Frankie and his stories. Buck knew Frankie loved San Francisco, Los Angeles, New York—exciting cities that fed his imagination, and in this wet, soft night with the streetlights fading, Buck knew he'd finish the story that began on that highway in Wyoming with Frankie and the girl.

The next weekend, jazz musicians from as far south as Hermosa Beach streamed into Georgia's jazz club. They started at five o'clock in the evening and went until six the next morning. It was a musical wake, and the tunes were melancholy at some times, but hard, fast, and joyous at others. He listened to the stories the musicians told about Frankie; his father was a famous piano player and Frankie idolized him until he left Frankie and his mother. They wandered around the United States until his mother remarried and up and left Frankie on his own. Buck wrote it all down and could hear the love and respect they had for his friend.

He walked through the fog and back to the hotel. He couldn't sleep, and opened a Kerouac novel.

Too strange, too subterranean, Kerouac had written before he had turned his back on the edge of the continent and headed east.

*   *   *

The first rejection came quickly: "Interesting characters but not suited to our style." He showed it to Jake.

"That's a nice one, cowboy," he said. "You haven't heard anything yet."

At a loss as to how to proceed, he made random changes and sent it out again. While he waited, he read and spent time with the other writers, trying to understand a process that was increasingly overwhelming him. What was he supposed to do now? Should he start another book?

Six weeks later he had two more rejections. It seemed that the more he wrote about Frankie, or about the wrinkled rhythms of jazz, or even about the residents of the hotel, the further away he was from a real story.

"You're a good writer," one publisher wrote, "but the story needs to come forward more."

One afternoon he found two pink message slips the switchboard attendant had left curled in his mail slot. They were both from Linda. She wanted him to call her. He folded them and put them in his shirt pocket. When he called her the next day, the phone rang several times and he was almost ready to hang up when Linda answered.

"Sorry I didn't call you sooner," he said.

"Georgia told me about Frankie. I'm sorry, Buck. Georgia said you were in the hospital. Are you all right now?"

"I'm okay. Hearing about Frankie triggered a bad attack, but the new medications are helping." How did she feel about Frankie's death? She'd known him before; wasn't she hurting as well?

"Can you come over tomorrow?" she said. "It has to be tomorrow because I'm leaving for New York the next day."

"New York? Why?"

"I have to go now. Will you come over tomorrow?"

Late the next afternoon he rang her buzzer and pushed through the door when it clicked open. She was not at the head of the stairs.

"Hey," he called, and walked toward the living room. Three large suitcases were in the middle of the room.

"Buck," she called from the bedroom. She was sitting on the edge of the large double bed, talking on the telephone. The white satin comforter was folded back. Two smaller pieces of luggage were on the bed. She pointed to a small chair in the corner and Buck sat on the edge. His boots looked like pieces of the ground against the pale rug. He coughed.

She was clearly angry at whomever she was talking to, and when she hung up and looked at Buck he could see she'd been crying. Her mouth was drawn tight, and her eyes were swollen.

He sat forward. "What's going on?"

"I look a mess, don't I?" She ran her hands through her hair. "Come on." She took his hand and led him into the kitchen. "Do you want something to eat? I might have something for a sandwich."

Her casualness startled him. Gone was the studied elegance that had unnerved him before. He sat on the stool. She took a bottle of vodka from the freezer and poured more than a shot into a cut-crystal glass. She took a beer from the refrigerator and sat at the table.

He took the beer. "Thanks."

"I want you to do me a favor, Buck. I have to go to New York. It seems that"—she took a swallow of vodka—"the person I left to run my gallery in New York got creative with the account books and I have to get back before I lose the gallery." Her voice cracked and she took another drink, nervously ran her fingers through her hair.

He didn't know what to say. Here was a woman he'd known only as controlled and composed. What could she want from him?

"I want you to stay here while I'm gone."

He coughed up the beer he'd just swallowed.

"That reaction is a bit stronger than I'd expected."

"You want me to do *what*?"

"Think of it as babysitting my apartment while I'm gone. Get the mail, collect the papers, and sign for any packages that might come, that sort of thing. Here." She gave him a sheet of paper. "I've made a list. You don't need to worry about the details of the apartment or any of that."

She hurried to the bedroom to answer the phone, and he took his beer and walked to the living room. The city spread before him. A sparkling city of light. The apartment was perfect for an artist. Solitude and beauty would surround him. He could fix what was wrong with his novel, or maybe start a new one.

Linda came in. "You can bring your typewriter and tons of paper and work over there." She pointed to a table in the corner. "Or in the kitchen since you seem to like it there." She walked nervously to the window as if some answer lay outside, then turned and faced him. "I have a cot that you can put up here by the window." She looked distracted. "If you'd feel more comfortable."

She went back into the kitchen and he heard her fixing another drink. He wondered offhand how much vodka she'd had. She came back, sat in the chair and leaned back. She seemed to have finally run out of nervous energy, but something more was wrong.

"What else?" he said.

"What?" She looked at him.

"What else is wrong? Something else must be wrong to get you this upset."

She looked down the hall toward the kitchen. "A painting is missing. A valuable one. When my assistant looked for the insurance coverage, she discovered the embezzlement."

Buck leaned forward, looking at his worn-out boots against the pale rug. He barely had an idea of embezzlement, but he could appreciate losing something valuable, and he understood her anxiety.

"You'll stay here? I don't think I'll be longer than a week, two at the most. Maria is coming with me for the first few days. I've left her phone number on the sheet I gave you. You can always call her if you need help."

He said he'd let her know and left. Outside, walking home, he wondered why of all the people she must know, had she asked him? He wanted to go back to the residence club, pack his bags and typewriter and move in, and tomorrow he'd have a whole new view of his novel, of his life. But he knew he wouldn't have any new views. There was only one story, only one truth, and he hadn't even gotten close. He'd written about Frankie and a girl standing in the dust just outside Cheyenne because something about the moment made him remember Ray and Lorrie. The ache he tried to ignore through jazz, the constant revisions and rejections, were because he'd left the real story in Eagle Springs. He had written a novel and it might be published. It just wasn't the one he needed to write. The more he wrote about what others had lost, the more he was avoiding all that he had lost, and the more he needed to go home and find the part of himself he'd left behind.

It was late afternoon when he walked the Montgomery stairs he'd climbed so often and rang the bell. She knew immediately. They went to the living room.

"I can't do it, Linda. I'm sorry for the trouble you're having, but I can't do it, and I'm sorry because I'd help you if I could. You've been a good friend to me." He swallowed hard.

She lowered her head and he hoped she wasn't crying, but her shoulders were set and still.

"The fact is"—he coughed and stared out at the beautiful white city this morning shrouded in fog—"I'm going home. Back to Colorado. It's almost the same as you going back to New York. I've lost something and someone valuable. Some connection that I didn't know was so important and I think if I don't go back now . . ." He was almost afraid to say the words. "I might never have another chance."

GOING HOME

CHAPTER TWENTY-FIVE

It was dawn when the Greyhound bus pulled into the depot in Eagle Springs. The leaves in the acacia trees in Kiowa Park glistened from a morning shower. Buck stood outside the depot and looked at the park, the high school down the block, the ridge of mountains, and the snow glistening on the top of Kiowa Peak, and they were as he remembered them, but something was missing. Perhaps it was the fiction of innocence, of romance, that had changed. The surprise at the end of a street, the gift for narration that waited in the canyons and High Range, all gone. It was as if the town had fallen as silent of its own mythology as an old man staring inward at the loss of his past.

More like I've gone silent.

He stored his suitcase in a locker and pocketed the key. Outside, the high altitude forced his breathing and he pumped the inhalator as he crossed the intersection toward Wheaton & French. Across the street a black man pushed a long pole with a damp sponge up and down the glass, wringing the sponge out in a bucket near his feet. "Mo'ning." He nodded and started pushing the sponge back up the window.

"Morning." Buck looked in. The rich mahogany counters were polished and the perfume bottles shining.

"Open 'round nine. You're up early, mister."

"That I am. Don't work too hard."

"No sir."

Buck thought there was a time, not very long ago, when you'd never see a black man on the main street in Eagle Springs, even washing windows.

The streetlights were still flashing yellow when he pushed through the door of the Village Inn. A woman behind the counter looked up.

"Morning. Sit anywhere."

Buck eased into a booth. "Coffee smells good." He studied the menu.

"You're up early." She brought him a cup of coffee.

"Second time I've been told that this morning," He smiled. He ordered bacon, eggs, potatoes, and toast. "Might keep the coffee coming," he said.

A young woman came in and sat at the counter. She wore a two-piece teal colored suit and black pumps. She and the waitress started a conversation that suggested they knew each other.

He imagined her leaving her house or small apartment

early in the morning and waiting for a bus to bring her downtown. Maybe she had a child, a boy, whom she kissed lightly on the forehead before she left. She would set out his breakfast and leave a note telling him not to forget to drink his juice and milk and be careful at so-and-so's house. "I'll see you at five," she'd write.

By the time he left, the sun had risen above the High Range, the dampness had burned off, and Eagle Springs began to slide into its routine under a high blue sky. He could have walked to his house, only a few blocks away, or at least called his parents, but he wasn't ready yet.

A bus waited at the corner.

"Where you headed?" Buck asked.

"Bluffs."

Buck sat toward the back. Apparently the driver made his own schedule, since he kept reading the paper. On the sidewalk, people were hurrying to work. The shades were still down at the *Gazette*.

"Not many passengers," the driver said, finally pulling away from the curb. "We're going the wrong way to pick up the business crowd."

Buck nodded.

"Fine by me," the driver continued. "I hate to drive a crowded, noisy bus."

The bus stayed empty for several blocks until two college girls got on. They sat near the front, a few seats ahead of Buck.

Outside, the day was getting brighter. They passed the park. After the girls got off at the college, the bus swung right and wound through a development of single-story ranch-style houses with wide lawns just turning green.

"What time is it?" Buck asked, slipping his satchel over his shoulder. This didn't look like the road to the Bluffs he'd taken so many times.

"End of the line coming up." The driver shouted as though he had a busload of people. "Thanks be to God." He pulled to the bus shelter and opened the doors. "Nine thirty." He added.

A young girl with honey-colored hair that curled behind her ears was waiting at the stop. Her hands were in the pockets of her jacket, and a purse, its strap diagonal across her chest, pressed against her hip.

"End of the line," he said again looking at the girl. "This is a twenty-minute stop, miss."

"That's okay." She smiled at Buck and looked at his boots as he got off the bus.

A street sign read Prospect Lane. When he'd left there was no sign; it was just "the road to the Bluffs."

Why had he come here? He could have checked Pauline's last address in Denver before coming back to Eagle Springs. What made him think she might be here? Did he want to find her, or was he searching for something else? How many threads did he have to follow to find the answers to questions he had yet to ask, and would that be the story he needed to write?

Around a corner he saw Pauline's house. Besides needing painting, it looked out of place surrounded by the modern houses. A quietness settled around it that Buck found unsettling.

The street ahead was deserted except for a kid riding his bike in circles in the middle of the road. Buck walked down the narrow, rutted path to the back yard. The elm tree swayed and the leaves on the aspen trees twittered. Even the glider on the back porch moved slightly with a squeak that sounded like an old, lonely sigh. Red dust sifted above the hard, dry ground.

He climbed the three steps to the back porch and peered into the kitchen, empty except for the table still in the center of the room. He walked around to the south side, and peeked in the bedroom window.

"Pauline?" His voice was barely above a whisper.

He went around to the front porch, and stood helplessly, arms hanging at his sides. His breathing was short and strained. He used his inhalator and shoved it back in his pocket, listening to the quiet, willing her voice to call out.

"Mister?"

He jumped, knocking the rocking chair over.

"Geez, kid," he said. "You scared the hell out of me."

A rangy kid with dirt-brown hair and wide brown eyes was watching him. He looked about twelve or thirteen, and straddled a beat-up bicycle, one sneakered foot resting on the ground.

"Lady isn't here anymore."

"I see that." He stepped off the porch.

"What's that?" The kid pointed to Buck's pocket.

"Inhalator." The kid squinted at Buck. "For asthma." He whacked his chest and coughed. "Helps me breathe."

"Ain't nobody lives here anymore." He studied Buck. "What's your name?"

"Buck. You?"

"Johnny. I live at the end of the block. There." He pointed to the corner.

Buck nodded.

"Where do you live?"

He'd forgotten how inquisitive kids could be. "Used to live over on the north side of town, close to Boulder Avenue."

Johnny nodded as if he knew exactly where Buck meant. "Where'd ya get them boots?"

"You ask a lot of questions, kid." The kid waited for an answer. "A friend gave them to me." He almost wanted to add: *it was the lady who once lived here.*

"Had 'em long?"

"Couple years or so."

"Look beat-up."

Buck smiled. "I figure I've just about got them broken in. All beat-up like this?" He looked at the kid. "That's how cowboy boots are supposed to look."

The kid considered his sneakers. "The lady?" he said suddenly. "My mom said she was Indian and she killed herself. Nobody wants to live here. My mom says the house has bad spirits." He turned the bike around. "See ya, mister." The bike slid on the gravel before he righted it and pedaled fast down the street.

The hint of a spring breeze, mildly warm and soft, stirred the air as Buck watched the boy ride off. In spite of the warm wind, he felt a chill course through him so strong that he had to keep from shaking. Waves of nausea swept over him as he turned and began a shaky walk back toward town.

* * *

It still didn't take much to get the interest of the Eagle Springs Police Department. A cowboy slumped on a park bench drinking beer in the afternoon in Kiowa Park stood out, so it didn't surprise Buck to see the sharp toes of shiny black cowboy boots poking from beneath the crisp khaki trouser cuffs of an officer with the ESPD planted smack in front of him. He wondered what had taken them so long to find him, since he'd been sitting there most of the afternoon.

He concentrated on his boots. *The kid was right. They look like hell.*

"Afternoon, son. Everything okay?"

He wanted to say everything was fine. He was drunk as hell and if he was left alone, he planned to get drunker. He looked up. It was Officer West.

"Hey there, Officer West. I'm doing just fine, thank ya."

"Well, I'll be damned. Buck Malone?"

"Yessir." Buck put the beer bottle under the bench. He kept the brim of his cowboy hat low so Officer West couldn't see the wandering look in his eye.

"Didn't recognize you. Heard you went out West. California."

"Yessir."

"Back for good now, Buck?"

"Can't say for sure."

"Um hum." He waited. "Your dad doing okay?"

"Yessir. Right as rain." Buck squirmed, figuring West was debating between tossing him in jail to teach him a lesson, or calling his dad, who so far didn't know he was back.

"Reckon you forgot drinking liquor in public parks and most recreational areas is against the law here, Buck?"

"Yessir. That I did. Sorry." Instantly he missed California where he could do any damn thing he wanted to.

He noticed the park crew stringing lights through the acacia trees bordering the temporary dance floor. "Today Wednesday?"

Officer West looked toward the bandstand. "That it is. Sorry to say rock 'n' roll's taken over instead of the weekly square dances. Bunch of goddamn noise, you ask me. Rhythm and blues they call it." He lit a cigarette. "They play that crap in California?"

Buck looked at wire-haired kids jumping around on the stage, flailing tunelessly at their guitars.

"Tried to keep 'em out," Officer West said. "But that caused a bigger ruckus."

"How so?"

"We hauled a couple of 'em into the jail for disturbing the peace, rowdiness, that sort of thing. Didn't sit well with Art

Packer at the *Gazette,* who squawked about First Amendment rights. We released the kids to their parents. Now we can't do anything but plug our ears."

Something told Buck they'd try and do more whenever they could. Meanwhile, he was glad to hear Art Packer was still the editor.

Officer West took off his hat and wiped his forehead with a bright-white handkerchief. He stood for a minute as though unsure what to do about the music or about the clearly inebriated young man in front of him. "Believe you can get fixed up okay without my doing anything special right now. You see it that-a-way, Buck?"

"That I do, Officer. Appreciate it."

West didn't move. "Mind handing me that bottle of beer under the bench?"

Buck didn't even pretend surprise that it was there, and handed him the bottle. Officer West tipped his hat and sauntered off. Before he tossed the bottle in the green trash disposal he emptied the contents onto the lawn. It spilled through the sunlight like just-mined gold.

CHAPTER TWENTY-SIX

It was dusk by the time Buck arrived at Lyle's house. The familiar slice of light from the studio fell on the lawn near the back. It was oddly comforting. He crossed the porch and turned the knob. Lyle still didn't lock his door.

"Hey?" Buck stood just inside the living room. "Lyle?"

Hurried footsteps echoed in the hall, and then Lyle was there in his jeans and paint-smeared T-shirt, his hair still a crisp white crew cut, his body trim, maybe holding a hint of heaviness.

"Hey," Buck said again. "Look like you've seen a ghost."

"Feels like I have." If Lyle was surprised, his voice didn't sound it.

"Sorry. I should've called."

Lyle moved into the living room. "Have a seat." He pointed

to the couch, and sat in the chair opposite.

The room looked the same. The battered coffee table piled with books and newspapers in front of the couch, and the desk pushed against the wall. But nothing felt familiar. Had he changed that much? He'd made a mistake. He should have called his parents first.

"I went to Pauline's house," he said. "It was empty. I don't know what I was expecting. Actually, I thought she was still in Denver. There was a kid, about twelve, riding his bike in the street and he told me nobody would buy the house because there were bad spirits in it. He told me"—he took a deep breath, and felt his chest tighten—"that his mother said the Indian woman who lived there killed herself." He looked at Lyle. "But he's a kid. What the hell does he know?"

Lyle sat back. "I didn't have your address, Buck. I called your folks but they weren't sure either. I wrote to you the day after Pauline died, but had no idea where to send it."

Buck's breath came short and fast, the cough building with the wheeze. He pumped his inhalator. He needed a pill to relax the chest muscles but didn't have the prescribed medication. He lowered his head and coughed more and Lyle got up, went to the kitchen, and brought back a glass of water and an aspirin. "Sorry you still have that asthma."

"Comes and goes."

The bitter taste from the beer he'd had earlier soured his mouth. He needed to brush his teeth. His stomach lurched, either from hunger or fear. Since he'd felt fear before, he recognized it.

"When did it happen?"

"Not long after you left. Maybe two or three months."

Three months. Where was I then? Walking down Market Street? Standing at the edge of the continent staring at a blue ocean?

Darkness began to fill the room and Lyle turned on a light. "Why did you come home, Buck?"

When he was a kid, Buck used to pray now and then. The dumb kind of prayer kids say: *Dear God. Please take away my asthma, keep my folks safe, and don't let the "A-Bomb" land on Eagle Springs.* But he'd never taken to praying when he grew up, so he couldn't work up a prayer now when it seemed pretty clear he needed one.

"Don't know if I've got a good answer. I started thinking I couldn't go forward anymore in San Francisco, or any place else I guess, until I came home."

Lyle nodded. "Sam died not long after you left, and Pauline tried to make a go of it in Denver. I got her a part-time teaching job at the Art Institute and she was doing good work on her painting. Then she came back here. She began going to Spirit Rock to meditate, to comfort Sam's spirit, and help him through to the other world. She always felt she'd failed him, but she also wanted to connect with her roots. Even her paintings changed. She stopped doing large, abstract oils and started working up character studies of her people, some of them in colored pastels." He took a sip of his drink. "They were really good."

"She did one of Sam," Buck said.

"She started driving her pickup into the hills and sitting in the truck bed all day, painting. That's how she started, you know. Sitting in that truck."

"She told me about that," Buck said. "She said she learned about perspective from staring at the roads as they narrowed into the horizon."

Lyle stood up and took a step toward the kitchen. "From the way you look, I'd say you've already had enough beer, but I think I need a Scotch."

"Officer West confiscated what little I had left. I can manage one of those."

"How'd you manage to run into him?" Lyle asked.

"I was drinking in the park."

Lyle didn't argue. He went into the kitchen and came back with the drinks.

"I don't know what to tell you, Buck." Lyle's voice was weary, as though he wished he didn't have to talk about this. "The truth will be hard no matter how I tell you. We were supposed to meet to talk about putting on a small exhibition of her work here in Eagle Springs. She didn't call, and she wasn't home. I called Ruby but she hadn't heard from her either, so I thought she might have gone to Spirit Rock. It had rained the night before and I worried because the rock can get slippery, but Pauline knew how to manage climbing the monument." He took a long drink of the Scotch. "I found her body at the base of the rock. She was still breathing, but just barely. I got her into my car and raced to the ER, but she didn't make it."

"Sweet Jesus." Buck buried his face in his hands. He was shaking, his eyes blurred with tears, his breathing a steady, noisy, wheeze. He didn't move or look up at Lyle.

"I went back to the monument to get her truck. The police were there, looking up at the rock and at the damp ground. They said it could have been an accident or deliberate."

Buck looked up. "What did they mean by *deliberate*?"

"That she might have jumped off the rock."

"She'd never slip or fall from Spirit Rock. She knew that place better than she knew anything." Buck's voice was weak. "And she sure as hell wouldn't jump."

"I don't know what truth you need that will help you make things right, because I don't have any truth for you. I knew Pauline from the time she was fifteen years old, and I loved her all that time. Do I think she could have killed herself? Yes. This wasn't her only life. She was an old soul who'd passed this way before and most likely will again. She was curious, and to Pauline, death was a journey to the other side. But she was building a future, which makes suicide less likely."

Buck looked out the window at the black silhouette of the mountains in the distance, the only constant at this moment.

"Do I think that her foot slipped on the rock that was still damp? That it was an accident like the police said? Yes. She could have slipped."

"What about Perez?" he asked. "Was he back? Could he have had anything to do with this?"

"Ruby and I thought about that. We scouted around, especially in the little bars in the foothills and out by the Army base, but no one had seen him. We had no way to contact Ray, either." Lyle stood. "You look like you could do with something to eat. Hamburger okay?"

Buck sat at the table as Lyle started to fix dinner. "When did you get back?" Lyle asked.

"Early this morning. I didn't tell anyone I was coming home. Planned on getting a room in one of those motels off Highway 85." Buck shook his head. "Truth is, I wasn't sure I'd be welcome. My leaving was, well, not taken to kindly, dropping out of high school and all."

"How's your writing? Was San Francisco a good place for you?"

"I guess so. I finished a novel and sent it out, but at last count I had three rejections. An agent is looking at it now, though. He says he's interested."

"It's good that you produced something. Are you writing something new?"

He shook his head. He hadn't even thought about writing since he'd left San Francisco.

Lyle put the hamburgers on the table and poured two more Scotches. "That's not good," he said.

They ate in silence until Buck suddenly wondered about Pauline's truck.

"I have it. It's in the garage," Lyle said.

"And the keys?"

Lyle nodded.

"And the keys to her house?"

Lyle nodded again. "Ruby gave them to me. Asked me to check on it now and then."

"Appreciate it if you could let me have those keys, Lyle." Buck heard the insistence in his voice and regretted asking.

Why had he assumed he could take ownership of her truck, her house?

Instead of handing over the keys, Lyle said, "You need to call your folks. Since I don't imagine you want to move back home, you can stay here until you figure out what you want to do. But going to Pauline's house right now isn't the best plan."

"You been there?"

Lyle nodded. "Ruby didn't want to go alone."

Buck sat back in the kitchen chair and drank the Scotch, hoping the stronger drink would narrow his perspective, and at the moment that was what he wanted. Besides, Lyle was probably right. Going to Pauline's would scatter what little reason he had. Maybe it wouldn't hurt to at least go home.

"You might splash some cold water on your face. If you feel like you can drive, you can borrow my car, but steer clear of Officer West." He handed him the keys to his car.

"Thanks, Lyle. I'll be careful."

The sun had dipped behind Kiowa Peak. Night would fall quickly. He parked the car at the corner and stayed there, looking at the house. He saw the familiar tree-shaded porch and one wicker chair near the railing. The dining room shades, tinged a dull yellow from the light inside, were pulled halfway down. He wondered if, at this hour, his father would still be working in his basement workshop.

He hesitated. This was a bad idea. *Between the drinking and all that Lyle had revealed, he, should sift through everything first.*

He couldn't wait. Not just because they'd hear one way or

another he was back, but because he owed them after leaving the way he had.

When he'd left, he was a seventeen-year-old kid. He wasn't the same now, but they would always see him as a kid. Any common ground they once had as a family had slipped away, and he wasn't sure he had the will to get it back.

He knocked lightly on the door, and suddenly his mother's face, small and older than he would have anticipated, was looking at him through the screen door. Immediately he was sorry he'd hurt her. Not sorry he'd left, but sorry his leaving had so visibly hurt her.

"Buck!" She pushed open the screen door and then he was in the living room, with the familiar smell of furniture polish, and the light pushing through the half-pulled shades and his mother's arms around him. Her body felt frail beneath her flowered cotton housedress.

"I just got back, Mom. Sorry I didn't call first."

"Come in. Let me look at you. You're so thin. Here, sit beside me." She clutched his hand.

His father came up from the basement where he had been working. He stared as though he couldn't believe the young man sitting in his living room was his son.

"Buck?" He stood in the doorway, both shock and surprise on his face.

"Hey, Dad." He stood and they both made a feeble attempt to shake hands. Buck sat back down on the couch. "Sorry I was never great about letter writing."

"You know me," his mother said. "We're not a letter writing family, but I always thought you'd write if you needed anything."

"Truth is, your mother has arthritis in her hands and she can't write real well."

"Charles, please."

"Even has trouble cooking and such."

Buck looked at her hands, folded on her lap. The knuckles were swollen and some fingers stiffened into awkward positions.

"I didn't know, Mom. I'm real sorry. Are you seeing a doctor?"

What if something happened to his dad? Could she manage on her own? From the look of her fingers he wondered if she could turn pages in the books she loved to read.

"Charles exaggerates, as usual. Please tell us how you've been. Where are you staying?"

He hesitated between telling him he was staying at the motel or at Lyle's. No matter what he said, they'd want him to stay here, but he couldn't.

"Have a chance to stay with Lyle for a while."

They were silent, as though waiting for someone to tell them what to say.

"Came about on the spur of the moment. I finished a novel in San Francisco," he said quickly. "Sent it out to some publishers. Still a chance one of them will accept it."

When hell freezes over.

His father's face was without expression, and Buck wondered if he was remembering their meeting at the emergency room when Pauline was there, or the solemn afternoon Buck had packed his clothes and left.

"How is it you're staying with Mr. Samuels?" he asked.

There was no good answer. "It's just temporary. I'm going to see if Art Packer will take me back on the paper, or maybe start out fresh in Denver."

"I'm happy for you, Buck," his mother said. "If it's what you want, then that's good."

He told them about San Francisco and that he'd had some luck with his writing but his father's expression made him stop. Nothing had changed.

Buck stood. He'd been there scarcely an hour.

"Please stay for dinner, Buck?"

"Maybe another time. Need to get myself settled a bit. You still make that good meatloaf?" He smiled against the tears blurring her eyes. "I'll come by for dinner some night real soon. Good to see you, Dad." He shook his father's hand.

Walking down the familiar street back to his car, he realized he hadn't asked his dad what he was working on, if his shoulders hurt from bending over the workbench, or if he still listened to pop music on the radio while he worked.

He drove north out of Eagle Springs until he got to Castle Rock where he went into a run-down bar, and ordered a beer.

Staying in Eagle Springs won't prove anything. I should've stayed in San Francisco. Not one damn good thing has happened since I've come home.

He had two more beers, started Lyle's car and headed to

the Horseshoe Tavern in the hills above Sand Creek. Like most of these little mountain bars, the place was half empty. A girl sat alone at a table in the corner. She looked up when Buck came in and tried to hold his gaze, but he headed for the bar.

The bartender gave him a whiskey with beer back. He gave him the second one also, but stopped at the third.

"Had enough, cowboy." It wasn't a question.

"'Kay," Buck mumbled. "Jusgimme a beer."

The bartender put a beer in front of him.

"Last one, pal."

It wasn't closing time, but would be soon. These taverns in the hills closed early. A few cowboys wandered in and started pumping quarters into the jukebox. One of them danced with the girl.

Buck didn't want to leave. He nursed the beer until the bartender refused to give him another one, then he picked a fight with one of the cowboys. That's when the bartender gave the police a call. The charge was drunk and disorderly conduct, the disorderly part being that he didn't like being told he couldn't have another drink and was ready to fight.

Officer West sauntered in, tipped his Stetson back and considered Buck.

"When I took that beer away earlier this afternoon, son, I didn't intend for you to get yourself to the Horseshoe Tavern."

Reluctantly, but with no options, Buck was led to the police cruiser. At the station, he leaned against the wall while West booked him, but the wall felt like Jell-o against his back and he slid right down it with an inane giggle, landing on his butt with a pitiful thump.

"Whoa, there." Officer West had him up and in a cell almost before Buck knew he'd fallen. "This isn't sea level, Bucko. Better temper your drinking."

"Buck!" he yelled. "No damn 'Bucko.'" He curled up on the cot. "Gonna sleep now. Look for Ray tomorrow."

He raised up on one elbow and looked through the bars at West. "Snot-nosed kid don't know what he's talking about," he yelled. "Neither does Lyle. Buncha goddamn liars in this town."

"No need to shout," West pushed a mug of coffee through the bars and along the floor. "See if this coffee doesn't clear things up a bit."

"Ray'll tell me the truth." Waves of nausea rolled through him and he made it to the toilet in the corner just in time.

"Son . . ."

"Don't call me son!" Buck slobbered.

Officer West sighed. "Believe I'll give your folks a call."

Buck half staggered, half crawled toward him, grabbed the bars and pulled himself up. He was face-to-face with the officer, who took several steps back. "Now lisenofficer Guest . . ."

"West," he interrupted.

"Esactly. If you were me, would you want your folks to see you like thish?"

West hesitated. "You hungry?" West said.

"No. Lemme alone." Buck made it back to the cot, lay down, and watched the room spin in a collage of cement blocks, bars, and images of Spirit Rock and Pauline.

* * *

When he woke up, his dingy cell had the gray light of morning.

"How you feel?" Officer West was peering at him through the bars of the cell door.

Maybe if he had brought something to eat Buck's situation wouldn't seem so hopeless. Now he just wanted out.

"Where the hell are my boots?" Buck muttered.

"Don't worry. We got 'em."

Buck couldn't remember a thing from the time Lyle told him he could borrow the car to right now. His mouth felt pasted together beginning way at the back, and he was pretty sure he smelled. He didn't get up.

"You the only cop in town, Officer West? Seems I'm running into you quite frequently."

West didn't smile. "Bit short staffed these days," he said. "Besides, let's just say I've taken a special interest in you."

"Well, I appreciate that," Buck stammered. "Could you bring me my boots and I'll be leaving so you can catch up on some rest I reckon you need."

West didn't move.

"Please, that is."

West tilted his head toward someone standing down the hall without taking his eyes off Buck, and it occurred to Buck that to West, he must be some unsolvable mystery. A deputy appeared with the boots. He looked about Buck's age and watched him with something Buck hoped was close to wonder and not disgust. Officer West opened the cell door and handed the boots to Buck and stood in front of him while he pulled them on.

"Seems you can't hold your liquor too well, Buck. I don't recall you being a drinking man. Something you picked up out in California?"

"Won't happen again," he mumbled.

"Um hum. Don't mind my saying so, you stink. We got a little shower in the back for prisoners we let enjoy our hospitality for a night. You're welcome to use the facilities."

Buck scooped up his jacket and hat and thought a minute. It didn't make sense to go outside looking like he must look.

"Appreciate that. Believe I'll take advantage of your kind offer."

"What ya got there?" the young deputy asked, jabbing a chubby finger at Buck's satchel.

"Nothing. Just something I carry books in."

"Oh yeah?" His voice sounded vaguely interested. He must have been standing there while Buck had been pulling his boots on. When he spoke, both Officer West and Buck jumped a little, as if they'd forgotten he was there. "You're the guy who wanted to be a writer." He had a weird little gleam in his eye, and Buck decided he didn't want to know how he'd come by this information.

"I didn't want to be a writer." He was careful to control his voice. His head hurt so badly he couldn't afford to get mad. "I am a writer."

"Um hum," Officer West said again. "You head on down

and clean up. I expect you'll be heading on home to get some breakfast."

"Reckon. You haven't called my folks have you?"

West shook his head. "Won't be seeing you in here again, will I?"

"Hope not." Buck walked gingerly down the hall toward the shower.

*   *   *

Officer West had woken him early. By the time he finished showering and rubbing some dry toothpaste over his teeth, it was only seven in the morning. His stomach rattled for want of food, but he didn't want to go to the Village Inn. He walked back to the bus station, ate at the counter, and took his suitcase from the locker where he'd stowed it earlier. In the restroom, he pulled out a clean shirt and changed before making sure he had the keys to Lyle's car. A quick look in the mirror made him splash more cold water on his face, but it didn't help. He had some money, and decided to have a cab take him to the Horseshoe Tavern, where he hoped Lyle's car was still parked.

The cabbie didn't hide his reluctance to take someone who, despite his attempt to look presentable, still looked as run-down as his destination. He was somewhat relieved that Buck had a suitcase and told him he had to pick up his car. Once there, Buck asked him to park next to the Dodge parked at the side of the bar.

By the time Buck drove down the alley at Lyle's, the

sun had risen above the high range and a warm breeze was blowing. Buck pulled up behind a black pickup in the alley behind Lyle's house. It was Pauline's truck. Lyle was talking to a heavy-set kid with long hair tied back in a ponytail. He was leaning over the engine. **Boulder Mechanic & Garage Center** was lettered on the back of his shirt.

"Hey." Buck walked toward them. He saw **HermW** lettered on the pocket of the kid's uniform.

"Hey yourself." Lyle eyed his appearance. From his expression, he did not see the improvement Buck had hoped for.

"Think you can get it up and running, Herm?" Lyle said.

"Dunno. Needs plugs, rear brake adjustment; tires are flatter 'n' a pancake. Ain't been used for a while, eh? Oughta sell it for scrap and get a new one."

"Best you don't be thinking that way," Buck said.

"I can try and have it running but could be a week at least. I can send a tow truck in the morning if that's agreeable?"

Pockets of rust stains tarnished the black surface here and there, evidence of a desolate and lonely end. Buck thought it cruel that he couldn't at least sit in it, find some evidence of Pauline, however elusive. He didn't want it towed through town the way it looked now.

"That's fine." Lyle said. "Come by and pick it up this afternoon. Sooner we get it fixed, the better. Right, Buck?"

Buck shrugged and went inside.

"Sorry I didn't show up last night," Buck said when Lyle came in. He took a sip of coffee. "I had accommodations courtesy of Officer West." He paused. "Either that guy never sleeps or Eagle Springs has a one-man police department. Got your car back okay."

"I appreciate that." Lyle nodded. "I guess it was bound to happen."

"What?"

"That you'd do something stupid like get blind drunk. Feel like you understand things better?"

Buck shook his head. "Offer still open to stay here a couple of nights?"

"Might be able to offer you more than a couple of nights. I'm going to be in Denver off and on to work on the exhibition. The Art Institute's set me up with some lectures as well. You can keep an eye on the house if you've a mind to. You can have Ray's old room if you want."

"You're doing a lot for me, Lyle. I don't have a job. I can't even pay for my room and board. You sure about this?"

"Pretty sure. Mind if I make a suggestion?"

Buck got a glass of water and sat down again. "Shoot." He still had the shakes, not just from the night before but also from seeing Pauline's truck sitting just outside the window.

"Maybe you'd feel better if you started writing. Now before you get riled up, Pauline made me promise that if I ever had the chance, that is, if I ever saw you again, I'd be sure you get writing. I've got a beat-up Remington. You're welcome to use it."

"I have a typewriter." He took in the fact Pauline had confided in Lyle. "An Olivetti portable. Someone I knew in San Francisco gave it to me."

Lyle considered this information. "And you lugged it all

the way here from San Francisco?"

Buck nodded. "It's not heavy."

Lyle drummed his fingers on the table. Buck folded his arms and rested his head on them.

"You wrote your first book on it?"

"Yeah," came Buck's muffled reply.

More drumming on the table. "Must have been a pretty good friend to give you a typewriter."

Buck was quiet. Lyle waited.

"Friend of a friend." He looked, bleary-eyed and tired, at Lyle. "A woman. She was a friend of Frankie's." At the mention of Frankie's name, his chest tightened. He coughed, but there was no wheeze. "She was okay. At first she scared me a little. She was beautiful. Everything about her was perfect and polished and her apartment looked the same—perfect and polished. Her name was Linda."

"Was the novel about Frankie and this woman?"

Buck got up and took a beer out of the refrigerator without looking at the time. "Want one?" he said to Lyle.

"Sounds like I might need one."

"It was more about Frankie. I met him on the bus going to California." He tipped the bottle back and the beer tasted good sliding down his throat.

"He played jazz piano and was damn good."

A storm was brewing above the high range. San Francisco began to feel like a parenthesis in his life where everything was separated from the present, exposing the past to greater scrutiny.

"*Blues for Frankie* was the title." The wind had started gusting outside. "Linda read it and thought the reason it was hard for me to write was because I'm writing the wrong story."

"What do you think?"

"I think she was right. Now I just need to find the right story." He took a swig of beer. "Just maybe not right now."

Thunder broke across the mountains and rain started to push against the screen. Lyle got up and closed the door. "Frankie must have meant something to you, otherwise why'd you write about him?"

Somehow, despite his condition and his grief, Buck understood not just why the novel wasn't right, but why he'd come home. "Because he made me think of Ray."

"Tell me about the woman."

"Linda was a friend of Frankie's. She had an art gallery in New York. I didn't want to get involved with her. I spent a lot of time wandering around the city, almost like I was learning how to be alone and I liked it that way. But Linda was interested in my wanting to write. She gave me the typewriter." He rubbed his face. "Toward the end, I began to feel sorry for her."

"Why?"

"At first she seemed so sure of herself. She was beautiful and rich, and seemed to have it all, and she was interested in my writing. We'd sit in her elegant apartment on Telegraph Hill and she'd read it out loud." He pictured the two of them sitting in her apartment.

"It was strange to hear my words being read aloud and,

in a way, it made me believe I could write. Things went bad in her gallery in New York and I saw how vulnerable she was under all that glamour, and I felt sorry for her. She wanted me to help her out, and I didn't. Just like I didn't help Pauline."

"Once you ditch all that guilt," Lyle said, "maybe you'll know what you want to write about."

Later, Buck sat on the back porch steps and stared at Pauline's pickup until it turned into something other than a black truck, until it became a way out—not out of Eagle Springs again, but out of the trance he'd been in since coming home.

* * *

At the end of the week Herm pulled Pauline's pickup to a stop at the curb. Lyle and Buck stood on the porch looking at it. It gleamed like obsidian, although in some places the black wasn't as glossy and some dents were visible. The sun's rays bounced off the polished chrome. It looked beautiful.

"Herm, you did a hell of a job," Lyle said. "Looks like new."

"Wanna test her out?" Herm tossed the keys to Lyle.

"Yeah. Just like new. Thanks, Herm," Buck said.

Herm walked to a car that had followed him. "You boys have a good time now."

Lyle drove the truck around the corner, back up the alley, and parked it in the garage. When he came into the kitchen, he handed the keys to Buck. They were fastened onto a beaded key holder: the key to the truck and the key to Pauline's house. Buck put them in his shirt pocket and snapped it shut.

CHAPTER TWENTY-SEVEN

Near the end of his second week back, Buck went by the *Gazette*. It was late in the day and he squinted, coming from the bright sunshine into the dim, interior light. A woman in her mid-thirties was typing and looked up when he came in.

"Hey," he said.

Her light brown hair was pulled back and a blue blouse matched the color of her eyes.

"Can I help you?"

"Wondering if I could speak with Art."

"Is he expecting you?"

"No, ma'am."

She watched him for a minute and Buck couldn't blame her. He hadn't been doing much to keep himself looking good. He kicked at the floor with his boot and considered leaving. "He knows me," he added.

"Okay. May I have your name?"

"Buck Malone."

"Oh. You used to work here, didn't you?"

"Yes ma'am. Long time ago it seems. How's it you know that?"

"I've seen some of your stories and articles in the files."

Buck nodded. "Still have the stories?"

"I think we might have some of them." She paused. "I'm Art's wife, Ellie. Have a seat, Buck. I'll tell Art you're here."

"Appreciate it."

He flipped through the latest edition of the *Gazette,* and then looked up to see Art on the other side of the counter. His hair was mussed, as though he'd been running his fingers through it, and tortoise-frame glasses perched on his nose. His brown eyes looked serious but he smiled. "Buck Malone. I'll be damned."

Buck walked to the counter. "Great to see you Art. You don't look any different."

"You do. Come on back. Ellie's just putting on some fresh coffee. Can you sit awhile?"

They talked until late-afternoon shadows darkened the office and Art turned on the desk lamp. Art said he'd met Ellie at a journalism class she was taking at the college. "Love at first sight," he said. "Did you finish your novel?"

Buck nodded. "Rejected three times. I tried to do revisions, but I'm never sure how or what to revise."

"Tell me about your novel."

"I can't. Writers, editors who read it said I was a good writer, but there was always something off."

"Do you know what that might be?"

Buck swallowed some coffee. "Yeah. I met a woman in San Francisco. She gave me a typewriter and that's how I got going. She said maybe I was having trouble because I was writing about the wrong thing. What I had was good, she said, but I began to wonder if what I needed to write about was Eagle Springs."

"Have you started that story? About Eagle Springs?"

"Nope. Haven't been back long enough. I'm just trying to get my bearings. Guess I'm waiting to see what happens with the manuscript I wrote in San Francisco. A buddy of mine at City Lights Bookstore in San Francisco sent it to an agent he knows in New York. I haven't had much luck with it so far."

A telephone call interrupted them and gave Buck a chance to look around the once-familiar office. It looked different and the same: small, musty, with a dim light streaming from the transom window above Art's slanted worktable.

Art picked up the conversation. "I like your friend Linda's idea that maybe you're not writing the right story. A lot happened to all of you here in Eagle Springs. Maybe that's the story you really need to write. Every small town has its story, and you were writing about some of that when you wrote about Queenie Dawson. Those weren't bad pieces. They might not have worked then, but work on them more and maybe we can run a series. As for the *Gazette*, as long as you can tell the difference between a subject and a verb, you can write for a paper. I'll be able to pay you more, but even that won't be much. You can have your former desk over there. Pretty much set your own hours as long as you make deadlines. In your spare time, it's okay with me if you want to use the typewriter and paper to write here once you've finished the work for the paper."

"I can use my typewriter," he said.

"That a yes?"

"Guess I can give it a try."

Art's voice and expression turned serious. "There's a couple more things I guess I should mention, although Ellie would probably rather I didn't. Might be just as well if you don't wind up in jail again, or get caught drinking in Kiowa Park."

"Doesn't look like a great start if my one night in jail is already around town."

"Just to me. As editor, I check the police blotter every day."

"Congratulations, Buck," Ellie said, ending the lecture. "We have a part-time high school girl, Carrie, who helps us. She sits at the desk in the outer office."

"Thanks, ma'am." He nodded.

""Have you kept in touch with Lorrie?" Art said.

"Nope."

"She's coming back to Eagle Springs in a week. Seems she's suddenly Hollywood's newest blonde. Or so the tabloids say. She never came back to finish high school. Her mother took her to Hollywood and Lorrie was discovered by some director." He tossed a copy of the *Hollywood Reporter* across the desk. Buck looked at a small square Art had circled.

Just when Hollywood thought it couldn't take another blonde, along comes Lorrie Raymond, a beauty from Eagle Springs, Colorado.

Buck didn't have to guess where the last name had come from. He put the paper on the edge of the desk. "I'm glad she got her dream," he said. "How long ago did this happen?"

"Maybe a couple of years. We're just hearing about it now. She was probably in Hollywood when you were in San Francisco. It's up to you, but I'd like you to work up something about Lorrie. How she got started acting, what kind of girl she was. The kind of thing local folks would like to hear about a hometown girl who makes it in Hollywood."

"How come?"

"The movie company is planning publicity here for her first movie, seeing she's from here and all."

*   *   *

That night, Buck put the key in the ignition of Pauline's truck and backed it out and down the alley. He made it to the end of the block and stopped. No fragrance of lavender traced through the cab, no wind blew her dark hair in the space between them. He was mistaken. This couldn't be Pauline's truck. He drove around the block and parked it in the garage again. The kitchen light flipped on when he slammed the garage doors shut. Lyle stood silhouetted in the doorway.

"Mind telling me what you've been doing the past week? Place smells worse than the Silver Dollar saloon."

"Sorry." Buck tossed his jacket on a chair. "Guess I got wrapped up in other things."

He filled the sink with warm, soapy water and started washing the dishes stacked there.

Lyle leaned against the counter watching. "What other things?"

"I was thinking about the meeting with my folks. I know you think it's important, Lyle, but I can't find a way back into their lives, and I don't want to. In San Francisco, I was damn lonely at first. I wandered all over the city, and went to the beach where I just stared at the Pacific Ocean. When I came out of those first months, I was different."

"Don't worry about it. At least you saw them. What else happened?"

"I talked to Art Packer."

Lyle picked up a towel and started drying the dishes. "How'd that go?"

"Pretty good. He's taking me on with a salary. Not much, but I'll see how it goes."

"That's good news, Buck. You've always been too hard on yourself. Give this a chance."

"Art's already given me my first assignment. Interview Lorrie Rathburn."

"Lorrie? What's she got to do with this?"

"Seems she's coming to Eagle Springs doing publicity for her first movie. Art wants me to interview her since I knew her before. She has a new name too. Lorrie Raymond."

Lyle shook his head. "I'll be damned."

Buck looked out the window. The wind blew heavy, dark, clouds across the sky. Another major hailstorm was on the way. Suddenly, he wanted Ray to be here, or at least to know he was alive.

"I'm glad for Lorrie," Buck said. "She has what she said she always wanted. To be an actress in the movies, to come back to Eagle Springs famous." He paused. "It'll be good to see her."

"Lorrie had it rough here," Lyle said. "All you kids did, but she had it really rough with the abortion and all. I hope she has what she wanted."

"Why do you say that?"

"Is writing what you want, or is it what you need? Before you interview Lorrie, which by the way I think is a good thing, you might try and look at what she has now and ask yourself if it's what she needs."

The back screen door banged in the wind and the hail came down hard. Buck rushed to close the door.

"Think she picked Raymond as her last name to remember Ray?" Buck asked.

"Maybe," Lyle said. "Maybe she still isn't over Ray."

Buck looked at the mountains. They were steady and certain. "I'm not over Pauline. Why would she be over Ray?"

* * *

He drove past the Canyon Road cutoff to the Seminary, and toward the center of Three Rivers. Nothing had changed.

The red-brick arcade still bustled with activity, and kids stood on the bridge behind the arcade pitching rocks into the river. Buck turned down the gravel incline to Ruby's and pulled into the parking lot. Two trucks were parked near the door.

He sat in Pauline's truck waiting for the wave of memory to subside. It was all here. The first time he'd danced with Pauline, the night he'd sat with Lorrie trying to convince her to give back the compact, the fight with Perez.

He pressed his head against the steering wheel. *Please help me, Pauline.*

A cowboy came out of the bar and headed toward his car. He took a long look at Buck before getting in and driving up the incline to the road. Buck got out and pushed through the door. Ruby was cleaning the bar, her back to him, and a cowboy sat at the end.

"Hey, Ruby."

She spun around, cloth in hand. He heard her gasp from across the room. A glass fell. "Lord God. Buck."

"Yep. All six feet of me."

She came around the end of the bar and the cowboy was suddenly interested in a woman he knew as a friendly bartender now embracing a young man.

"Lord God." She leaned back to look at him. "You look like a man, if I can say that."

He smiled. "Guess it's true. I'm not a kid anymore."

The cowboy paid and left. Ruby posted a "Closed" sign on the door, then went behind the bar and poured two Scotches.

Buck sat at a table. "Place looks the same, Ruby. I just got back. I'm staying with Lyle until I decide what to do."

She put two glasses on the table and sat, tipping her glass to his and they both drank.

"Pauline told me she believed that your move to San Francisco would free you to find yourself and write."

"What happened, Ruby? What the hell happened? Some kid had a story that Pauline had killed herself but I don't believe him and Lyle, well, I can't get much from him."

He took a drink. "Pauline wouldn't do that."

"I don't know much more than anybody. Lyle called me and said he'd found Pauline's body at the base of Spirit Rock. It looked like she slipped because the monument was still damp from rain and because she was lying close to it. He called the police and that was what they figured. I heard those damn fool rumors about suicide too and you're right, Pauline was never one to give up."

"Do you believe she slipped and fell? She'd been climbing that monument all her life. What other rumors and stories did you hear? Did something happen to make her afraid?" *Oh God. Please don't tell me she was afraid and alone.* "Ruby," he said. "Please don't tell me she was afraid and alone," repeating aloud his thought.

"I'll tell you what I know, but first you eat."

"Can't eat."

"That's what you always used to say." She smiled and motioned him to her apartment in the rear of the bar where she lived now.

They ate tamales in quiet, holding their memories close.

"There was some talk that Perez had been seen," Ruby said. "But nothing came of it. If he was here, I know he would've come by to see if she was working here, but no sign of him."

Buck poured some more Scotch into their glasses. His heart was racing. He pumped some medicine and took deep breaths.

"You still bothered by that asthma?"

"Not as bad. Might have outgrown it somewhat. It got better in California. It's the stress that's getting me now. So everybody, including the police, think she slipped?"

"Buck, as hard as it is for me to say this, you can't dwell on what did or didn't happen. What we believe, or whatever we think we know, it just doesn't matter now."

They moved back to the bar and she took the sign down and flicked the switch that lit up the neon light outside. "You heard from Ray?" she asked.

He shook his head. *Whatever happened, Ray doesn't know any more about it than I do.*

CHAPTER TWENTY-EIGHT

He let himself into the office using the key Art had given him, and settled at his former desk. He would have expected a feeling of ease, of familiarity at this moment, but he felt only a sense of disconnect. By the time Art came in, the wastebasket overflowed with crumpled yellow sheets.

"Trouble?"

"Not sure I can write about Lorrie. I never really understood her to begin with."

"Maybe you understand her more than you think. Buck, I don't want to pry but maybe if I ask you a question or two it will spark a thread you can follow into the story."

"What's on your mind?"

"Wasn't she mixed up with a friend of yours? A Mexican boy? Didn't she get pregnant?"

"What'd you bring that up for?"

"It's called getting in front of a story so you don't get slapped around by it later. I think there are still people in town who remember the trouble the minister's daughter got into. Just something you might keep in mind. You knew Lorrie and the fellow. How do you feel about what happened to them? What you already know might help you understand Lorrie better so other people can see her differently." He shuffled some papers. "Use the material you wrote about the Seminary. I hear they're planning some publicity shots there."

Buck reverted to his San Francisco habit of walking and looking for ideas. He walked around downtown and finally sat in the park facing the empty band shell, remembering the night Lorrie was crowned Miss Rodeo Queen of 1956, and how excited she was that he was going to write about her in the paper. It didn't seem important now.

Back at the *Gazette* he wrote sentences, words, anything that would get him writing. He filled a sheet of foolscap, reread it, and typed it up on the Remington only to toss it in the trash with the rest. Was it true he had nothing real to write about Lorrie? He'd said nothing about the effect her mother's drinking and her father's apathy might have had on Lorrie, or the even stronger illusion she had that Ray Perez would give her the love she thought she wanted.

I didn't tell the truth about Lorrie before, he thought. *But maybe I can now.*

*   *   *

After a restless night, he left early for the paper. Art motioned him over the minute he came in.

"Lorrie Raymond is arriving in Denver next week, then coming here. I want you to go to Denver and interview her."

He felt a flutter of excitement at the idea of seeing Lorrie. "Any idea when she's going to be back in Eagle Springs?"

"Not yet." Art pushed a Teletype message across the desk. "But you'll probably have to talk to this guy to arrange to see her. The *Denver Post* is running the story tomorrow."

Colorado's own Lorrie Raymond married Hollywood director David Nash in a celebrity-filled ceremony at the Sands Hotel in Las Vegas, Nevada, yesterday. Nash is producer and director of Raymond's first film, "The Far Mountain." Publicity stops include Chicago, Denver, Salt Lake City, Los Angeles, and Raymond's home town of Eagle Springs.

Buck laid the notice on the edge of Art's desk while the idea of Lorrie married settled in his mind. Was she finally over Ray? Did marriage and a movie career mean she'd found her life?

"Well," he said. "Lorrie was always full of surprises."

* * *

Buck left the *Gazette* phone number in case David Nash, or anyone associated with him, called back to arrange a meeting with Lorrie. He started scanning archived issues of the paper, and glancing at old police blotters, making notes of possible ideas. He began to see that the more he'd written about Frankie and Linda and San Francisco, the more he'd lost Eagle Springs and Pauline and Ray and Lorrie. Now Lorrie was coming home.

It was in the afternoon, with the shadows long and the sun hitting the top of the wall near the ceiling, that he came on the stack of old police blotters. Casually, he riffled through them, skimming the truncated items until something caught his eye.

Jan. 27, 1957. 10 p.m. Disturbance at Bluffs. Arrested A. Perez for drunk and disorderly and attempted vandalism of single-resident home on Prospect Street. Booked overnight.

Buck's hands were shaking. He bent his head between his knees, taking fast breaths, and pumped his inhalator to calm himself. He couldn't collapse now. He gulped cups of water from the cooler and rested his head on the desk until his breathing eased. He read the report again, then pulled it from the stack and jammed it in his satchel. Had Perez been here when Pauline died? When he came to the month of March, the month Lyle said Pauline had died, he looked at each entry carefully. There it was, written in the same uneven handwriting as the one he'd just read.

March 18, 1957. Morning. (approx. 10 a.m.). Indian woman's body found at base of Spirit Rock. Undetermined cause/time of death. Contact: Lyle Samuels, friend of deceased.

The anonymity of the report on Pauline should have stunned him, but it didn't. A dead Indian woman wouldn't call for much copy. No details were given. Not even her name, age, condition of body. Hadn't Lyle provided all this? Was there another report? He took this one and put it with the notice about Perez's return.

He kept looking and there, buried on page three, was a short piece.

Pauline Moon, a twenty-eight-year-old Indian woman and local artist, was found at the base of Spirit Rock just north of Seminary Road. A black pickup was nearby. The cause of death is inconclusive but police theorize Moon may have slipped while climbing the monument, which was still wet from a rain the previous night, and as a result of the fall, suffered a fatal concussion.

The phone rang. Buck listened as someone on the other end said it wouldn't be possible to permit a private interview with Miss Raymond. News conferences would be held in Denver and Eagle Springs.

* * *

The decision to drive Pauline's truck to Denver rather than take Lyle's car came to him so quickly that he didn't have time to second-guess himself. The drive north gave him the space he needed to think about the police reports. Perez must have been in Eagle Springs when Pauline died. Had he come after her again once she left Denver and returned here? Was she running to Spirit Rock to get away from him? Did he catch up with her there? Buck couldn't push the thoughts out of his mind. Did she feel all her chances were gone for the future? He couldn't bring himself to accept any conjecture as truth, either that she killed herself or that Perez had a hand in her dying. The only truth was that she was dead.

He stopped at Castle Rock and had a beer in a run-down bar at the edge of town. She'd been alone, again. It didn't matter that she hadn't tried to keep him from leaving; the point was, he'd left.

Maybe if I'd written, he thought, *so she'd at least have known how to get in touch with me.* But it was no good. No matter how or what he tried to understand about what had happened, the reality was he'd never know the whole truth. Whatever he knew would be what he chose to believe, but it wouldn't be fact.

He had a second beer and gave himself over to seeing Lorrie in Denver.

He parked the truck a few blocks from the hotel. A dusty black pickup pulling up to the swanky Brown Palace Hotel would call attention that he didn't want. He gave a swipe to his boots and was glad he'd worn a clean shirt, jacket, and jeans when he crossed the elegant lobby to the front desk and asked the clerk for Lorrie Raymond's room number.

The clerk looked at him as if he were joking. A lanky cowboy, complete with Stetson and boots in the elegant lobby asking for Lorrie Raymond, Movie Star. "Sir?" he said as if he'd surely misunderstood.

"Lorrie Raymond. I'm an old friend of hers up from Eagle Springs. Buck Malone. She's expecting me."

Later he would be amazed at how easy it all was. The clerk picked up the phone, and Buck heard him say, "Miss Raymond? There's a Buck Malone here at the desk to see you. Hello? Hello?" The clerk put the phone down. "I believe she hung up. Sir."

"Do tell." Buck smiled and crossed the lobby, reaching the bank of elevators just as Lorrie emerged, and Buck marveled at how she seemed to shine as she ran at him, throwing her arms around his neck.

"Oh, Buck." And he held on. "Come on," she said after a moment, pulling him into an elevator. She pressed *Mezzanine* and they got off, quickly finding a deserted corner.

"Lorrie, you look prettier than before, if that's possible." They stood close to each other and Buck was amazed at the joy he felt seeing her.

"Isn't it like you to just walk up and ask for me like that?" She smiled at him and he took his cowboy hat off. "Good Lord! Are you still wearing cowboy boots?" They both laughed.

"Actually, I'm back in Eagle Springs now and working at the *Gazette*. Art Packer gave me a steady job. He knew we know each other and asked me if I'd interview you."

"Oh, so that's why you're here?"

"Only partly. I wanted to see you again. If I don't get an interview, I don't care."

She sank into a chair in the corner. "How will we ever catch up?"

"Maybe we don't need to," he said. "Just start out fresh now." But as he said the words, he couldn't see that happening.

Her hair was blonder, short and styled in deep waves, and her diction was careful and modulated, her expression cautious, even furtive, as she glanced around the foyer. It was clear that people would begin looking for her any minute.

"My truck's a block away," he said. "Want to make a run for it?"

She peeked around a corner. "Do you think we can make it?"

He shrugged. "What's the worst that can happen?" He regretted it immediately when an expression of fear flitted across her face. With a shock he realized that for all the surface glamour, she was uneasy. "If you want to, I'll be sure we make it." She looked at him for a second.

"Okay," she said, and her voice was small, the way it was when she'd told him she loved Ray.

They went through a door behind the meeting rooms and took a service elevator near the kitchen, then hurried out a delivery door, suddenly finding themselves in the bright sunlight of Seventeenth Street.

"Come on." They ran the block and a half to his truck.

"Oh, Buck," she laughed once in the truck. "That made me think of all the sneaking and running around at the Seminary that summer."

"Where should we go?" He started the engine. "I know some out-of-the-way places in Denver where we can talk. Cheesman Park's pretty big, doubt anybody would see us there. Maybe a little restaurant out on Colfax?"

Her face was in profile as she stared straight ahead and he couldn't gauge her expression. "Well, we're already crazy. David will have the police looking for us before we hit the outskirts of Denver."

Did she want to leave Denver? "I don't want you to get in trouble. We can sit here and talk, or arrange to meet up again tonight in Denver or at least in Eagle Springs when you get there."

"No." She curled her legs under her just as she'd always done. "Believe me, there's no way I could get away alone, here or in Eagle Springs."

"People watch you a lot?"

She looked at him, her eyes serious. "Actually a lot of people rely on me." She ran her fingers through her hair as if emphasizing what she said. "You know, agents, hairdressers, that kind of thing."

He checked the rearview mirror nervously.

"It's okay, though." She smiled. "I'll call David from Eagle Springs and make up some story."

That was how Buck ended up on the narrow highway going home again, this time with Lorrie. He drove slowly to avoid attention, and at the fork of the Cottonwood and Eagle Rivers, he headed northwest toward the foothills and Mesa Road.

"Isn't this Pauline's truck?" Lorrie said suddenly.

He cracked the window open. He wished he could whistle. He wished he smoked. Anything to bring nonchalance into the moment, take his mind off the feeling that whatever they were doing wasn't going to come out well.

"Yeah."

"Did she give it to you?"

"Might say so. Have you heard from Ray?"

"Why would I hear from him? Besides, he'd never contact me after my mother threatened him with prison." Buck saw a frown crease her forehead.

"Did you know that, Buck? She told me if I ever went near Ray again she'd make sure he'd go to prison for what he did to me."

Buck didn't speak, but he remembered Mrs. Rathburn's violent anger and her threats.

"It wasn't Ray's fault," Lorrie said. "He didn't even know I was pregnant until that night."

He gripped the wheel. He was the only one who knew that both he and Ray had known Lorrie was pregnant, even that she might seek out an abortionist, and neither one of them had done anything. For the first time since he'd picked her up in Denver, he felt sadness and guilt, recognizing that he'd failed Lorrie.

"You were at the hospital that night, weren't you?"

He nodded.

"I guess I was in pretty bad shape, I don't remember. They said I could never have children because of the abortion." She waited. "But that's okay. I never really wanted kids. Buck—" He heard excitement back in her voice. "Isn't that the cutoff to Monument Lake?"

"Yep," he said.

"Let's go there, Buck."

"I'm not sure about all this."

"But I might not have this chance again."

The same words he'd said to Linda when he'd left San Francisco. He turned onto the cutoff.

"Okay," he said. "But there isn't much time. I can get you back to Denver before midnight and they might not hang me at noon."

"Time for what? For you to ask me questions that everybody thinks they already have the answers to? Besides, you were never great at putting pieces in the *Gazette* for me."

"I'd never write anything bad about you. Besides, back then I didn't know anything about writing for a newspaper." He wasn't sure he knew much more now.

The cutoff wasn't really a road, more a widening through the dunes. He ground the truck to a stop at the side of the road and killed the engine. The lake was close enough to walk to, even if the path was rocky.

"We're supposed to walk?" she said.

"Lake's dead ahead. " He couldn't help but smile. She was

the same Lorrie. "If you want to see the lake, I guess so."

They sat in silence for a moment, Buck trying to fathom the fragile boundary between who they were and who they'd become. He felt entwined in events he wanted to be free of, yet here he was with Lorrie and after all that had happened, it was just the two of them.

He got out of the pickup. "Come on," he said.

He crossed a dune that rose abruptly in front of the truck. Ahead, Monument Lake lay like a deep blue memory, and he felt whole and incomplete simultaneously and wondered how that was possible. The air held the sweet smell of the lake, and evening would come early here when the sun dipped behind the High Range.

The door of the pickup slammed behind him. He should have waited for Lorrie to catch up, or gone back to help her. It wasn't easy walking through the heavy sand and rough gravel, and there was no clear path.

Just then Lorrie came over the rise and paused, and in that split second, when the wind caught the full skirt of her pale green dress and raised it slightly to reveal her slim tan legs and when she raised her arm to shade her eyes and look for him, she was Lorrie again and his heart ached for whatever he expected of her, for whatever betrayals she'd felt because of him.

She walked delicately, as though tracing an intricate pattern on ice rather than maneuvering through rough sand, toward the edge of the water. She'd taken her sandals off in the car, and now their thin yellow straps wound around the fingers of one hand, and the rhinestones sprinkled across the top glittered like tiny mirrors in the fading light. The water scalloped around the edges of her bare feet and then she did something that brought everything from that summer back to him. She clasped her hands behind her back, the sandals dangling lightly from one hand, and swayed slightly back and forth, the way she had that night at the square dance in Kiowa Park, as if she were listening to an inner song, and just as he had realized years-ago, he knew he'd never really understand Lorrie.

They sat on the sand and she told him that Ray had brought her here one summer afternoon.

"We sat over there." She pointed to the far shore. "That was the first time Ray kissed me." She tipped her head back and looked at the sky. "He always looked so beautiful to me."

A breeze came up. "You cold?"

She shook her head. "What happened to Ray, Buck?"

"I don't know. I got one letter from Fort Ord in California. I should've tried to find him when I was in San Francisco but he would have been gone by then."

The sun slipped behind the high range and the early-evening light rolled across the plains toward town. The sky turned navy blue, then dark, and the new moon began to rise in the distant eastern sky.

"We better get going, Lorrie. Forget about the interview. I'll make something up."

To get to the highway north, he needed to drive through town. As they neared Kiowa Park she asked him to pull over.

"Might not be good to get out, Lorrie. Unless you want to be recognized."

She opened the car door and headed toward the park. He followed, looking around nervously.

"Sure, I want to be recognized. What's the point of being famous if you can't be recognized?" She stared at the stage. "That seems so long ago, when I won that Miss Rodeo Queen contest."

"Didn't you like it?" He was glad the park wasn't crowded.

"Sure. It was fun. Okay, one last thing. Giuseppe's pizza. Can we? Please?"

Getting back to Denver was becoming a problem he hadn't anticipated. He stopped at Giuseppe's, ordered a pizza, and called Lyle.

"You might want to be prepared for a visit from Eagle Springs' finest," he said. "I drove to Denver to see Lorrie, maybe try to interview her there."

"Are you calling from Denver now?"

"No."

"What's that noise I hear?"

"I'm in a restaurant. Giuseppe's."

"Sweet Jesus," Lyle said. "Is Lorrie with you?"

"Yep. Waiting in the truck. Now before you get riled at me, she wanted to come down here. I planned heading directly back to Denver. The truth is, Lyle, I think Lorrie and me need to talk."

"Well, of course she wanted you to take her there, and of course you think you both need to talk." Lyle's voice was tight. "Since when do you do whatever Lorrie Rathburn wants?"

Buck paused, taking in the gaiety of Giuseppe's, the tables of young people and college students, all as it had been before.

"Actually I've always done what Lorrie wanted, Lyle. I admit I got carried away when I saw her today, but it was fine to be together again." The waiter waved to him to pick up the pizza. "Okay, it was stupid. But I'm still going to Pauline's—"

"Wait!" Lyle interrupted. "You're taking Lorrie to Pauline's?"

"I know what I'm doing, Lyle. I'd appreciate it if you wouldn't share any of this with the cops, though."

"Get her the hell back to Denver tonight, Buck. If her husband finds out you've taken his wife and star on a trip down memory lane, you're likely to wind up in serious trouble."

"I'll do that."

Before he left, he bought a six-pack of beer even though what he really wanted was some of Lyle's Scotch.

* * *

"Are you sure this is all right?" Lorrie said as they pulled down the path to the back of Pauline's house.

"No." He turned off the engine and sat in the truck, just looking at Pauline's house. "But I'm not keen on eating pizza and drinking beer in the park or in the truck."

He got out and walked toward the back door. Lorrie followed at a distance. Amazingly the door, a little loose on the hinges, opened with only slight pressure. He flipped the light switch. Nothing. "Naturally no lights." He put the pizza on a chair. "Wait here." He went to the truck and found a flashlight in the glove compartment.

Lorrie waited on the porch and with the dim glow of the flashlight, they made their way into the kitchen. Lorrie found some candles in a drawer, some half-burned down, and a small box of matches. In the candlelight they sat at the kitchen table eating pizza and drinking beer and she talked about her life in Los Angeles.

"I like Los Angeles more than I thought I would, when I lived here. There's always so much going on, so many people. The light seems different, and sometimes the sun looks so old. There's a wind called the Santa Ana. It's an angry wind, not like the Chinook here. It burns down the canyons of the San Gabriel Mountains, and people just collapse on strangers' lawns, watching the palm trees whip the fire. I drove to the edge of the mountains one night with a boy and we sat in his car and watched it. We ate apples out of a paper sack."

"Who was the boy?"

"Oh, I can't possibly remember." She walked to the open back door and looked through the screen at the mountains in black silhouette. "He might have been a boy I met at the Playhouse."

"Your memory of him sounds nice. You must have liked him."

She'd taken her sandals off and curled her bare feet beneath her.

"Sure. I must have."

He'd thought they had so much to say, yet they were as

silent as the house that surrounded them. Only Pauline's spirit moved as delicately as his own breath.

"What about Ray?"

She sipped her beer. "What about Ray?"

"You ever think about him? Now, I mean?"

The candlelight shadowed her face, fixing it with a softness and a sense of mystery. She looked away.

"Sorry," he said. "Guess that's none of my business." He opened another beer for himself. "Forget it."

He heard a noise outside and jumped.

"What's the matter with you? Afraid of the dark?"

"Just jumpy, I guess."

What did he expect? That she'd declare her love for Ray after all this time?

"You haven't told me a thing about you, Buck. What about your novel? Was it about us? All of us, I mean? That summer? I went to San Francisco to study acting. I was there for about a month and wanted to see you, but didn't know if you were there, or how to find you."

He told her about San Francisco. Not about his days and nights of wandering, or about his loneliness. He told her he loved its Bohemian life style, the creativity he found in jazz, the hours of talking with the other writers. But he didn't tell her about Linda or Frankie because suddenly he didn't know what to say about them. He'd convinced himself San Francisco was the story.

He cleaned up and checked outside to be sure they hadn't been spotted, half expected Lyle to come walking up the drive.

Lorrie wasn't in the kitchen when he came back and he

hurried into the living room. Not there. He turned toward the bedroom. She was lying on Pauline's bed with the quilt over her, sleeping, her bright blonde curls against the pillow. He sat on the edge of the bed, remembering all the nights he'd slept there with Pauline, remembering the night he'd found her, beaten and raped by Perez, and how that had begun the end of their affair. He lay down next to Lorrie and slept a hard, deep, dreamless sleep.

*   *   *

Dawn edged across the mountains. Lorrie stood looking out the window. She had covered Buck with the quilt and now she came and sat beside him, running her hands across it.

"Sam gave this to Pauline," Buck said, wishing his tongue didn't feel so thick.

"It's beautiful," Lorrie said. "I think Pauline would be happy to know you're here, Buck. Not just in Eagle Springs, but in her house."

He sat up and she carefully folded the quilt.

"What about you, Lorrie? You say you like California and Hollywood, but are you happy?"

She ran her fingers through her hair. "Don't worry about me. You were always worrying about us, Buck. About me or Ray or Pauline. Besides"—she stood and straightened her clothes—"I have everything I ever wanted. Why shouldn't I be happy?"

He pulled on his boots. "Wish I had some coffee. Maybe

we can pull off at Castle Rock."

They were quiet on the drive to Castle Rock. She sat close to him and at one point, rested her head on his shoulder and slept some more and he thought that in all the years he'd known her, he'd never felt this close to Lorrie. No matter what she said, he was convinced that she would accept this life, happy or not, as the right one for her.

At the restaurant Lorrie called her husband, made up some story and said she'd be at the hotel by eight. Buck could tell by her expression that the conversation wasn't going well.

He called Art and asked him not to print anything in the paper about Lorrie gone missing overnight.

"She's with me, Art. We're on our way back to Denver. Everything is fine. I know this is one of those situations you probably didn't want me to get in. If you want to fire me, I'll understand."

He dropped Lorrie off at the back entrance to the Brown Palace. They held hands, then embraced, and Buck said he hoped she wouldn't get into too much trouble.

"Blame it on me, Lorrie. Tell them I kidnapped you."

"Now that would make a good story," she said as if she were almost considering it. "I can manage David. He doesn't want to do anything to hurt me." She gave a bright smile. "I'm his ticket to fame and fortune."

She asked him to come to Hollywood and see her, but they both knew he wouldn't. She got out of the car and walked around to the driver's side, leaning in the open window and kissing Buck, her lips lingering on his before she stepped back.

"Yes," she said. "I did love Ray. At that time I believed he was all I had, but when it came to his marrying me I wasn't sure about his feelings so . . ." She lowered her head. "I had the abortion."

And then she was gone, the jewels on her sandals flashing in the morning light as she went in the door.

Buck left immediately for Eagle Springs. Once at Pauline's, he took the Olivetti out of the case and put it on the kitchen table. There was still enough light to type something for Art.

August 1957
Star
By Buck Malone
The journey from Eagle Springs to Hollywood isn't easy.
It's more than a train ride.

He tossed it out and started again.

Star
The journey from Eagle Springs to Hollywood begins in the mind of a young girl. She isn't dreaming about fame and fortune but about love, or maybe the way a boy's lips might feel against hers. It begins in the things she whispers to herself at night, or in the curves and angles of the word she traces in her notebook.

It begins on a summer night, maybe a night like tonight,

when she's crowned Miss Rodeo Queen of 1956 and she dances to a slow Western waltz with a cowboy, and she wants that night to go on forever because it's proof of something indefinable and she wants to hold on to it. The journey is like every journey taken in America. It's inevitable. It's forbidden. It's impossible. It's a whisper, and home becomes just the place a person is meant to leave. California is the edge of all that promise and mystery, the proof of what's possible. The Pacific Ocean, scalloped against sandy beaches like a lace tablecloth on your mother's dining room table, is the pact between then and now, just as the Santa Ana winds are a threat to that pact. California is a neon woman, a script, and the words: "Lights! Camera! Action!" California is a state of mind. It's everybody's history, sooner or later. But then, so is America and Eagle Springs. So Lorraine Rathburn is coming home, even if her name is Lorrie Raymond now, and she's not a Rodeo Queen, she's a Movie Star. Lorrie is that girl who believed in her whispered hopes, who held her inevitable and forbidden desires close. Lorrie is the girl who will discover that part of the bargain is in the coming home.

*   *   *

He made the bed, cleaned the kitchen and folded the quilt, which he put in the truck with his typewriter. He parked in the lot behind the *Gazette*, relieved no one was there as he dropped the news item in Carrie's in-box. Then he drove to Spirit Rock.

It was just after ten and the sandstone was a vivid ochre shade in the morning sun. He thought he found the spot where Lyle might have discovered Pauline's body. He looked up at the monument and remembered how she had once tried to get him to climb to the top but in the end she'd had to pull him up the last few feet and he'd collapsed in a fit of wheezing. *We laughed at my silly-ass inability to climb*, he remembered.

This time he made it. He lay on his back staring up at the high, beautiful blue Colorado sky. Above him a hawk circled, searching the edges of the wind. It soared down and up, up and down, again and again, until it caught an updraft and was swept high where it glided effortlessly, parallel to the face of the mountain, looking for a place to land. Buck watched it circle in an ever-narrowing pattern and then, in a final display of power and grace, spread its huge wings for balance until it settled on the edge of a cliff, and he remembered what Pauline had told him never to forget: it's always better to land than to circle endlessly.

THE END

ACKNOWLEDGMENTS

First thanks must go to my wonderful "team," Derek Szempruch and Ashley Fontanetta of UpStage Group-San Francisco. Thanks to both of you for making my dream come true and for your friendship. Thanks to Michael Correy, graphic designer, and Paul Thomason, editor.

I'm happy to thank my two mentors and teachers, Caroline Leavitt, cheerleader and editor extraordinaire, and Masha Hamilton, whose grace alone was worth the price of admission. Thanks to my many teachers in UCLA Writing Program online, and Gotham Writing classes online.

To my many readers, virtual and non-virtual, who read my drafts and patiently talked with me, you also helped my dream come true. Thanks to Kelly Cozy for sharing volumes of valuable knowledge with me. Thanks to Lauren Baratz-Logsted, Rosemary Bledsoe, Dana Nojima, Brigitte Thorpe, Tina Balog, and Katharine Yee. Thanks to the knowledgeable members at Backspace, especially the wonderful Karen Dionne—thanks for your honesty, Karen. Very special thanks to Galina Gorodetsky. Special thanks and affection to my dear friend, Manfred.

Recognition to my locations and time period: to 1956 for being an interesting period, to Colorado Springs and Denver, to the Soaring Sixties, and to San Francisco for jazz and for being the best place to live.

ABOUT THE AUTHOR

Diane Molberg is the author of numerous poems that have appeared in literary journals and anthologies. Her most recent publication was the short story, "Fedora." She taught literature at San Francisco State University for several years before devoting herself full-time to writing. She has led frequent discussion groups in several venues including Book Passage in Corte Madera. She lives in San Francisco, California, and is currently working on a second novel. "If I Go" is her first novel.

CPSIA information can be obtained
at www.ICGtesting.com
Printed in the USA
FSOW02n0721130815
9655FS